# "Are they all dead?"

Bolan nodded. As an afterthought, he picked up a pair of empty water bottles and cut open a vein on two of the bodies. He hoped the blood samples would reveal what types of toxins were used to turn humans into weapons.

"Who were they?" Rudd asked.

"Someone's pawns," the soldier replied. "Most likely, they were kidnapped tourists, harmless people sparked to insanity by some biochemist."

"Who'd do such a thing? And who'd let them loose here, where there's just kids?"

"If there's a clue in the blood, I'll use it. I'm going after them," Bolan stated grimly.

"Alone?" Rudd asked.

"Alone. With an army. It won't matter. I'm going to find the people behind this," the Executioner said.

# Don Pendleton's Mack Bolan®

## Grave Mercy

A GOLD EAGLE BOOK FROM

# WORLDWIDE®

TORONTO • NEW YORK • LONDON
AMSTERDAM • PARIS • SYDNEY • HAMBURG
STOCKHOLM • ATHENS • TOKYO • MILAN
MADRID • WARSAW • BUDAPEST • AUCKLAND

Recycling programs
for this product may
not exist in your area.

First edition September 2011

ISBN-13: 978-0-373-61547-6

Special thanks and acknowledgment to
Doug Wojtowicz for his contribution to this work.

GRAVE MERCY

**Printed in U.S.A.**

Age after age, the strong have trampled upon the weak; the crafty and heartless have ensnared and enslaved the simple and the innocent...

—Robert Green Ingersoll
1833–1899

I have witnessed the innocent being ground into the earth by heartless monsters. Enough! They will be avenged.

—Mack Bolan

# CHAPTER ONE

Mack Bolan, running at full speed, speared his foot into the door of the laboratory and was stopped cold. Usually the Executioner's 220-pound frame and the forty pounds of gear he wore were more than sufficient to easily splinter a door. Bolan grimaced under the impact as he rebounded from the heavy panel. It took a few steps for the soldier to recover his balance. The stench of incinerating heroin was heavy in the air, impenetrable cloying clouds obscuring the burning processing tables sprawled throughout the long room. The soldier's brilliant, tactical mind was unaffected by the airborne opiates, as his face was masked. He doubted that he'd been physically affected by the gases filling the room, so without muscular impediment, he realized that the door was reinforced. Under the usual set of circumstances, such a kick would have loosened the crossbolt from its mooring in the doorjamb, but the door was locked from the outside, which made sense.

No drug lord wanted his drug processors to have a free way out when they could slip packets into their mouths or other orifices. Locking the lab from the outside was a means of control. Only Long Eddy himself made the profits, not some emaciated, poor, jittery lackey with a rectum full of heroin-stuffed condoms.

That's why Bolan kept a 12-gauge shotgun—a Masterkey—under the barrel of his rifle. He triggered the stubby blaster, and a cylinder of lead powder turned the locking mechanism to scrap.

With a push, the door flew wide open. Even as the first shafts of sunlight and fresh air rolled in through the crack, Bolan realized that he'd made a mistake. With a new supply of oxygen rolling into the burning laboratory, the flames flared even hotter. The process was called a backdraft, and it was one of the most terrifying traps that professional firemen could walk into.

The Executioner had made a mistake—he was only human—and now his nerves were screaming at him, announcing the harm the blast of superheated air around him was causing. It was survivable. The heat rose, air rumbling behind him and igniting under superheated force. His legs pushed, long limbs releasing coiled energy as he sprung out onto the sand, trying to push himself prone and let his heavily protected back and boots absorb most of the damage that vomited into open air. Flames seared the back of Bolan's head, his hair curling up and snapping off instantly, his scalp singed. Something struck him hard between his shoulder blades, the Kevlar back of his armored, load-bearing vest and the trauma plates inside sucking up much of the force. Something hot and painful seared across his right shoulder, flesh parting under the impact.

Bolan hit the sand and buried his face in it as the gush of superheated air created a vacuum. The walls of the corrugated aluminum and plywood laboratory crumpled inward, the implosion crushing the building like a beer can. Twisted, and spewing smoke in the sand behind Bolan, the Jamaicans' drug laboratory was history. He knew that he had left wounded enemy gunmen inside, and by now, those people were dead. There was a pang of regret. While he was known as the Executioner, Mack Bolan wasn't a cruel man. The wounded he'd left behind were knocked out of the fight, no longer a threat to him. They'd have received medical aid once the battle was over, just small fry who didn't deserve to suffer after they'd been put out of the fight.

It had been Long Eddy who'd set off the conflagration, and the dreadlocked crime lord had little concern for the people under his command. Right now, the Jamaican was racing along the beach toward a long pier where a couple of cigarette boats had been moored. His legs looked skinny and now completely black in contrast to the pristine white shorts that flapped above his knees like a skirt.

Bolan surged to his feet and whipped off the mask covering his nose and mouth, the collar of his blacksuit grinding painfully against the tender skin on his neck. He realized that his right shoulder wasn't responding, though his hand was still clamped around the pistol grip of his M-4 rifle. He tried to pull up the muzzle of the weapon, and he knew that his nervous system had shut down, trying to suppress the pain of his injured arm.

Tentatively, Bolan reached to his shoulder, feeling the hard edges of broken glass shards sticking out of his deltoid and right biceps. One particularly large spear was jammed into the muscle just below his neck and behind his collarbone. He let his head droop, then his eyes locked on Long Eddy as the cop murderer leaped into his boat.

"Jack!" Bolan called over his throat mike. "I need a pickup, fast!"

"I saw the lab go up just now," Jack Grimaldi, one of Bolan's oldest surviving friends and allies, answered. Instants later, the bulbous form of a Hughes 500 helicopter rose over the trees, its downward rotor wash buffeting the Executioner with heavy winds.

"Jesus, Sarge!"

Bolan threw the M-4 onto the floor of the passenger cabin, then dragged himself into the back seat. "Do you see Long Eddy's boat?"

"You need medical attention first. You're bleeding like a stuck pig," Grimaldi countered.

"I've come this far to bring down Eddy, I'm not going to let a couple of flesh wounds stop me from finishing the job," Bolan said. "Go."

Grimaldi was torn between obeying his friend's order and concern for his health. "Take care of yourself while we catch up, damn it. I don't want you bleeding to death—this is a rental, after all."

It was one of those rare moments when the Executioner would have smiled, suppressing a chuckle at Grimaldi's smart-ass remark, but the pain of wrenching off his load-bearing vest had overridden that bit of levity. The blood-smeared ballistic nylon shell dropped to the floor in a clump, and Bolan could see multiple deep gouges and burns where shrapnel and flame had tried to reach him. He gently touched his shoulder again and felt for the biggest pieces of broken glass. There were four jagged shards, and he'd have to take care of them before peeling himself out of his blacksuit top.

The largest piece of glass had plunged into Bolan's shoulder muscle and come out far too easily for Bolan's taste. He grimaced as he saw bits of human tissue— his muscle fibers to be exact—clinging to the blast-sharpened tip. The soldier let it tumble out into the wind. The other three pieces were smaller, but Bolan had to explore the wounds with his fingertips. He felt the ragged gash, wincing as he carefully advanced deeper into the rift of flesh, looking for any remaining bits that might not have come with the big shard. The cut was wide, and deep, so the soldier reached into a pocket of his vest for a packet of coagulant powder. The moment the compound hit the cavity of his shoulder wound, it turned into a semisolid gel that conformed to the shape of the injury, sealing off severed capillaries and damaged veins.

It wouldn't last long, but Bolan could hold on long enough. Now that he'd stopped the bleeding, he plucked out the other square pieces of glass. A splinter at the top of his right biceps slid out with sickly stickiness, but none of these lesser lacerations were going to be a problem. The soldier slapped gauze and tape on the smaller cuts, then laid a thicker pad of sterile dressing on top of the shoulder wound, with medical tape sealing the clotting agent in place.

"Sarge, that boat must be rocket-powered," Grimaldi said. "I've got this baby up to 110 miles per hour, and he's still holding his distance."

"Are you saying you can't catch up with him?" Bolan asked, shrugging into the bloodied load-bearing vest. He winced as the shoulder wound took the pressure, but the field dressing would stay in place, ironically thanks to the added weight. A fast pat-check showed him that he had three magazines left for the M-4, and the Beretta 93-R stored in a holster clipped to the side of the vest. Usually the Executioner liked having a shoulder rig for the sleek 9-mm pistol, but with heavy kit like the armored vest, he didn't have space beneath the shell to fit his holster straps.

He zipped up the armored vest, tugging on its side vent straps to accommodate the lost layer of clothing. He didn't need his gear bouncing and jiggling around, possibly doing more damage to his injured arm. Bolan flexed his right hand, then bent the arm a few times. He had movement, enough to handle his weapons, but it would be a temporary thing. He'd taken serious injuries before, and experience taught him that anything more than a few minutes of activity would sap the strength from the wounded limb.

Bolan transferred the M-4 to his left hand. While he was born predominantly right-handed, years of warfare had made him ambidextrous. He was glad he hadn't taken a bullpup rifle into this fight because he didn't have the time now to shift an ejection port for left-handed use. The M-4, as it was configured, was relatively friendly to left handers, especially with its selector switch and magazine release on both sides of the receiver. He adjusted the holographic scope atop the weapon, adjusting it for his "off-side" eye, knowing that the settings for his normal use would be way off target for his left eye. The new parallax was perfectly aligned now, enabling Bolan to put every bullet where he needed it to be.

He put Long Eddy in his sights, the red holographic dot centered on the Jamaican's spine. Bolan pulled the trigger, but the physics of the helicopter and the cigarette boat over choppy waves sent his bullets careening over the side of the speedy watercraft. The tall Jamaican whipped his head around as fiberglass was chewed by autofire so close to his spine. Though there was no magnification on the holographic sight, Bolan knew that Long Eddy was shouting something. There was someone else on the boat.

"Jack! This has got to end!" Bolan roared. Grimaldi checked over his shoulder. Even through the dark visor of his pilot's helmet, the soldier could see the look of concern on his friend's face.

"You're hurt!" Grimaldi called back, but already the sleek helicopter nosed down, its bulbous front locked on to the rapid, dartlike boat. "Too hurt for close quarters!"

"But not hurt enough to accept collateral damage," Bolan growled. "He's got someone down there."

Grimaldi's sigh hissed over their intercom. The Executioner knew that the pilot, his faithful friend through countless wars, had given himself over to the orders he had received. The two men had been working with re-

lentless urgency in an effort to stop the Jamaican drug
dealer, especially since Long Eddy had taken captives.
For a brief few minutes, before Bolan had turned the
heroin lab into a blazing funeral pyre for contraband
and bandits alike, he had been under the impression
that he had rescued all but one of the USO performers
who were contributing their time and effort to American servicemen engaging in humanitarian aid in Haiti.

It had been a reckless firefight in an arena where
there were plenty of volatile chemicals, but the one
hostage that the Executioner had thought he'd failed
was a young woman whose stage name wasn't much
different from the one she'd used when they'd first
met in Japan. Punk singer Vicious Honey, despite her
nearly anarchist lyrics and music, was still an artist
who gave her all for the U.S. military. With the thought
that Honey might have been dead in a ditch somewhere, Bolan had shut down and became an unstoppable killing machine. Only the blast of burning lab
chemicals hurling him to the sand had snapped him out
of his numbed warrior state.

For a moment Bolan wished that he'd still been in
that war fury, as pulled muscles, bruises, burns and
lacerations were weighing heavily on his shoulders. A
flash of the familiar mix of pink-and-blond hair appeared in the cockpit of the speedboat.

"She's alive!" Grimaldi spoke up. "But you already
knew that."

"Get me close," Bolan said, discarding the M-4.
In the tight quarters of the racing watercraft, even its
compact length would be too unwieldy. This fight was

going to need speed and brutality, so the Executioner drew his Beretta, removing its blunt suppressor so it would move even faster in his grasp. He wrapped his right hand around the handle of his combat knife, his teeth gritted as he knew that violent activity wasn't going to do his injured arm any good.

Pain and convalescence were going to have to wait until a life was saved.

Bullets peppered against the bottom of the helicopter as Grimaldi swung the aircraft close enough for the warrior to jump. With a kick, Bolan hurled himself toward Long Eddy and the renegade Rasta who held Honey by the back of her neck.

For a brief heartbeat the world came to a stop, the roar of the rotor, the chatter of autofire, the rush of wind. Bolan was free from gravity, sailing to a spot between the tall masts of the cigarette boat's airfoil spoiler. Even as he hung weightless, traversing from air to watercraft, he saw Honey's blue eyes lock on him with recognition.

The shock of the diving Executioner left Long Eddy's man staring at him, agape. Long Eddy himself, clutching the wheel of the boat with one hand and a sawed-off shotgun in the other, was also frozen in surprise.

The audacity of Bolan's attack had bought him vital moments as his waffle-treaded boots slammed hard into the fiberglass shell between the spoiler's supports.

Long Eddy recovered his wits, swinging up his shotgun up as Bolan pushed himself forward. Honey twisted, lowering her head, making herself even smaller than her petite five-foot-one. The Rasta struggled to keep Honey's head up with his forearm under her chin, the Uzi in his other hand still aimed up toward the helicopter. The Executioner knew that he was going to take some pain, but he had committed to this, his lightning-fast mind plotting out the angles even as his forearms uncrossed.

The knife in his right hand struck the barrels of the stubby shotgun that Long Eddy raised, steel clanging on steel just a moment before the twin 12-gauge shells within detonated, launching their payload. Struck with twelve .36-caliber pellets just above his ribs, Bolan willed himself past the pain that slashed him from shoulder to right hip. The Beretta 93-R's extended 6.5-inch barrel touched the captor in control of Honey, and as soon as Bolan felt that spongy contact, his finger closed on the trigger.

A 3-round burst tore through the gunman's face, emptying his head of brains as if it were a gore-filled piñata. Honey snaked herself loose from the dead man's grasp, pushing herself away from Long Eddy, who was still in the fight.

His shotgun's payload expended, the Jamaican drug lord sneered and whipped it around like a club, the hot double-muzzle slicing open skin on Bolan's cheek. The twin barrels and their wooden furniture continued swinging after the bloody impact, cracking against the soldier's left wrist. It was almost painful enough for the Executioner to drop his Beretta, but all it succeeded in doing was stopping the gun from aiming at Long Eddy. The only weapon Bolan had was in his right hand, and his right biceps had taken two pellets from the shotgun, the bare limb pouring blood from the injury. Agony seemed to be crushing half of his body, but the Jamaican drug lord was looking to make a far more impressive dent in his adversary's skull with the empty shotgun.

It felt as if Bolan were pushing his knife-wielding fist through molasses, muscles screaming at him to stop even as the double-bladed dagger's tip struck Long Eddy in his chest, between the fourth and fifth buttons of his vividly colored shirt. There was resistance as the knife encountered a Kevlar vest underneath the linen shirt, but Bolan pushed hard with both legs, using their tremendous strength to add to the penetration power of the knife. The Kevlar's ripping gave way to the squishy parting of flesh and the grinding rustle of bone cut by steel.

Blood poured over Long Eddy's lower lip, his big brown eyes bulging in horror.

"Fuck...er..." Eddy gurgled as the Bokor Applegate-Fairbairn fighting blade twisted in the man's chest, tearing arteries and bronchial tissue.

Bolan didn't respond except to bring up the Beretta. A stroke of the trigger left the would-be king of Jamaican crime without half of his face and skull. Bone snagged the knife blade between ribs, and Bolan didn't have the strength to yank it out. He simply released the blade's handle, and Long Eddy's corpse toppled backward over the rail, gangly limbs flying in the air as he struck the water.

Honey had figured out how to work the throttle and

had killed the boat's engines, then turned to Bolan. "You came for me?"

Bolan nodded weakly, collapsing into the pilot's seat now that the danger was over. Less than a hundred yards away, black dorsal fins broke the surface around the splashy froth where Eddy had gone into the Caribbean Sea. "It let me take care of two birds with one stone."

Honey chuckled nervously. "What do I call you now?"

"Friend is good enough," Bolan answered. The trembling young woman gave him a tight hug, her eyes clenched shut so she couldn't see him silently redden as she aggravated his broken rib.

"They were going to sell us," Honey whispered. "The bastards were going to sell us."

Bolan stroked the frightened young woman's hair. "You're too rebellious to be for sale, Honey. You'd have found a way out."

Sooner or later, Bolan was going to have to start the engines and head for land, but right now, he had to soothe a young woman's trauma and recover enough strength to pilot the craft. Above, Jack Grimaldi orbited the Hughes over the speedboat. With luck, Bolan would have a week or three to recover from the injuries he received today, but Long Eddy, the King of the Caribbean, was dead.

Bolan put enough breath together for four words as he watched a shark swim past, a gangly leg in its jaws. "Long live the king."

# CHAPTER TWO

Three couples were entwined in each other's arms on the bobbing yacht that was anchored at sea. They were watching the Caribbean sunset, yet seemed more interested in their partner's curves and supple warmth.

It was an idyllic interlude, the soundtrack provided by an MP3 file pumping out tropic island tunes over the yacht's sound system.

Pierre Fortescue felt a pang of regret for ruining such a perfect romantic vacation, but it was quickly subsumed as he remembered that these were Americans, the people who had withdrawn their approval and allowed the Duvaliers' ceaseless control of Haiti to disappear. Since the end of Papa Doc's and Baby Doc's reign, Fortescue's home nation had fallen into a sewer pit. The worst insult was when the earthquake that he and the rest of his cult had prayed for was misread as the punishment of God against the nation that had bartered their freedom to the Devil.

Fortescue snorted. The gods that he and the Black Avengers spoke with predated the quaint humanist concepts of a supreme being weak enough to let his son be nailed to a tree. The *loa* were no sniveling pacifists, no way in heaven or hell. When the Fortescue family's first Haitian ancestors called them down, their vengeance against France was a total emasculation that had allowed the British, an insane emperor, the Nazis and now the Muslims to overrun them and bring them ruin. The *loa* didn't caress their enemies, they scourged the fools until they were hollow echoes of their former selves.

France was but one crippled victim of the dark lords of voodoo. And now, America and Haiti would feel the harsh caresses of voodoo magic.

The motion of the yacht wasn't sufficient to make it hard for the tall, dark-skinned Fortescue to hop up, grab the rail and haul himself over. There were two young people on the deck, a swarthy young man with black hair, nuzzling into the neck of a young blond woman who looked emaciated except for a pair of swollen breasts too large for her bony torso.

Fortescue, crouching out of sight behind the deckhouse, sneered as he realized that those were probably some of the best breasts that money could buy. Typical whites—so frightened of having an ounce of body fat on them, and yet they were envious of the voluptuous curves of healthy women.

One of his fellow Black Avenger raiders had slipped aboard as he observed the scene, then opened up a small duffel to retrieve the inoculator pistols. Fortescue loaded the first twin-dart cartridge into the breech of the inoculator. The tiny weapons were designed for dealing with animals, and had been stolen from a Florida wildlife ranger station.

Fortescue walked onto the bow, staying low so as not to betray his position, yet craning his neck to see if there was any semblance of alarm on the part of the two couples on the port deck. They, like the couple closest to him, were oblivious to the presence of dark raiders on their craft. Fortescue cleared his throat, and the man looked up in his direction.

Fortescue could see that the young man was a Hispanic, and the young Latino grunted as Fortescue's first dart caught him under his pectoral muscle. The dart wasn't actually an anaesthetic but a quick acting paralytic. The dose froze the young man, rendering him inert, yet not strong enough to stop his lungs. The blonde woman was about to squeal when Fortescue punched his second dart into her, striking her in the stomach. He wasn't certain that if the dart had struck one of those silicone-inflated bags on her chest that it would reach her bloodstream.

The blonde stiffened in paralysis, the paralytic effects of the tubocurarine hitting her like a ton of bricks. The toxin was one of the main chemicals from the primitive jungle poison curare. The young woman's eyes widened with horror as she was unable to move. She was too small, too light, for the dose of toxin that Fortescue had put into her, but as long as her diaphragm was paralyzed, she couldn't make noise. It was better to let her die here, on the yacht.

The young man beside her was strong enough that his chest still rose and fell, lungs working despite the complete loss of strength in his arms and legs. He'd likely survive the dosing with tetrodotoxin, leaving him mentally malleable. It wasn't as if a scrawny, ninety-pound girl would have provided as much of a threat as a 180-pound man, not with the plan proposed by Morrot, the Black Avengers' leader.

Blue eyes looked up pleadingly at Fortescue. The young woman looked as if she wanted to move her lips, minor twitches, but the power of the tubocurarine was just too much for her. It would take upward of a minute or two more for her to suffocate. The young man twitched, able to influence his own body that much, staying alive. He could sense his lover's distress, or at least see that she had stopped breathing.

Fortescue rested his hand on the paralyzed young man's chest, checking for a heartbeat. You'll forget her quickly enough, he thought. It was a pointless gesture, the youth couldn't hear his thought, and he really didn't care about his torment, but that brief show of compassion was something he felt the urge to give.

As soon as the Haitian had his dart gun loaded, he nodded to his companion. A third of their number was waiting in reserve, ready to hit anyone who wasn't put down by Fortescue and friend's darts.

Four quiet puffs of $CO_2$ launched their pointed, toxin-laden missiles with stealthy quickness. The two young couples were rendered immobile with little fuss or muss. One of the young men struggled, his lungs failing due to an unforeseen bout of asthmatic response, but two losses abovedeck were little loss to Morrot's operational plans. Fortescue waved his assistants on to scoop up the unconscious ones, ignoring the flopped corpses on the decks.

"How many belowdecks?" Fortescue asked.

"Register says three crew and another couple," his

ally, Cornelius, said, looking at the laminated paper. "Do we take the crew?"

"They're strong and will be useful," Fortescue said. "Besides, these men aren't true believers. Just because they share the same skin color means nothing. They are pagans, adherents to heathen gods."

"They think the same about us," Cornelius answered. "So, it's only fair."

"It is unconscionable that they consider us savages, worshipping carcasses impaled to planks or a burning shrubbery," Fortescue replied. "When we make our move, their world's streets will run with their blood."

Cornelius's smile was broad and infectious. "Blood shed by their own hands."

Fortescue nodded sagely. "Reload, and we'll head belowdecks. Get Gallad."

The three Black Avengers headed below the deck.

THE STRAPS CUT into Guillermo Rojas's wrists as consciousness returned to him, his arms twitching futilely in response to his feeling of restraint. Rojas wanted to turn his head, but a leather thong across his forehead and gripping his chin kept him still.

All he could remember was Stephanie, her gorgeous blue eyes alit with horror, foam streaming over her lips. Then there was the black shadow, wielding a strange, sci-fi-looking handgun, that reached out to touch his chest, as if to soothe his worries over the gurgling, drowning girl who trembled beside him. Rage and grief spun in his strap-bound chest, his fury an impotent storm as he didn't know where the midnight-skinned marauder was, and grief over the sweet, blue-eyed creature he'd fallen for. Stephanie Coulton, tiny and privileged, had found him as beautiful as he'd found her, and had brought him down for a spring getaway despite her father's disgust that she was consorting with someone that the man felt was destined to be a pool boy or a gardener, not her social equal.

She'd loved him, she'd defied her father, and now he knew what her face looked like when her lungs shut down, jammed with histamine. He knew the symptoms of bronchoconstriction well—Rojas was a medical student, only a year away from his first internship. His mind reeled as he searched for a reason why he'd just lain there, helpless as she died, suffocating.

His mouth was dry, and he wasn't able to speak. His pharmaceutical knowledge simply wasn't enough to determine what had happened, but he was certain that it wasn't any form of anaesthetic. No "knockout drug" acted so quickly against a person, but he knew that there were toxins out there that were used for rapid incapacitation. He'd been present at emergency intubations, and knew anaesthesiologists utilized drugs that caused instant paralysis—which was why intubation teams acted instantly when the patients were given their injections. As soon as the subject went limp, the intubation tube was put down the windpipe and into the main bronchial tube.

Such a drug acted instantly, and was capable of stopping someone's breathing, indeed it was counted on to prevent reflexive movement during surgery. Handled right, it could render a big man like him immobile, easily captured, but a dose that would leave him helpless was far too much for a girl who was half his weight. Muscles frozen, Stephanie was doomed the minute the toxin hit her bloodstream.

A fingertip caressed his cheek, and Rojas grimaced as his effort to turn was again stymied by the rig that held his head in place. Tendons cracked as they tried to move a completely immobilized head.

"The first one awake, good."

Rojas tried to open his mouth, but he finally figured out the dryness in his mouth—a leather "tongue" was stuffed into it, and it was part of the multistrap system that held him immobile. All he could do was murmur past the gag.

"Yes, so sorry about not allowing you to speak, but unlike my favorite visionary, I do not care to listen to the wails and laments of my experiments," the voice said, a lilting French accent weighing heavily on his words. His timber was deep, its resonant echo making Rojas imagine that it came not from a throat, but a bottomless gullet that would be more at home on a shark.

Rojas snorted, trying to trumpet out some form of sound. His eyes craned to see the shadowy man flitting in the darkness at the edges of his peripheral vision. His chewed on the leather pad that gagged him until his teeth started to hurt.

"Such fire. I appreciate it," the French-accented shadow man said. "It gives me a challenge."

Rojas's blood chilled at the ominous sound of that statement. Dark brown eyes swiveled in their sockets, grasping for more than a blurred glimpse of the smear of motion that possessed the doom-laden French accent that taunted him. Fingernails scratched along his jaw-line, and the young man caught a glimpse of the man's digits, callused and long, bearing the color of straight, strong coffee.

"Oh, you want to see me?" his tormentor asked.

Rojas managed an affirmative sound.

A face loomed into the light over Rojas's left shoulder. The shadowy figure bore a distinguished face that was handsome with middle age's wisdom and grace, his broad, flat nose the only sign of any imperfection as the bridge had an odd kink in the middle of it. Rojas almost felt relief that it was a fairly normal-looking man, not some chimeric predator, when dread snuck into his heart, a frightened tingle that zipped through his chest and rolled down his arms to his fingertips. Something on the other side was wrong, horribly wrong.

The man stepped out from behind Rojas's chair and turned toward him. The oversize, milky-white eye glared out of the fused mass of flesh that was the remnants of what used to be human features. The eye, three concentric rings of varying hues of white, glared at him, and Rojas would have kicked and screamed had he retained any ability to move. Instead, a high-pitched whine blared through his nostrils, the closest approximation of a scream of horror that he could manage with a mouth stuffed with leather.

"My name is Dr. Morrot," the man said.

Rojas had initially thought he'd awakened to a nightmare, a fever-dream where Stephanie had died slowly and horribly and where he had been kidnapped by monsters. He realized that the first of his waking moments were a respite of peace compared to the wave of insanity washing over him. Bound helpless in front of a deformed madman with a nausea-inducing orb where an eye should have been, tormented by a voice that belonged to a devil, not a human, Rojas's arms, laden with lean, strong muscle, flexed against his restraints, but they didn't budge. His legs tried to kick, to twist, but they, too, were thwarted by the trap that Morrot had placed him in.

Rojas could hear that others in the room had begun to awaken. Their nostrils blared and bleated as they made an effort to speak, alarm filling those nasal sounds as they realized that they, too, were immobilized.

Morrot leaned in, licking Rojas's shoulder. "Mmm. The salty taste of fear, accompanied by the buttery scent of panic. Of course, the smell is really a byproduct of the body's elimination of potassium, but as a medical student, you already knew that, right, Mr. Rojas?"

Rojas wanted to bellow, to throw that trivia back into Morrot's ugly, misshapen face. He'd wondered if he were free, if he'd have the courage to punch this spindly figure standing in front of him. However, the baleful eye glaring unblinkingly at him, sagging in its socket, was as paralyzing as the dart that had taken him on the yacht.

"Good morning, children!" Morrot boomed, his slender arms spread wide. Now that the disfigured doctor had stepped back, Rojas could see the man in full. He wore a short-sleeved, olive-colored T-shirt that was covered by a maroon-and-purple-stained butcher's apron. The slender limbs were deceptive in their thinness, as Morrot was a tall man, easily six foot six, and those arms were corded with muscle that flexed with every movement. The horrible damage to the left side of the man's face extended down his neck and to his upper left arm, stringy tendrils of skin spiderwebbed over a raw, red surface.

Around him, Rojas's companions from the yacht let out their fright in any way they could, from guttural throat constrictions to piercing whines through nostrils. Morrot seemed to bathe in the captives' fear, letting it wash over him like a refreshing drizzle breaking up a steamy, hot and ugly day.

Morrot took a deep breath, then lowered his gaze to the prisoners as a masked assistant, wearing a white coat and scrub pants approached him, carrying a tray laden with syringes. "It's time to open your minds and say 'ah.'"

Rojas and his companions tried to scream past their gags, but all that came out were panicked whines through their noses.

THE YOUNG PUNK rocker paused as she stood beside the idling Jeep, regarding a convalescing Mack Bolan as he swung in a hammock. He could still taste the hint of cherry on his lips, the silken softness of her pink-and-blond hair a fresh sensation on his fingers. Honey's dark red lips pursed as she blew him a kiss.

Bolan casually caught it with his good hand, and he returned a salute to the tough woman. The driver of the Jeep leaned on the horn to get Honey's attention, eliciting a middle finger for him. She gave one last lingering look to the soldier, then jumped into the back.

Tires ground at the dirt road, kicking up a cloud that did nothing to hamper the verdant slashes of color beneath a sky as crystal clear blue as a painting. This place was paradise, so close to the beach that he could smell the salt of the sea and gentle rush of waves. Children carried surfboards from a small hut, waving to the soldier as he reclined in the hammock.

Bolan waved back to the kids. Honey had arranged for him to stay with a friend of hers, Anton Spaulding, at the Jamaican surf camp he owned. Spaulding was an exceptional host, laid back and gentle, the epitome of the surfer lifestyle, having built his dream home in the pleasant, peaceful woods.

Spaulding walked toward the hammock, clad only in blue-and-white palm-frond-patterned surfer shorts. His skin was browned from constant exposure to the sun, his hair a dirty blend of sun-bleached blond and dark brunette that fell haphazardly over his forehead and ears. His blue eyes gleaming over a broken nose.

"Shame to see her go," he said, leaning on one of the trees holding Bolan's hammock.

"She has things to do. Better things than looking after me," Bolan replied with a chuckle.

Spaulding smirked. "I don't know. Looked like leaving was harder for her than pulling a tooth."

"Wasn't easy for me, either," Bolan said. Glass

clinked, and he turned to see Spaulding hold up a pair of beer bottles.

"I'm not sure if these will go well with your painkillers."

Bolan smiled. "I try to limit the chemicals that go into me. Alcohol, too, but…"

"When it's time to relax, you got the beer."

The two men chuckled. A convulsive twitch of muscle over one of Bolan's healing ribs sent a spark of pain rushing through him. Still, it was a worthwhile exchange. With a twist, Bolan rolled out of the hammock. The stitch in his side started to fade as he accepted the beer bottle.

"Finally moving now that Honey's not around?"

Bolan shot a glance at Spaulding. "What, you're going to be my nursemaid now?"

Spaulding shook his head. "No way, man. But she must have threatened you to keep you lying down."

"Combination of threats and pain."

"When do you think you'll be out to join us in the butter?" Spaulding asked.

Bolan had to remember he was at a surf camp to decipher that the bronzed young man was inquiring about when Bolan would take a few spins on a surfboard. "Once I don't feel like I'm being kicked in the chest when I laugh. And by then, I should be on my way out of here."

"It'd be a shame."

Bolan frowned. "Trouble finds me easily. It'd be a shame if it landed here."

Spaulding began chuckling again. "This place is

as far from trouble as you can get. That's why Honey
dropped you off here."

"I hope so," Bolan answered.

# CHAPTER THREE

The crystal clear waters of the Caribbean ocean felt good.

Though Mack Bolan continued to feel the lingering ache of his broken ribs, he was still capable of kicking his feet as they dangled off of the back of the surfboard. He was propelling himself through crests and furrows in the water, aiming the tip of the fiberglass "plank" at oncoming swells.

The soldier had surfed a few times between missions. The sport was one that was easy to pick up, but one of those things that took a lifetime to master. Bolan's excellent conditioning and agility put him above the rank of rookie. The twenty-first-century board he was on was even more accommodating to his aching form as it was lightweight, but designed to support more than the weight of slight-limbed youths. Bolan could easily lift this plank, and it was shaped so that it could keep him afloat with any balanced weight on top.

The exercise provided by his efforts at balance on the fiberglass hull was at once gentle on his tender ribs yet invigorating to his shoulders and abdominal muscles. Arms and legs, constantly flexing to make the most of his momentum when the wave caught him up and hurled him on, were eating up the exertion, re-strengthening their too-long-inert spring-steel tautness.

As Spaulding soared past, hurtling along a "left"—a wave that's tube extended from right to left—he gave Bolan a thumb's up before he ducked down, letting the cresting wave form a pipe over his head. The soldier had seen the man tilting, pushing against the rising concave of the wave, seeming to defy gravity as he ground along the wall of water. Once inside the pipe, Spaulding was in a world that had to be experienced to be appreciated, a tunnel of serenity where a man or woman could disappear for a slice of time that seemed to last longer on the inside than outside, embraced by the ocean's enormous power without any of the punishment of its potential death grip.

Spaulding glided along the Jamaican shore, where there were no flesh-rending reefs, no bone-shattering rocks. Here was a place where the youngest students—known in the sporting community as "groms"—and veteran surfers could frolic. It was where this particular, injured soldier could rehabilitate without risk of exacerbating his injuries.

Bolan had finally picked up one of Spaulding's spare boards when Martin Rudd had shown him the physical rejuvenation qualities of surfing. Rudd had been a winter extreme sports photographer, a man who had skied and snowboarded down untamed mountainsides, skirting trees and boulders in search of a new day's shot of adrenaline mixed with the majestic glory of snowcapped mountains splayed out in front of him. That ended when Rudd, skiing through a gap of boulders, snagged the tip of one ski on a jutting rock and spiral-fractured his right femur. Left with one thighbone an inch shorter than the other, Rudd had expected never to take to a slope again.

Now, the forty-something "extreme" sportsman had found renewed strength and freedom on the pounding surf, enough to get him back onto mountainsides, if not doing stunts, then at least able to keep up and photograph the new wave of somersaulting snow devils. Rudd still suffered from a permanent limp, but it was from the disparate lengths of his legs, not because of the pain of a now fused and healed femur. The truncated leg had been allowed to heal, regaining much of its lost might and vigor.

Bolan had first followed Rudd into the butter five days before, but the soldier had one pang of regret though he was no longer subjected to searing pain like a knife in his lungs after doing wind sprints on the sand. The injuries that had kept him here for this brief span of heaven were no longer a hindrance. He easily hoisted young groms onto his shoulders as they begged to see the world from eight feet in the air. Staying here for more than another day or two, healing, was no longer an option.

The Executioner hopped to a crouched position, his feet and hands on the board as he settled his balance, the sleek shell maintaining its forward momentum as it rushed into the coming swell. As he steered the board by gripping its smooth sides, he got the right angle and rose to his full height. His mass pushed the board against the opposing force of the coming wave, and in

a heartbeat, he was lifted effortlessly onto the crest.
The power of the ocean beneath him was akin to an
Asian elephant he'd ridden in Thailand when battling
a Chinese heroin ring. Like that powerful pachyderm,
the wave didn't notice Bolan's added mass, continuing on its course without pause. In the Thai jungles,
he had been able to steer the beast through a den of vicious Chinese gunmen, the mighty elephant carrying
him like a living tank through the battle.

The ocean, however, dwarfed that seemingly endless might, accepting no commands from knee prods
against its neck. Where Bolan had been only barely
able to direct his pachyderm on its charge of destruction, the Caribbean Sea accepted no commands, took
no orders. Instead the soldier had to aim the surfboard,
his sharp eyes and instincts feeling for furrows and
paths of least resistance as the wave rose behind him.

It was exhilarating and humbling in the same pri-
mal instant. Bolan had the freedom of a winged god,
yet was at the mercy of cosmic gravitational vortices
that hurled the Earth and the moon around the sun at
millions of miles per hour. Balanced precariously, he
skimmed over the surface of the ocean as swift as an
arrow, mere pivots of his hips enabling him to adjust
his course, compensating for gravity and the swelling
sea beneath him. It wasn't true flight, just like his para-
chuting or his free falls, it was "falling with style" to
quote one movie. Still, with the wind in his face and
the sea at his back, he hurled along, arms spread to
take in the sun and the breeze, drinking in the wonders

of the Earth before the wave's push and gravity's pull overwhelmed the delicate balance.

He finally ditched into four-foot-deep water, the incompressible fluid cushioning his torso and head as he dived in, pulling up before he dug his face into the sediment at the bottom. Behind him, the neoprene leash around his ankle connecting him to his board yanked the fiberglass hull into his ankle and shin. His lower legs no longer sparked sharp jolts of pain from the glancing impacts as the board cracked on them. Bolan's bruises had developed into "surf bumps" days ago.

With a shrug of his long arms and strong shoulders, he propelled himself to the surface. The right shoulder's cut had long since closed, and the skin fused shut without fear of opening up again after its two-week reprieve. One stroke had brought him up to suck in air, and he twisted to grab his board, scrabbling on top of it. A deep intake of air no longer was an exercise in masochism. There was still pain, but it was a dull, throbbing pulse, telling Bolan that the flexing bones of his ribs were almost good enough for him to return to duty without fear of physical failure.

A day, two at the most, and the Executioner would launch himself back into action.

Spaulding had been right, Bolan mused as he kicked out to meet more swells. It would have been criminal to have lived in this stretch of Earth where land, sea and sky intersected to form the surest proof that the universe didn't solely exist to punish humanity. Joy and mercy were rare sights in the spheres where the Executioner traveled, and he could easily have fallen into the fallacious trap that reality held only cruelty and suffering. Even a minute basking under this sun, smelling this forest, listening to the hushed whispers of this surf, had washed away the caked layers of cynicism that had threatened to darken his heart of hearts.

Life was good here.

Bolan couldn't feel disheartened by the duties that pulled him away from this affirming environment. The tranquil peace, broken only by the laughter of children and the crash of waves was a reminder of the things that he fought for.

This gentle realm was the spur for the Executioner's War Everlasting. The violence that Bolan brought to bear against the savagery of criminals, terrorists and other violent predators was a firebreak. He was the wall between civilization and the corrupters who looked for an easy way to feed whatever their greedy hearts desired. A week among kids and beach bums had renewed his touch with humanity. It returned faces to what could have too easily become an abstract concept of innocence, and enabled him to return to the shadows around the world, stalking those who'd bolster themselves with pain and suffering.

Bolan mounted the surfboard, dangling a leg on either side of it as if he were riding a fiberglass horse. He ran his fingers through his wet black hair, cool blue eyes scanning the horizon where the sky drooped to meet the Caribbean Sea.

It was beautiful, another glorious sight in a world full of them. Though Bolan would soon have to leave, he kept a realistic appreciation of the seascape. He had been on every continent in the world, and had visited most of the major island chains, summoned to engagements against murderers and conquerors on every one. This was far from his first visit to Jamaica and given the piracy, drug smuggling and other pursuits of the criminal mind, the Executioner would once more come back to the island nation that held this small cradle of placid joy.

His fighting energies had been built back up, and they were trying to rush Bolan's injured parts to heal so that they could turn themselves toward productive ventures in the Executioner's endless crusade to protect all that was good and civilized in the world. He was thinking about the hints and whispers of trouble that hummed in the daily news, clues that would be far more blatant if Bolan had access to the threat matrix gathered at Stony Man Farm, a plug-in roster of unrest and violence that were symptoms of diseases to which he had to bring his cleansing flame.

The most blatant bit of news was the discovery of a yacht found adrift, no crew on board, and no signs of violence. Several young college students, here on spring break, had disappeared without a trace. It was nothing new in Jamaican waters as the fabled "pirates of the Caribbean" had evolved over the centuries, trading in their flintlocks for M-16s and their rowboats for Zodiac rafts with high-horsepower engines on the back. There were other small news passages about a couple of fishing boats that had gone missing. However, since the crews weren't made up of beautiful, young American tourists, the news agencies didn't care about them. It had been two fishing trawlers, their combined crews at thirty, also gone as if snatched by the ghosts of the sea.

One part of Bolan wanted to kick his surfboard out past the breakers and carve some more waves, but the Executioner was already mentally organizing a map approximated from the missing fishermen and tourists' last-known locations. He'd call to confirm his estimations, either pulling in favors from local law enforcement, or in a last resort, taking his inquiries electronically to the Farm to get the cyberteam's assistance. The only other snarl in his plans to take war to the mystery kidnappers was that most of his gear had gone back to the States with Jack Grimaldi while Bolan recovered from his wounds. All he had with him right now was an Atomic Aquatics titanium dive knife in a sheath strapped to his right calf. The closest thing to firepower that he possessed were two 9-mm Beretta pistols in a lockbox, hidden from view of both children and gun thieves looking to make some money on the black market. Normally, Bolan would have tried to keep the discreet little Beretta PX4 Compact concealed, but shirtless and without a belt for his drawstring-waisted surfer shorts, he had no options.

Luckily for Bolan, among surfers, dive knives in calf sheaths were about as common as cell phone holsters in New York City.

It still wasn't the kind of arsenal that the Executioner would need to blitz a piracy operation, but Bolan could take his first steps, making do with weapons acquired from his enemies. Low supplies did little to slow a Bolan blitz, such as when he was living hand to mouth with barely enough money to buy gunpowder to make his own ammunition.

Another wave broke over his thighs, Bolan and the board bobbing in the water. A few more waves wouldn't hurt, and in fact, they'd complete his regimen of exercise for the day. Then, after toweling off, the soldier would have a chance to begin his research and equipment assembly for this night's stalk. He'd be done in time for sunset, the Executioner's time. Then he could hunt through the shadows, using darkness as his most powerful ally in dealing with the foes who outnumbered him, but rarely could outfight or outplan him.

For now, the sun was out, and as a wise man had once said, there was no disinfectant like daylight. Any effort to find the parasitic hijackers and kidnappers during normal hours would prove to be inefficient.

The Executioner admonished himself. Too often, professionals had found themselves in deadly situations, bleeding and or dying because they were "in the white," a level of awareness that was a total lack of preparedness or consciousness of surroundings. Living that way was a sure means of finding oneself in the path of a knife or a bullet. Bolan had only survived all these missions, all these wars, because his mind was sharp, his senses peeled and his reflexes primed to go.

Movement had tripped Bolan's instincts, the preliminary rustle of foliage indicative of a man crashing through a forest. Peripheral vision and hearing had picked up on that, and to Bolan, they were as obvious as signal flares. He turned to spot the source of the crashing—a haggard-looking figure that emerged onto the sand.

Bolan took in the details of the man, and with spine-stiffening realization, he saw the machete dangling in the newcomer's hand.

With a kick, Bolan freed his foot from the board's leash. He speared into the surf with lightning quickness. Even as he swam to shore, powerful chest and shoulder muscles exploding with force that thrust him to land, another detail came to the forefront of his thoughts.

The man's eyes.

They were blank, unfocused, even though his lips were peeled back from his teeth in an enraged rictus.

Bolan had encountered chemically reprogrammed opponents before. They were driven by their orders, sanity ripped from their drugged minds. The poor, brainwashed zombies felt little pain and even less restraint, using every ounce of their strength at such a rate that even when they recovered from their altered mental states, their bodies were wrecks.

Because of that wild abandon, their strength pushed beyond their normal limits.

Even at his strongest, Bolan was hard-pressed to deal with these blank-eyed murderers.

The Executioner dug his feet into the sand, pushing toward the man. He would make no excuses for failure.

Not when children were in the path of a machete-wielding maniac.

THE CREATURE THAT HAD once been Guillermo Rojas winced as the first rays of light poured in from the opened doors of the shipping container on the back of the truck. With that first touch of day, he burst through the door with savage fury and speed. He didn't notice the harsh gravel that sliced the soles of his feet.

What he was aware of was the extra weight in his right hand. Memories were few and far between in his chemically landscaped brain, but he recognized the object as a fearsome weapon, almost as long as a sword. He didn't know the word for it—he had no more words for anything. He did remember the depthless joy he felt when he had sunk such a thing into human flesh, a cathartic jolt of vengeance that rolled through him.

More thoughts coalesced in his fevered mind, clearing through his fog of madness. Pain and terror washed over him in unyielding waves, phantom memories of injuries inflicted at the hands of people—blacks, whites, men, women, adults and children. All of their faces and appearances were associated with agony and impotent horror. His only anchor was a single voice cutting through the omnipresent nightmare.

"Kill them!" the resonating voice boomed. "Kill them and end the fire in your blood!"

Rojas understood only two words, but they were all he really needed now. He had to lash out and destroy everyone because they were all a part of the torture he'd been subjected to. All the addled medical student knew was that humanity as a whole had turned on him, scourging his flesh and sanity. He also had a hint, a feint trace of another loss, a beautiful golden angel.

That pushed Rojas forward, and he staggered on, hearing the lilt of music and bubbling laughter of joy. He knew the sounds of the creatures who had left him to suffer unspeakable horrors.

What Rojas hadn't seen were his fellow brainwashed assassins, two more men and two young women, all wielding machetes. The five of them charging toward the surf camp's sounds. Rojas had been programmed to ignore them, his psyche masterfully twisted so as to allow Morrot's killers to work in groups without attacking each other. Injected with amphetamines and twisted by a multimedia assault that filled them with false memories of a living hell, the people were no longer human. They were dedicated attack dogs, no longer possessing pause or reason.

The trees and foliage between Rojas and his prey were little impediment to him. Despite branches and blades of tall grass gouging his chest and legs, he barreled through the undergrowth. The others were slower, or simply taking the path of least resistance.

Nothing would keep him from the bloody revenge he sought.

Not even the man who charged out of the water, naked except for surfer shorts and a black sheath on his leg.

Rojas opened his mouth, releasing a wild screech, raising the machete to attack.

# CHAPTER FOUR

Any doubt that Mack Bolan possessed that the machete-wielding Latino was reduced to an animalistic state disappeared when he released an unholy howl that split the air, turning the heads of a half dozen kids lounging and listening to music on the sand. Running through water and in wet sand felt like trying to pull his feet out of the tendrils of a hungry octopus, but his long legs gave him enough of a stride to reach the edge of the water.

The attacker's maniacal eyes flitted toward the prone children who weren't aware of their danger. Bolan knew he only had a few moments to stop him.

"Over here!" he called, the boom of his voice pinning the drugged man's dead, cold eyes to him.

Another bestial hiss erupted from him and he swung his machete toward Bolan. In any confrontation between human and terrain chopper, the foot-and-a-half-long blade won every time, so Bolan didn't bother with blocking. He sidestepped, avoiding the swing that started from above the attacker's head and ended up slicing only air.

Bolan considered drawing the Atomic dive knife, but he could see that his opponent was young and despite his scratches and blank gaze, it was possible that he was an American. It didn't take much more than a gauge of his age to realize that this could be one of the kidnap victims, and as such, one of the many innocent lives that he'd sworn to protect.

In the Executioner's world, there was no such thing as an acceptable loss. Once the machete reached the nadir of its arc, Bolan lunged, putting both hands around his opponent's forearm. With a hard yank, Bolan pulled the man's face into his left shoulder, letting the uninjured joint take the brunt of the collision. Jaws snapped shut with a sickening crunch and the drugged maniac's eyes rolled in their sockets.

Such chemically enhanced foes were mostly immune to the pain of conventional punches, bullets and blades, but the Executioner was a master of all manner of combat. As such, he knew the weak points of the human body, and the trunk line of nerves just under the ear and behind the jaw was one such place that even in a haze of painkilling amphetamines would stop a person with one blow. The would-be killer jarred into submission, Bolan turned his attention toward disarming him.

A shriek from behind—the spine-chilling wail of a terrified child—turned him away from his attempt to render his attacker harmless. Two more figures rushed into view, blades held over their heads. Suddenly the Executioner found himself outnumbered, and his concern for the suffering of his opponent disappeared. With both hands holding the man's forearm still, he knifed his knee into it. With a snapped ulna and humerus, the man's grip on the machete disappeared.

That accomplished, Bolan released the limb and brought his left elbow up hard, another crashing blow across the man's jaw that threw him into the sand, senseless and barely mobile.

He turned to see a growling young woman with ratty black hair rushing in pursuit of a ten-year-old boy, her intent to bury her blade in the kid's back. Her rage was so focused on the youth that the Executioner was able to catch her by surprise, hammering his right forearm across her throat in a clothesline maneuver. The healed stab wound released a spike of complaint, and it felt as if the young woman had run headfirst into his ribs, but at the end of the collision, she was flat on her back and Bolan still stood.

She screeched in frustration, her blank, feral gaze locked on the man who'd stopped her. She still held on to her machete, but Bolan hopped over her and landed one heel hard into the inside of her elbow. The joint popped loudly, and she, too, was disarmed, but clawing, jagged fingernails sliced into the warrior's right thigh, planing off ribbons of dermis.

Bolan cracked his heel against the young woman's jaw, feeling it dislocate under the force of his back kick, and while it cut off her animalistic growls, she was still reaching up with her left arm to hook her gnarled fingers into his crotch. He sidestepped her effort to geld him and gave her another kick, this time to her temple. Even as he did so, he caught sight of his male attacker in his peripheral vision, bursting up from the sand in a rampaging rush.

The Executioner turned and met the man's charge

with his right elbow striking him in the collarbone. Through his arm, Bolan could feel the snap of his opponent's clavicle, and the drug-crazed killer stopped as if he'd struck a brick wall. Even stunned from Bolan's countermeasure, the man lashed out blindly with his left hand, fingers reaching for Bolan's face where they could tear skin and burst one of his eyeballs. The soldier straightened his right arm, a palm strike deflecting those blinding fingernails as he hit the man's other forearm hard.

A wail of frustration all but split open Bolan's right eardrum, leaving the soldier wide open for his attacker's next tactic. The Executioner grimaced as teeth tore into the skin of his right shoulder, splitting flesh and releasing a torrent of blood down his biceps.

With a grimace, Bolan brought up his left palm, jamming the heel of his hand between the eyes of the attacker. It took every ounce of precision not to strike the man in the nose and drive splinters of bone into his brain, but even so, the young Hispanic was going to feel the effects of his concussion for a long time. The blow literally lifted his attacker off Bolan's shoulder and sent him crashing into the sand.

The young woman he'd clotheslined took the brief moments of scuffle as an opportunity to rise into a crouch. Her hand was nearly around the haft of her machete. Bolan regretted the need to cripple her, but she was determined to carve up a fellow human being. He kicked her in the wrist, snapping it like a twig and knocking her into the sand. Her howl was not of pain, it was too forceful, and her bared teeth were poised to rip open Bolan's calf. He pivoted and snapped his heel into her forehead with the same force he'd use to kick open a locked door.

If she survived, she'd need plenty of physical therapy to use both of her hands again, and Bolan wasn't certain he'd restrained himself enough to avoid giving her brain damage. She was still, for now, and that was all that mattered because there was a third killer on the loose, a fourth and a fifth now in view.

It was as if someone had released a pack of velociraptors onto the beach, bestial shrieks filling the air. Bolan was already bleeding, though no arteries had been bitten, and he'd only dealt with a young man and an even smaller woman. He watched Spaulding wrestling with one of the attackers, a screeching little woman with dirty blond hair and thick legs that had wrapped around his torso.

The surf camp owner's face was a crimson mask, and his wobbly legs betrayed severe blood loss or head trauma—perhaps both. As it was, Spaulding was still fighting, holding one at bay while the other two, both young men, were on the rampage. A fourteen-year-old boy stood his ground between one of the assailants and two eight-year-olds. His courage was admirable, but the machete severed his right hand as he held it up to the drug-crazed berserker.

Bolan didn't have time to make choices, he charged the would-be killer who was about to take more body parts away from the teen. Three long strides turned into a leap, and Bolan hooked his arm around the head and neck of the machete swinger. Two hundred twenty pounds of lean muscle and hard-forged combat skill combined to make the flying tackle into an impact that hammered both men into the ground. Sand flew as the drugged assassin broke Bolan's fall, and perhaps more than a few ribs.

The crash was hard enough to spin the machete out of his hand, but that only meant that he had a meth-fueled wrestler on the other side of this fight. Bolan didn't see the looping left that whipped around and struck him in the back of his head. It was an eye-crossing blow, and because he hadn't loosened up to roll with the punch, it felt as if his brains were sloshing around inside his skull.

Despite the recent impediment, Bolan could see the berserker's right fist heading straight to his face. He lowered his head swiftly, swinging it into the on-rushing knuckles like a wrecking ball. Fingers cracked as they struck the hard curve of bone at his hairline. That was why the Executioner had used the heel of his hand and his foot on the foreheads of his prior two opponents—the head was a tough mass of bone while knuckles were relatively fragile. Even though his foe's right fist was now a useless jumble of bent fingers, Bolan felt the clawing fingers tearing at his nape and the back of his head. The short wisps of black hair back there were drenched with blood as nails tore skin.

"Enough," Bolan grunted as he brought up his knee and twisted his opponent down so that he took the kick between his shoulder blades. The heavy verte-brae around his spinal cord was more than enough to prevent the man from ending up crippled, but not by much. Breath escaped his lungs in a fetid explosion.

Bolan took that brief second to slam his elbow into the attacker's sternal notch. He tried not to let his anger over a crippled boy color his response, but the elbow chop struck the former machete marauder in his xyphoid process, another juncture of nerves and muscle that when struck properly could render a man helpless and breathless until he passed out. Too hard, and the target would die. Too soft, and with lungs full of air, it would just hurt.

The man bent backward over Bolan's knee froze, his mouth stretched like a landed fish's as it tried to suck in air, but foiled by unresponsive nerves and muscles. The soldier shoved the marauder off his knee and dropped him in the sand. His first instinct was to tend to the fourteen-year-old whose agonized screams echoed in his conscience, but there was another maniac on the loose with a wicked blade. He moved away from the Jamaican boy reluctantly. He had to locate the fifth of the attackers.

The Executioner turned when a strangled death cry escaped Spaulding's throat. The dirty-blond psychotic was fighting to rip her chopper out of Spaulding's skull where it had gotten stuck. Bolan charged toward her, knocking her off the latest addition to his collection of the friendly dead. She couldn't have been half of Bolan's weight, so when he shoulder-blocked her in the upper chest, it was like a freight train flattening a compact car. She flew off Spaulding, landing ten feet away, not in much condition to do anything more than gasp for breath.

He took a half of a second to evaluate her condition. Her hands were folded up into the air, twitching at the end of her forearms. Any movement now consisted of involuntary spasms as he'd knocked her completely senseless.

That would do, for now. Bolan had one more menace to stop.

A strange pop filled the air, and the Executioner turned to see Rudd holding his surfboard up, the fifth attacker's bloody machete lodged in its body.

Bolan broke into a hard run, his long legs pistoning against the sand. Blood rushed, a torrent of thunder rolling through his brain at the same breakneck speed he charged the man attacking Rudd. It was a battle of wills between the two. The machete had been rammed into the surfboard's fiberglass frame, and the drugged killer was trying to rip it free. It would be only instants before the assassin decided that the struggle wasn't worth it, and he'd go at the surfer with teeth and nails.

Bolan had been on the receiving end of those savage attacks. He didn't doubt that Rudd would end up with his throat chewed out or his eyes burst.

At the last moment, the soldier lowered his head and shoulder-blocked the drugged berserker in the small of the back, the force of his impact hurling the brainwashing victim ten feet past Rudd, landing him in the surf. The splash of water over his body didn't do anything to clarify the killer's mind as he leaped back to his feet with unnatural speed and strength. Bolan knew that a tackle like he'd given this man would have left anyone else writhing in pain. Even Bolan's shoulder ached from that contact.

"Well, come on!" Bolan shouted at the blank-eyed man. He couldn't have been more than twenty-one, but he appeared to have been on a football team. The youth in front of him was as big as the Executioner, and had a thicker musculature, making the soldier think of a linebacker. Tanned and blond, he was undoubtedly an American, and this one would be strong enough to twist Bolan's head off his shoulders thanks to the chemical cocktail that had reduced him to a feral, froth-mouthed berserker.

Bolan had tried muscle, and ended up slamming into a brick wall, jarred himself by the very impact that had saved Rudd. Pure strength wasn't going to be enough to end this conflict because if he struck any harder, he'd kill the young man. It was time to outfight, using his intellect. He summoned up his best "drill sergeant" voice and taunted the berserker again, "Kill me!"

That order spurred the linebacker-size attacker to charge, blind rage spurring him on. Bolan threw himself at the charging drug-crazed assassin, but he aimed low, striking the man across the thighs and flipping him head over heels. The berserker tumbled into the sand, throwing up a cloud, and the thud that resounded from his fall was a powerful drumbeat. The big killer's eyes were now unfocused, dazed from the crash, and Bolan didn't waste a single moment, scissoring his legs around his neck.

With all the leverage and strength of his calves and

ankles pressing on either side of the marauder's neck, Bolan had him locked in a true sleeper hold, not pinching the windpipe shut but pressing the knots of bone around his ankles against blood vessels that fed the brain. Deprived of fresh oxygen, the killer's fevered brain faltered, losing consciousness even as the berserker clawed at Bolan's shins.

The soldier grimaced, but with a proper sleeper hold applied, the would-be murderer was slumped, out cold in the sand.

"What the hell is going on?" Rudd asked, his voice shaky.

"Check on Antoine. One of these crazies chopped off his hand," Bolan ordered.

Rudd paused, blinking at the bloodied and battered Executioner in front of him.

"Move it!"

Rudd's senses returned to him and he rushed to the badly wounded teen's side. Bolan knew that he'd have to find some form of cord to apply a tourniquet to the stump; direct pressure wasn't going to work.

Luckily, the maniacal assassin had a belt on. Bolan whipped it out of the unconscious brute's belt loops and started to stagger to Antoine's side.

The only warning that the Executioner had of an attack were the grunts and pants of the attacking woman. For Bolan and his finely tuned reflexes, that was more than enough. The young woman had murdered Spaulding, so a gentle response wasn't in the cards. She was within a few feet when her throat released the shrill beginning notes of an animalistic howl, but Bolan cut it off with a raised elbow that exploded her nose and tore her cheek open.

She hit the ground, and Bolan sighed. He'd let his emotions get the better of him, and now a brainwashed young woman was disfigured, bleeding and unconscious in the sand. He tore himself away from his self-reproach.

A boy needed medical attention, and Bolan's battlefield first aid was going to keep him from bleeding to death.

BEFORE BOLAN returned his attention to the flattened, defeated machete-wielding marauders, he'd already encountered a terrible death toll in this attack. Spaulding was one of course, but there was a mother and two children slain in the violent rampage. The woman, named Anna, and her eight-year-old son were hacked apart, Anna's life given as she provided a living shield against the rising and falling edge of the murderer's blade. Her courage and sacrifice were in vain, sadly, as the machete's merciless steel severed her left arm as it shielded her son's head, taking off the limb and crushing a cruel crease in the boy's face.

Bolan looked at the horrific carnage, his gut filled with bitter defeat. He didn't look too hard, but he realized that he couldn't tell where mother ended and son began, their dark, crimson-stained skin torn apart, muscle and bone so pulped and splintered that it was as if a demonic elephant had stomped a puddle into their bodies. Dread and loss were crippling emotions, but the Executioner was far too human, too humane, to be able to bottle up and dispose of those feelings. Instead, he buried them, making them the spurs that stuck into his soul that would be there to prod him along should his strength begin to fail.

Dread and loss were abstract, unfocused ideas that he couldn't use. Pain and righteous anger, however, were the flint and steel that would ignite Bolan to go one more step, endure one more injury, throw one more punch. The horrors of this morning turned from peace to panic were the kindling, the firewood that would fuel his hunt for justice.

The last victim, a little girl whose age he couldn't even guess, had been so violently assaulted that blood has sprayed along the sand for twenty-five feet. From the churned, bloody sand, he could tell that it had been four of the maniacs, not the one who had cut through the trees to the beach, who had grabbed her up. Her screams had disappeared into the mix of those of other children.

Bolan saw a small, rag-stuffed doll splattered with blood and he stooped to pick it up. All the while, he re-proached himself for being to gentle with his attacker as the doll's owner was being attacked.

He cast the reproach aside after a moment. He had been on alert, but his senses had only so much acuity. He couldn't see through walls or hear the sound of the vehicle that had dropped off five armed people in the grip of chemical fury. It was a basic law of physics—the intervening strip of trees was too thick, too much of a barrier to keep him from noticing that, and even if he did know, Bolan had only his knife.

There were wounded besides Antoine, the young man who'd surrendered a hand in defense of others. Bolan and Rudd had tended to cuts and bruises after ensuring that the boy wouldn't bleed to death, but now Rudd stumbled around, shell-shocked by the horrors he'd experienced. A call through to the police and for an ambulance received an answer that the small surf camp would have to wait as a beach resort two miles up the road had been the victim of similar violence.

Bolan knew that the carnage on the scene at a more crowded pleasure spot would have been horrendous.

"Rudd," Bolan called, "help me check on the attackers."

"The girl is dead," Rudd said, his words coming out of his mouth in a slurred mush.

"The one who attacked you?" Bolan asked. He winced as he realized that he'd applied far too much force to her, but in the wake of Spaulding's brutal murder, he'd let slip his kid gloves. Still, she'd been a victim of chemical reprogramming, a drug-fueled rage that had been inflicted upon her and the other four, turning them into marauders who barely felt pain and had required skeletal fractures to stop them.

Bolan stopped at another body, a killer who had gone down with a twisted arm and a kick to the head. He was a local, a young man who was all lean muscle and long limbs. The soldier checked for broken bones in the neck, but the only signs of what had killed him were dried crystals flaking at the corners of his mouth, leftovers from the froth and foam that had burbled up when his body succumbed to a hormonal overload.

The big American wasn't a coroner, but he'd seen people killed by overdoses of drugs and it would be a good guess that the machete-armed invaders of this beach haven had all succumbed to massive heart attacks brought on by the chemicals pumped into their veins.

Five corpses, each of them brought down by the Executioner's hands in such a way that they would *live,* snuffed out by the same strange fuel that had driven them to attack.

"Are they all dead?" Rudd asked, cringing at the sight of them as Bolan stacked their limp forms together.

Bolan nodded. As an afterthought, he picked up a pair of empty water bottles from a nearby recycling bin and cut open the veins on two of the bodies. He'd have to collect blood samples and hope that Stony Man Farm could supply him with someone who'd run toxicology screens. He wanted to know what kind of chemical cocktail had been utilized to turn humans into weapons, and with that bit of knowledge, he'd be able to narrow the focus of his search for the perpetrators.

"That's grisly," Rudd said, looking at Bolan draining blood into a bottle.

"No more than what they did," Bolan said.

"Who were they?" Rudd asked.

"Pawns of someone. Most likely they were kidnapped tourists," Bolan answered.

Rudd's brow wrinkled. "Tourists?"

"Harmless people sparked to insanity by a biochemist of some sort," Bolan added. "I tried not to cause them too much pain, but they were too violent. Even so, the measures I took against them should have left them with long-term injuries, not dead. Their hearts gave out after I rendered them unconscious."

"Who'd do such a thing?" Rudd asked. "And who'd let them loose *here,* where it's just kids?"

"That's what the bottles are for," Bolan told him solemnly. "If there's a clue in the blood, then I'll use it."

"You're going after them yourself?" Rudd inquired.

Bolan nodded. "Alone. With an army. It won't matter. I'm going to find the people behind this."

Rudd nodded.

Bolan took a deep breath. "It's not a job I want. But I have a feeling that this was a test run. More people are going to be released on wild rampages. More innocents are going to die. I intend to end it as fast as possible."

Bolan stalked off to get his satellite phone to contact Stony Man Farm.

Rest and recuperation was over. The chase was on.

# CHAPTER FIVE

Morrot leaned on the desk, peering down at the tablet monitor that relayed footage from a digital camera video strapped to the frame of a remote-control airplane. The tiny little diesel-motored plane had long, wide wings that were shaped like those of an albatross, complete with the exact dimensions, enabling the craft to hang in the air with a minimum of fuel supply.

He looked at the group that he had released early, the one with his favorite subject, Rojas. He'd dropped the group near the Spaulding Youth Surf Camp to add to the horror—it was a place where children were in abundance. The news would find itself drawn to the slaughter of innocents. The remoteness of the little camp also ensured that Rojas and his friends would escape into the woods, free and wild murderers who would stalk and hunt for days, maybe even weeks, giving Morrot a continuing menace in the background while he strove to create more of his magnificent monsters.

Morrot had kept the camera in the air over the first surf camp to make certain that things were going according to his plan. From a height of hundreds of feet, but with a high-definition, long-range zoom camera, he was able to see Rojas taking a direct approach to the beach where the sounds of children playing had drawn him.

And that's when the tall man on the surfboard did something Morrot had never expected—he charged a machete-wielding berserker without even pausing to pull the knife from its calf sheath. In moments, the black-haired surfer had flattened Rojas and turned his attention to one of the women.

All told, the savage squad he'd released onto the Spaulding Youth Surf Camp had been eliminated in the space of two minutes by a single combatant. There were wounded, there were dead, but one lone human had stood against five people whose nerves had been numbed to pain and whose strength had been boosted by chemical-induced ferocity.

"Should we turn the other group back?" Pierre Fortescue asked, watching the same video feed on a monitor of his own.

Morrot shook his head. His mismatched eyes were locked on the screen, looking at the man who had stood for only a brief moment over the unconscious form of the woman. "There won't be anyone like him in the resort."

"Who is he?" Fortescue asked.

Morrot could only see the man from the top down, but his shoulders were broad, and his arms were long and wrapped in corded cables of muscle. He was of European descent, despite the darkened tan of his skin. "That man is a professional soldier."

Fortescue glared at the shaman, but subdued his spite before Morrot took notice. Fortescue himself was the son of one of the strongmen in the old Haitian guard, the Tonton Macoute. The Macoute wasn't only a cadre of highly trained gunmen, it was backed by ties to superstition and the skills of *houngans* like Morrot himself. Though Fortescue hadn't been one of those elite, murderous soldiers, he'd been taught by his father and had sharpened those skills in exile, being a hired gun for various Jamaican gang members.

The implication of Morrot's words made him bristle, but Fortescue was nothing if not smart. If he'd said or done anything in response to the accusation, Morrot would find a reason and a way to eliminate him. Morrot was ruthless and too damned smart, and Fortescue wasn't the kind of man to take unnecessary risks. Showing his temper under the one-eyed voodoo priest's verbal abuse wasn't just a risk, it was an invitation to slow, painful death after a horrific road of pain and insanity.

"He took down all five. There were a few casualties, but nothing truly usable to increase the panic," Fortescue said, keeping his voice clinical and cool. "The delivery to the resort will have to bring in some major carnage to instill the proper panic in Kingston."

"There will be blood and terror," Morrot told him. "Do not worry, my friend."

Fortescue looked at the half-mutilated face of the scrawny shaman in front of him. If anyone could manipulate the nations of the Caribbean Sea, it was this dark-hearted wizard of mayhem and madness.

The promise Morrot made would be backed by his programmed-for-madness minions.

WHATEVER GUILT Mack Bolan might have felt at his inability to save lives at the Spaulding Youth Surf Camp was dispelled when he saw that the Pleasant Shore Resort, two miles up the coastal road, had been turned into an abattoir. Dozens were dead, and hundreds injured, many in critical condition. The local news was inundated and trumped by international press circling the Jamaican getaway like sharks now that they had smelled blood in the water, literally.

One of the hotel's swimming pools had been turned to the color of red wine, the badly mutilated corpses of two people staining what would have been crystal-clear water. The filtration systems were plugged by chunks of flesh, preventing the thinning of the murky pool. The work of five insane people in the resort, armed with machetes that could carve through flesh and bone, was brutally efficient. At the surf camp, their victims had been spread out, giving the Executioner time to intercept the berserkers. The crowds at poolside and on the beach had been caught unaware, and the violent fury released found dozens of targets.

There had been security guards on the scene, but Bolan knew that nothing short of a contact-range shotgun blast or a bullet right in the medulla oblongata would slow the attackers. Handguns were a poor substitute for true fight-stopping firepower, though the Executioner's skill with his preferred pistols had made him deadly enough to survive combat against opponents with bigger, more powerful guns.

As it was, the security at the resort wasn't equipped to deal with armed maniacs. It was there to prevent drunks from hurting themselves or harassing the other patrons. The hotels spent big money keeping the drug gangs from bringing their business squabbles into their backyard, and what handguns were available were just that—pistols. The United States military learned a long time ago, during the Moro uprising in the Philippines, the uselessness of a mere sidearm against someone who was on painkillers and in the grip of fanatical rage. The machete-wielding killers would have died from their wounds, but for the fifteen minutes of fury that they were still operating, they were rampaging machines, lashing out at everything.

It had been the Executioner's training that had carried the day at the surf camp, and even then, there had been casualties. Too many for Bolan's taste, enough to feel that he'd failed at the standards he'd set for himself. Bystanders were to be protected at all costs, even to the point of catching a bullet in the chest. He'd never staged a battle where civilian noncombatants were on hand, and in instances where others had been endangered, Bolan had done his best to attract attention to himself.

The blood samples that Bolan had collected in water bottles sat in the little humming refrigerator, a box with a door and its sides and front covered in plastic sheeting colored to look like wooden paneling. He'd transfer it to a cooler to take it to a laboratory for examination, but even refrigerated, the blood and the chemicals within weren't going to last forever. Within twenty-four hours, natural enzyme breakdowns could erase traces of some toxins and drugs. Freezing the blood was an option, but then again, there was the problem of crystallization of water affecting the chemical makeup.

Bolan's laptop screen flickered to life, an incoming call from Stony Man Farm jarring it from sleep mode. Barbara Price, her face illuminated by her monitor's bleak, harsh light, appeared in the web camera chat box. She was mission controller at Stony Man Farm, the installation that was home to the nation's elite antiterrorist teams. Bolan sat in front of his own camera, dressed in a black T-shirt and khaki-colored cargo pants. Price's eyes flicked left, then right, noting the straps of his shoulder holster in place.

"You're aware of the attack in the resort," Price said.

"I caught a preview. It looked like someone wanted to release my marauders into the wild after they tore up a camp full of unarmed surfers and other kids," Bolan answered.

Price pursed her lips in a frown before speaking again. "You said you'd suffered casualties."

Bolan didn't answer.

"Hal and the President have been going over this. They know that you're in the region, but they aren't certain that the situation warrants your involvement," Price said.

Bolan still remained quiet, his slitted eyes providing the only sign of a response, a show of annoyance that the Sensitive Operations Group and the White House were able to dictate where and why the Executioner would take action. He finally spoke. "They don't have to be. *I'm* certain."

Price nodded. "Hal knows better than to deny you your choice of operations."

"I've got refrigerated blood samples from the berserkers I encountered. Is there a lab handy where I can get this looked at?" Bolan asked.

"We've been checking local laboratories and most in the country don't have the kind of toxicology skills you'd need," Price replied. "But we have help in the area."

"Hospital ships off Haiti," Bolan surmised. "U.S. Navy? I don't want to pull personnel off of the relief effort."

"No problem in that regard. We have someone on hand who is a trained medic," Price said.

"Is Cal coming to pick me up himself, or do I meet him on the ship?" Bolan asked.

"A navy helicopter's coming to get you and the samples to meet him," Price replied. "Since there's no need for forensic toxicology, the facilities on board the aircraft carrier devoted to that won't take away from things."

"Good," Bolan returned. "What's my cover?"

"Colonel Brandon Stone," Price returned. "We've already set it so that you can be armed on the carrier, but you do have to carry concealed."

Bolan shrugged. "Even military brass can't be armed on a Navy ship."

"Not everyone believes in the inherent goodness of the U.S. Armed Forces," Price replied. "Unfortunately that includes many commanders in the Navy, the Army…"

"I'll deal with it," Bolan said, tugging on a BDU overshirt, concealing the Beretta 93-R in its holster. As a soldier in the field, and years of interacting with servicemen abroad, the soldier had learned that the Pentagon policies about disarming troops when not in direct contact with the enemy had lead to countless being left vulnerable to ambushes. The death toll, thanks to those policies, was high, a level of loss that caused suffering among families at home and crippling deficiencies among active-duty personnel.

"The helicopter is coming to the camp, correct?"

"The less you have to travel with the blood before it can be brought to the lab, the better," Price told him.

Bolan nodded. "ETA?"

"Ten minutes."

The soldier looked up from buttoning the jacketlike uniform blouse. "I'll be ready. Any news on who is claiming responsibility for the attack?"

"No word per se," Price said. "Though the zombie-like rage exhibited by the attackers have people talking about voodoo. Someone leaked videos through the internet and they have hit cable news stations."

"That may be the point," Bolan replied.

Price tilted her head. "How so?"

"Phoenix, Able and I have had plenty of encounters with real-life voodoo zombies over the years," Bolan said, referring to Phoenix Force and Able Team, Stony Man's two action units. "Some were just makeup and bulletproof vests while others were people whose minds were destroyed by traditional *houngan* treatments, either as cheap slave labor or purpose constructed."

Price frowned. "No one is taking responsibility because the targets of this attack will know who was behind it."

"It could be part of the local Jamaican drug war, trying to fill in the void I recently knocked in the status quo," Bolan added. "Or it could be something political, because I can't see the cocaine cowboys on this island making a mess of their target demographic."

"Tourists looking for nose candy and herb," Price said.

Bolan nodded. "If they scare off tourism, a lot of their local dealers lose customers. With no income, they can't bribe the hotels to let them hang around and deal, and the addition of violence in the hotels makes them really out of luck."

"That doesn't mean that the local gangs aren't helping in some manner," Price said. "Someone would have to provide ingredients to the chemical cocktails that set off the berserkers."

"Calvin and I will look into that if we get a chance," Bolan told her. "I'd prefer to have him working with me here in the islands because he fits in better than I do."

"That's part of the reason why Calvin is riding a Tomcat to the carrier out of Langley AFB," Price said.

"He's not on hand yet?" Bolan asked.

"By the time your helicopter drops you off, he'll be on deck," Price replied. "They caught a tailwind off the coast of Georgia. Do you want any other help?"

Bolan shook his head. "If the President doesn't think this situation warrants my attention, I'm not going to pull in any more official Stony Man personnel than Cal. And how did he get free?"

"He took some time to meet with an old SEAL buddy," Price replied. "Building more unofficial relations, so to speak."

"What does the buddy do now?" Bolan asked.

"Security firm," Price said. "So now, Phoenix Force has more friends in the New York area… just in case."

Bolan nodded with approval. "Shame to interrupt that."

"Cal made the call to me that he was going down to meet you," Price replied. "One helicopter transfer to Langley…"

"I'll be sure to tell him I appreciate this," Bolan said. "I hear the chopper coming."

"Striker." Price spoke up, her voice grown soft, losing its hard business edge for a moment.

Bolan looked into the web cam, knowing that it was the closest that he could get to looking into her eyes over their cybernetic link. "Barbara?"

"I'm sorry that your…time off…had to end this way," she said.

"No need to feel sorry for me," Bolan returned. "You may want to spare some concern for the men who caused the deaths of children."

Price looked down. She'd heard the icy grating in his voice, like a whetstone over a combat knife.

Mack Bolan was on the hunt.

CALVIN JAMES pulled off the oxygen mask and flight helmet before he crawled out of the rear seat of the F-14

Tomcat. The Mach 2 fighter had torn through the skies like a guided missile, delivering the former SEAL to the aircraft carrier in time to meet up with the Executioner. The pilot of the plane had pointed out Bolan's chopper, looking as if it were hovering still in the air compared to the breakneck pace of the long-range jet.

James was glad to be out of the cockpit. He was two inches too tall for the Tomcat at six foot two, and his legs and head had been squashed in on the supersonic flight. The aircraft had traveled for an hour at full speed, but an hour in the claustrophobic backseat was just too much for him. The only consolation was that James had ridden in planes too small for him before and had learned how to bend and twist so he wouldn't end the flight with muscle cramps.

That's what he'd told himself as he rubbed his neck, wincing as sleepy shoulder muscles protested at the excessive stretching.

A crewman withdrew James's duffel from its small storage locker just behind the seat. There wasn't much inside it other than for a case containing his personal Beretta 92-F, two of his favorite knives and a Glock 26 backup pistol, with holsters and accessories for everything. Price had informed James that clothing would be provided at the other end of the flight, so his combat gear would be all he needed.

The captain, Timothy Bannon, was waiting across the deck, observing as his crew tended to the newly arrived Tomcat. With a simple turn, Bannon would be only moments from the bridge in case of an emergency. This carrier was his responsibility, and he hovered over it as if he were guarding his own toddler. Bannon was six feet even, with broad shoulders, and his baseball-style cap couldn't conceal the clean-shaved sides and back of his head. Blue eyes, looking out from blond, nearly invisible eyebrows, scanned the tall black man who approached him.

"Calvin Farrow," James introduced himself, using one of his cover names. "Permission to come aboard."

Bannon extended his hand. "Permission granted. The Justice Department needs my ship?"

"Just a small part, sir," James returned. "We have a man coming in by helicopter, and I need to take a look at the blood samples he collected."

"So you'll use our sick bay, rather than take up room on a hospital ship," Bannon surmised. "We're not doing anything on board, but we do have a good phlebotomy laboratory. Sadly, it's something that's needed in the modern Navy."

"Mandatory drug testing, among other things," James said. "I know the kind of stuff that people get into on duty on a carrier. Amphetamines to stay on extra duty when coffee stops working…especially for pilots."

James could tell that he'd struck a sore point with Bannon, but the former Navy SEAL had also struck a chord that resonated with the Captain. Both were Navy, and James's understanding of the unfortunate zeal of their fellow personnel was a salve to that soreness. "Here comes the chopper."

"The communiqué said that Stone is, well, *was* U.S. Army," Bannon noted. "Is he a good man?"

"There's not a lick of interservice rivalry in his

entire body," James replied. "You won't find a more staunch supporter of the military in the world."

"A real supporter? Or a war hawk?" Bannon asked.

James looked at Bannon. "Real. He didn't earn his colonel rank because of an accident of birth or a lot of money."

Bannon's broad shoulders relaxed. "Good. You see these ex-military contractors, and you start to wonder where their real sympathies lie."

"He's his own boss. This way, he gets to work without a lot of red tape sticking to him," James said.

The helicopter settled down, and Bolan stepped off. His black BDU top didn't match the digital camouflage BDU pants he wore, but the effect was a sharp blend, and the darker fabric was better at concealing the handles and bulges of his sidearms. If James hadn't known that the Executioner rarely went unarmed, he wouldn't have known that the man had at least two handguns and an assortment of other tools tucked away in pockets on his person. Bolan gave Bannon a sharp salute, then shook James's hand.

"I've got your presents," the soldier said.

James took the small cooler, giving its plastic side a soft slap. "Permission to head to your lab, sir."

Bannon nodded. "Granted, Farrow. Ensign, escort him, and get him there double time."

The ensign that Bannon addressed snapped to, and James turned, leaving Bolan and the carrier's captain to talk.

BANNON HADN'T exaggerated about the extensive technology in the lab. James not only had an assortment of regular and electronic microscopes, but there were centrifuges and spectrometers for looking at the chemicals within the bloodstream. The final item that James had brought on the flight, aside from his personal weapons, was his personal laptop, which had the spec-profiles of hundreds of drug and toxin combinations.

The Phoenix Force medic was also familiar with the kind of alchemy practiced by the "zombie lords" of the Caribbean, and thus would be able to direct the search for the kinds of atomic chains left behind in the blood samples. Fortunately, the blood hadn't been kept so cold that ice crystals had formed in its water content, making separating it into test tubes easier.

James knew that he was in for the long haul, and looked forward to the intellectual challenge ahead. He blanked the origins of the blood sample from his mind, burying his emotions over the violence the berserkers committed so that he could focus on the biochemical mysteries in front of him.

Once he narrowed down the origins of the maniacal tourist murderers, *then* James would switch into Phoenix Force commando mode and assist the Executioner in bringing hot lead and righteous retribution down on the murderous manipulators.

For now, the lab machines would hum and do their job.

# CHAPTER SIX

Fortescue handed over the folded bills to the informant. The man who'd been staying at the surf camp had been named Brandon Stone, and the informant had noted that a U.S. Navy helicopter had arrived to pick him up.

Morrot had been correct about the "professional soldier" description. One didn't get a quick ride from a Navy bird off a beach in Jamaica without some pull within the military. Fortescue recalled the speed and skill with which the man had dispatched five machete-wielding attackers while never once going to the razor-sharp scuba knife that he'd worn on his calf. There wasn't a military force on Earth that would have begrudged one of their own dealing with more heavily armed superior numbers with deadly force, even a club or picking up one of the fallen marauders' machetes. It was telling that Stone charged against them and used only enough force to render them harmless. Sure, some of the injuries on the dead, drugged minions had been long term—spiral fractured arms would have never healed even if their hearts hadn't exploded after they were rendered unconscious.

Fortescue remembered his hand-to-hand training, bought by his father and given to him at the hands of a former Spetsnaz commando. His reactions had been quick, his grace natural, strength remarkable, making the way of the empty hand easy to come by. The Russian had also taught him the use of the knife and skill with the gun, talents he'd honed as he'd worked long and hard for local crime gangs.

As such, Fortescue could tell the speed and power displayed by Stone was nothing short of elite, easily one of the most deadly human beings on the planet. Only one bit of extra force had been utilized, and that was on an attacker who had cut down a man in front of Stone's eyes. The clothesline strike was the kind of move that could have shattered the neck of the strongest man, and the way the woman had flipped and smashed into the sand, never to rise again, it was an attack that had been fueled by anger.

The informant had left him, and Fortescue slouched in the booth, a frown crossing his features. The inclusion of Stone was a wild card that few could anticipate. Morrot had made plans that would deal with the intervention of MI-6 or any number of conventional intelligence and counterinsurgency agencies. But a one-man army who had naval aircraft at his beck and call and moved as if his limbs were quicksilver flowing under his tanned flesh was something else entirely.

"He'll be tough," Fortescue muttered. "But he bled. Maybe he won't be so tough against more concentrated numbers."

There was also the "vampire juice" that Morrot had whipped up. It was a chemical cocktail that duplicated the painkilling effects of his zombification drugs, but left a man with his full cognitive abilities. Such a man, immune to pain and exhaustion, would be able to fight harder. Fortescue was fully aware that most people only utilized a fraction of their physical potential, slowed by pain to prevent overexertion. Fortescue had tried the solution, and his faculties had remained clear. With it, he'd been able to bench press twice what he'd originally been able to—a full five hundred pounds. A sparring match against three of his best men had ended with all three floored, Fortescue's assault far too quick for them to compensate. One had punched him, a blow that had left his cheek raw, as if it had been run across a cheese grater, and subsequent x-rays showed fractures on the cheekbone. The pain had kicked in only after Morrot's concoction had worn off.

The broken bones had healed since then, the pain of the face-breaking impact having faded, as well.

Would that kind of advantage be enough against the "professional soldier" on the beach?

Fortescue smirked. He, too, was a trained, capable combatant. With the "vampire" blood racing through his veins, he'd be unbeatable.

And just to be certain, Fortescue would bring along half a dozen of his best men, also powered up by Morrot's muscular jet fuel.

It might be enough.

MIKE CARMODY took another drag on his cigarette as he sat at the café table fifteen feet from Fortescue. The DEA agent was in Jamaica as part of the agency's effort to curtail the flow of heroin through the island nation, but it might well have been dropping a cork in the ocean for the hopes of stopping its ebb and flow. He'd received a phone call, though, this morning from a high-up Justice Department contact who told him his assistance was needed to get some intel about some specialized illicit chemicals and toxins running through Kingston.

A North American of African American descent, Carmody was comfortably unnoticeable when out in the bright light of day, and when it came time to reach into the shadows for that hard, grimy information, he would play a role that kept him from being an obvious intruder in the Kingston underworld.

As such, he wore plenty of bling, chains and rings glimmering around his neck and fingers, a dark blue silk shirt open down to his sternum and sunglasses that would have been a bargain if bought for $1000. It was the look of a man who wanted to emulate the more well-groomed rappers of the east and west coasts. The style also happened to look at home in nightclubs that catered to those who bought entertainment for an evening along with a liquor bill running into the thousands of dollars and a closed-off VIP room where women debased themselves just to have the slightest brush with wealth and power, no matter the origin of the blood money.

Carmody may have been comfortable in the silk shirt and linen slacks and cream-white Italian leather shoes, but he wasn't comfortable with the act he had to put on while doing "business" in Jamaica. He knew that the world would look at him as an exemplar of one of the worst stereotypes of black American organized crime. He fought to stifle that revulsion, and ninety-nine percent of the time, he succeeded quite well. His mission was to protect children and teenagers from the kind of slow death and mind rot that heroin addiction inflicted upon countless people.

He took another sip of chilled beer, watching a familiar face leave Fortescue's table, pocketing some folded bills. It was Eric Rambeau, one of the men he regularly tapped for information, and he could see that the scrawny little snitch was in a hurry.

Carmody dropped a few twenties on the table and took off after Rambeau. If there was the chance to figure out what was going on, it lay with the informant. Rambeau's head would be a good resource to tap. And if money didn't do the job, Carmody didn't mind.

If he had to get rougher to tap that brain, he'd tap it off a brick wall.

FORTESCUE WATCHED the American black man toss money onto his table and leave, obviously intent on following Rambeau as he left the outdoor café. It didn't take too much imagination to recognize the man as either a narcotics agent or an East Coast dealer who wanted Rambeau's take on the local underworld. The concept of narc seemed stronger here, as most of the dealers who wandered down to Jamaica to get their heroin leads weren't the type to get up and go on their own after a man. They had entourages of bodyguards and yes-men. He caught a quick flash of a pistol in a shoulder holster, something that passed so quick anyone who wasn't a professional would have missed it.

Fortescue looked over to the table where Romy and Bertrand were sitting. The two next generation Macoute were sharp-eyed and quick-witted—they would have been useless to Fortescue otherwise. He pointed to the man who'd gotten up and gone after Rambeau. Romy tilted his head in question, subtly asking by gestures whether the target was to be killed or to be observed.

Fortescue wiped his left eye in response, then tapped his ear.

They were to watch, only. Any further actions, they were to call him, and then decisions would be made. Romy and Bertrand were in motion as soon as Fortescue had tapped his ear.

Fortescue didn't believe in coincidences. For some reason, a man was looking at Rambeau, who had been tapped for information regarding Brandon Stone, the one-man army who'd torn through five machete-packing maniacs. Stone had gotten onto a Navy helicopter and disappeared into the Caribbean. The stranger had the look of a law enforcement or an espionage operative, and Stone had enough government pull to arrange for military transport within the space of an hour.

Romy and Bertrand would keep an eye on the stranger following Rambeau. If this had to do with Morrot's scheme, then the American would have to die. If he were just another piece of scum wanting cheaper product, the two Macoute would throw him a beating, but allow him to live.

It would all depend on how the man responded to their questions.

Rambeau had ducked into a storefront, heading to a standing, glass-doored refrigerator to pick up a cold drink for himself. Thin-limbed and with very dark skin, Rambeau fit the mold of snitch in Jamaica. There was no strength in those arms, so the slender man had to barter for his existence in Kingston's back alleys utilizing sharp ears, infallible memory and the ability to translate the actions of strangers. He worked for cops as much as he worked for the Rastas. Working both sides of the law allowed him an unusual freedom, as both sides tolerated him for what he could tell them about the other.

With a twist, he took the bottle cap off the cold glass bottle of soda and tilted it back. Chilled carbonation washed through his mouth with the first sip, and he felt relief at having survived another conversation with Fortescue. Fortescue was someone different from the police and the drugstore cowboys Rambeau had become used to. The Haitian was big, strong and seemed cold enough to have caused the drink in his hand to form ice if he'd stared at it hard enough.

The information that Fortescue wanted, how a man named Stone had come to the island, as well as how he'd left, was intel that Rambeau had gotten so easily, it was pathetic. The only way it could have been easier was if Stone had personally handed Rambeau his itinerary and pointed out its most salient points.

For the American to be that easy to trace with the alleged ties he'd had, Rambeau knew that it was a rotten trap. Stone wanted Fortescue and the Macoute agents with him to know where to find him. Stone was wagging his ass out in the wind like the wriggling tail of a worm in the water. The worm had been wound around a steel hook, and no doubt the American possessed something equally merciless and unforgiving to spear anyone who baited him.

Out of the corner of his eye, Rambeau caught a glimpse of a bulky shadow, startling him so much that his fingers slipped on the wet surface of the glass bottle and it landed on the ground with a hard crack. The snitch took a backward step when he saw Carmody. Rambeau knew that the American was with some agency or bureau, and he also knew that Carmody was big enough to handle Rambeau as if he were a rag doll.

"We need to talk," Carmody rumbled.

"I'd love to, but you'll have to wait until business hours," Rambeau replied. He pushed open the fridge door, forming a barrier between himself and the burly DEA agent. As if he were made of greased lightning, he whirled and darted toward the back of the shop. He'd put both hands on the counter and his feet had folded up under him, getting ready to vault the low wall between himself and freedom when his forward momentum was checked by Carmody's hand, clutching a fistful of his T-shirt.

Rambeau bounced backward, tumbling into the American's arms.

"Don't fuck with me, Rambeau," Carmody grumbled. "I don't like talking to you the same as you don't want to chat with me."

"Sorry, man," Rambeau replied. "Don't hit me."

"If I slapped you, I'd probably get splattered with all the shit you're full of," Carmody answered. "Come on."

Rambeau nodded nervously. Behind Carmody, he saw a couple more hard-looking men, and they didn't look as if they were watching out for the DEA agent's well-being.

Carmody saw Rambeau's eyes go wide at the sight of a new threat, and glanced out of the corner of his eye. It didn't take much to recognize two athletic men of paramilitary bearing. Their heads were too cleanly shaved to have had anything to do with the Rasta cocaine cowboys ruling the Jamaican underworld. For one, Rastafarians considered it a sin to cut their hair or beards, taking the example of Samson in the Judeo-Christian bible.

These two, at first glance, were as much outsiders as he was. Rambeau recognized them, however, which meant that Carmody was in trouble.

"Play along, or we're dead," Carmody snarled, still holding a fistful of T-shirt material.

"I hear ya, man," Rambeau returned.

Carmody dragged Rambeau out onto the sidewalk, transferring his grasp on the snitch's shirt to an iron clamp of fingers around the man's scrawny upper arm. Rambeau winced at the roughness, but the informant knew that anything less wouldn't be convincing to Fortescue's boys.

As they turned the corner into a space between buildings, Carmody pushed him to the brick wall and squeezed Rambeau's cheeks between long, powerful fingers. "I don't care about what those two want. I'm just looking for someone to deal with me, cheap."

"Ah, hell, you're up in their business," Rambeau whispered back.

"If you let it slip, both of our heads are going into a stew pot together."

Rambeau swallowed hard. "I'll keep my mouth shut."

Carmody clenched a fist as if to threaten him. "Talk all you want. If you save my ass, I promise never to manhandle you again."

With that, the alley entrance darkened with the presence of the two men.

"What the fuck do you want?" Carmody asked.

One of them answered with French-accented English. "For you not to be so rude to the skinny boy."

"I just want to know when the meet he promised me would come up," Carmody growled. "Jamaica's a nice place to stay, but I'm wantin' to make money, not burn it in some hotel."

The other man sighed. Carmody could see the shifting of chest muscles beneath the men's T-shirts. Their arms were covered by the long sleeves of their blazers, but the fabric pulled tautly across their torsos, betraying the physical fitness of the pair. It also told Carmody that any blows to their stomachs would be cushioned by rock-hard abdominal muscles. If he ended up on the wrong side of this equation, they'd beat him to a bloody pulp without batting an eyelash.

"Go make your money elsewhere," the second man told him. "Otherwise, you could lose something."

"You're not from around here, either," Carmody observed. "Though all your island gook sounds the same to me."

The first man moved forward as a blur. Carmody had been waiting for violence and he took a step to the side, deftly avoiding the fist that rocketed toward him. The DEA agent swung his forearm up and against the extended elbow of his attacker, deflecting the force of his momentum so that the Haitian would fall off balance. It was only a momentary distraction, but Carmody was able to pump his knee up, slamming the man in the lower stomach. The kick lifted the Haitian off his feet by a couple of inches.

Carmody tried to step out of the way of the falling, stunned assailant, but the second Haitian was on him like a shot. *That* showed training and deadly ruthlessness. Off balance and trying to back out of the spill of falling man in front of him, Carmody was unable to avoid or to deflect the second man's attack. The Haitian's forearm caught him across the side of the neck, 180 pounds of muscle focused on the juncture of arteries and nerves that kept the DEA agent's brain connected to the rest of his body. The blow turned Carmody's knees to jelly, and his head swam crazily.

It was all that he could do to brace himself against the brick wall to stay on his feet. It wasn't easy to hold himself up even with his arms splayed against the wall. Things became worse as the Haitian pressed his assault, driving the heel of his hand deep into Carmody's solar plexus. The air blew out of his lungs. The DEA agent brought both hands together around the attacker's wrist, holding on as tightly as he could. The Haitian's elbow rebounded off Carmody's jaw, the back of his skull rapping against the hard brick, but the DEA agent didn't let go. If he did, he'd be open to even more attacks. Pinning the enemy's hand was the only thing that gave him enough of a reprieve to recover from the chop across his neck.

The trouble with holding on with both hands was that he no longer had the leverage to stay on his feet. He was off balance once again when the Haitian pulled him forward. The DEA agent let go and pushed both fists hard into the Haitian's chest. The double punch would have carried more of an impact if he were at full faculties and with both feet firmly on the ground. As it was, the Haitian was still driven off guard, stumbling backward. Carmody reached out again, taking hold of his opponent's collar to keep his precarious balance and twist the Haitian around to his advantage.

The other man pushed up off of his hands and knees where he had fallen. With a twist, Romy spun his elbow into the soft flesh just above Carmody's right hip. Once again, the air exploded out of the American's nose and mouth and he buckled toward his surprised adversary. The man, Bertrand, took this opportunity to draw a fat little flashlight from his pocket. At only six inches long, it wasn't a club like the four and six D-cell lights carried by police and security guards, but the tiny torch was made of tough, high-tensile-strength steel.

Bertrand had been trained to utilize even this stubby little tool as a fist-load, and he proved it as he broke

Carmody's jaw with a single punch. The minilight's hard, hexagonal ring cracked as Bertrand once more lashed it against the DEA agent's skull.

Bright lights flashed inside Carmody's head, and he collapsed to the floor of the alley.

"What the fuck?" Rambeau shouted.

Romy struggled to his feet and took a handful of Rambeau's belt to drag himself to his feet. "Why are you talking to him?"

"Because he paid me a thousand bucks to get him a meeting!" Rambeau said. "And if you smack his cabbage again, he's not going to pay me the other four thousand."

"What meeting? Did he ask about Fortescue?" Romy asked.

"He didn't say anyone's name except mine and our mutual client," Rambeau said. "Trust me, I'm stuck here. Especially if I don't have this guy open up a billion-dollar pipeline. You ever piss off a Rasta for that kind of money? Ever?"

Rambeau looked down toward Carmody whose head was split open over his temple, blood pouring down to ruin his shirt. "Taking any more piss out of this guy is going to make him useless and cost me four long, cost a man whose idea of cost-cutting means a machete to the neck billions. When he finds out who fucked him over that means hell for you, too."

Bertrand plucked Carmody's shiny gold Desert Eagle from under his linen jacket, aiming it at Rambeau. "Who'd tell him?"

"You think I don't have contingency plans?" Rambeau asked. "Everyone I talk to has the potential to kill me. If I don't make insurance for myself, I'm dead five thousand times over. So I left notes that if I end up dead, the last people I met that day probably did it. And you lot and Fortescue, you're the ones with the target on your head. You shoot me, my patron and a hundred of his closest psychopathic friends show up with a mad-on."

"We can take Rastas," Bertrand said.

"If you have time to prepare," Rambeau replied. "They'll show up on your doorstep tonight, ripped out of their skulls and carrying more guns than the French Foreign Legion, and still be smart enough to avoid getting in close with you lot."

Romy pushed Bertrand's aim to the ground. "If we get heat, Rambeau…"

"You'll get heat," the informant told them. "I got intel on your boy Stone *way* too easy. He wants you to jump him."

Carmody looked up from the ground, his head drenched with blood.

Romy scowled at the pair. "You're lucky we don't have time for you."

Rambeau nodded. "Too true."

The Haitians left and Rambeau took care of the injured Carmody.

# CHAPTER SEVEN

Mack Bolan left Calvin James to his biochemical investigations and took Captain Bannon's offer of a quick flight back to Kingston. The two men had conferred as to the amount of assistance the aircraft carrier could provide to the Executioner and his struggle against the madman who released armed maniacs against unarmed tourists and Jamaican civilians. Bolan rarely asked for much more than access to spare ammunition and aerial transportation, though Bannon said that he had both Marine Force Recon and Navy SEALs at his disposal. He felt like giving in to the temptation of having elite teams of commandos at his beck and call, but the feeling had disappeared in an instant.

Those teams would be held in reserve only until the last moment. The Executioner wasn't one to endanger even the most trained fighting men in the world on a mission he'd undertaken. Certainly they were more than capable of handling superior numbers through marksmanship and carefully selected firepower, but he hadn't worked with these teams, so operational integrity and continuity wasn't going to be in their favor.

Bolan worked his own way, and as such, he couldn't bring himself to push the Marines and SEALs to his standards of action.

Bolan felt the vibration of his cell phone against his thigh and he took it from his pocket. It was the Farm, which meant something had come up in the hours he'd been aboard the carrier, getting updated on the resort attack, acquiring equipment and ammunition. "Striker."

"We have a hit, literally," Barbara Price announced. "We had a friendly asset in Kingston. Mike Carmody."

"I remember him," Bolan said. "DEA agent. Did a tour of blacksuit duty. Is he all right?"

"He's in an ER with skull and jaw fractures," Price reported. "He looks like he'd gotten run over by an angry rhinoceros."

Bolan grimaced. This was exactly why he refused to involve more people than necessary in his War Everlasting. Carmody had been a big man who excelled at hand-to-hand combat and marksmanship, and now he was suffering from a beating that could easily have left him with brain trauma. It hadn't even been a case of Carmody following the Executioner into the fire, and already there was collateral damage. The dead from the Spaulding surf camp had the potential for added friendly dead hanging around him, more lives that added to the river of blood that threatened to drown him in his nightmares.

Bolan pushed the guilt from his mind in the quick instant it had popped up. "He'll live?"

Price cleared her throat. "They just want to make certain there's nothing that can cause a stroke or aneurysm. He's under observation."

"You certain that it was in relation to inquiries about me?" Bolan asked.

"We don't have any solid details, but there is some-one who is waiting with Carmody. One of his informants," Price said.

"Give the pilot a landing spot, and I'll be at the hospital, if Carmody's man is still hanging out there," Bolan requested.

Price was quick to answer. "The informant is still at the hospital. Carmody's contact at Justice didn't give me any identification on the guy, but the informant did say he'd wait for help."

Bolan took down the coordinates so that the pilot could set him down at a helipad on the hospital campus, and he transferred the information to the Navy fly-boys running the chopper.

RAMBEAU RECOGNIZED "Brandon Stone" from the description that had been given to him by Fortescue. Though the Jamaican hadn't personally met the big American, there was no overlooking his military bearing or the intensity of his features. It didn't hurt that Bolan was a tower of lean, powerful muscle with short black hair and cold blue eyes that were an unmistakable part of the description that "Stone" had released to make himself tastier bait for Fortescue's hunters.

Bolan walked up to Rambeau, extending his hand. There was no challenge in the handshake, which impressed the little informant. Quite often, when first encountering Americans, they tried to show their strength by applying a death grip that ground knuckles and carpal bones against each other. Of course, that matched the supreme air of confidence that radiated from the man as if he were a lighthouse on a dark, foggy night.

"Stone," he introduced himself.

The Jamaican nodded. "Rambeau."

"What happened to Carmody?"

This Stone didn't beat around the bush, Rambeau thought. "He caught up with me and wanted to ask a few questions. That's when the two Haitians jumped us."

"Haitians," Bolan repeated. He pulled his cell phone and fired off a text message to Calvin James as he worked in his laboratory. It was a quick, two-word transmission that the black Phoenix Force medic would understand. "Black Alchemists."

Bolan returned his attention to Rambeau, even as he was typing the text. "Sorry about that. How did they know to jump Carmody?"

"They didn't," Rambeau answered. "They followed him because he was following me. I'd just had a meeting with their boss."

"Who's that?" Bolan asked.

Rambeau rubbed his fingertips together. "Half price because I like Carmody and I don't want to piss off a guy like you."

Bolan had already anticipated having to pay for information. He took a pair of folded hundreds from his pocket and handed them over to Rambeau. "I pay all of my debts."

"The only name I received from him was Fort,"

Rambeau replied. "I've tried to dig a little deeper, but there isn't much other than he was a contract worker for some of the Kingston rough boys, and that he has a strong military background. Apparently, he's hard and a consummate professional. That's all I know."

"But he's on edge enough to turn his attention toward you and Carmody," Bolan said. "I must have shaken him up."

"You know that was your plan, Stone," Rambeau answered. "You were subtle about it, but you're nothing but chum in the water, looking to bring the sharks out of the reef and into the open."

"Not quite the analogy I would go for," Bolan said. He reached into his pocket and withdrew more money. He handed it over, and Rambeau noticed a small business card folded into the bills. "Get on the blower to Fort and let him know I showed up to look in on Carmody."

"What if Fort sees this as a trap?" Rambeau asked.

"It won't matter. He's looking for me, and I was dropped off alone from my chopper," Bolan said. "All you have to do is tell him the truth, excising this little conversation."

Rambeau nodded toward the duffel bag resting by Bolan's leg. "Want me to tell them about your kit?"

Bolan shrugged. "Go ahead."

"Where do you want this sprung?" Rambeau asked.

"Somewhere that civilians wouldn't be caught in the cross fire," Bolan said. "The hotel on the business card."

Rambeau sighed. "I'm not sure if Fort will like the

fact that he's coming after you in an abandoned building."

"You don't have to sell it, Rambeau," Bolan told him. "You just have to lay the breadcrumbs for him to my door. I'll take care of the rest."

Rambeau looked at the card. "You got clangers down there, Stone. I wish you luck."

"If you knew that I made myself bait, you know that I make my own luck," Bolan said. "Get moving. I'll look in on Carmody, then go to my hotel. Call them when I'm on my way."

Rambeau offered a half smile, then shook the soldier's hand. "Hope to see you again."

"No," Bolan answered. "You don't."

With that, the big American walked past Rambeau and stepped into Carmody's hospital room.

BOLAN PAID the cabdriver to be quiet and keep the partition closed while he was being driven to the hotel. The driver had started to protest about the destination, offering other places that would provide him with a kickback. Five hundred dollars cut that off quickly, and now the Executioner sat in the back of the cab, cell phone to his ear, listening to Calvin James calling from the lab.

"Thanks for letting me in on the Haitian connection. I found traces of tetrodotoxin once I knew what to look for in the mass spectrometer," James said.

"Anytime," Bolan answered. "Trouble is, puffer fish extract is the last thing that could make someone get up and rampage. The people I fought were in full fury mode."

"I'd found a mixture of powerful tropane alkaloids in significant amounts," James said.

Bolan frowned. "Like scopolamine or atropine?"

"Exactly. I can't narrow down the exact alkaloids utilized, but someone's been to the Datura supermarket in Colombia," James said. "I'm pretty certain that the stuff got here because the dealers found religion."

"Not necessarily from Colombia, but I get you on the 'finding religion' bit," Bolan said. "We might be looking at a modification of ayahuasca, and that's available from Peru to Ecuador. Ayahuascan shamanism is becoming popular enough to be recognized and known by the English- and Spanish-speaking worlds, but the itself is getting a lot of scrutiny from various governments because of its hallucinogenic effects and negative health connotations."

James chuckled. "If you know that much, why call me in?"

"Because if I looked at the readout from a spectrometer, I couldn't tell salt from pepper," Bolan answered. "However, I do keep my eye on potential new drug crazes for the exact same reasons the cartels pay attention to new chemical and pharmaceutical advances and discoveries. If they can make money with it, they'll also kill for it. And when they kill for it, that's when I have to act."

The driver turned his head, curiosity kicking in. Bolan knew that he hadn't really bought the man's disinterest, in fact, he was counting on the cabbie to corroborate Rambeau's intel. "Fort" would be thorough, and that meant pulling info in from every source, including the taxicabs.

Whoever the Haitian was, apparently his professionalism was keen, which made him at once dangerous and predictable. Fort was dangerous because he'd be skilled and capable, and most likely quite able to adapt to any failure of plans in the field. However, military training was something both men shared, and Bolan could anticipate counters to his plans. Fort would know that "Stone" was a militarily trained pro, as well, and as such, Bolan would have to be careful that he didn't underestimate his foe's awareness. Professionals had set plans of action and a good enemy strategist could match Bolan move for move, just like chess masters able to run an entire game in their minds from the first few moves.

The Executioner was no stranger to opponents who were both deadly and skilled. He'd be pressed by their abilities, but his mind was a battle computer that had not only theoretical knowledge but the experience of countless battles.

"So have you done enough to sow your driver?" James asked.

"Get in touch with me when I'm at the hotel," Bolan answered. That was, in effect, Bolan's affirmation.

James chuckled in acknowledgment. "Have fun."

The call disconnected, and he slipped the cell back into his pocket. Bolan knew that James didn't really believe that the Executioner enjoyed chewing squads of angry, violent men into hamburger with the assorted tools of his trade, but it was the closest to shorthand for the Phoenix Force pro to tell him to take care of business. Though he'd likened his conflict with the Haitian "Fort" to a chess game, this was a serious engagement. Bullets would fly, people would die. *Fun* had no part in this equation.

As they pulled up in front of the hotel, Bolan sized up the externals of his battlefield. The building itself, while dirty and smeared with graffiti, was structurally sound except for several broken windows. There were overgrown wild shrubs along the face of the hotel, with tree limbs actually having bent in through some windows. The Executioner had noticed this place during his operation against Long Eddy. He'd only made a momentary recon of the joint, just in case he needed a location for future work in Jamaica, specifically Kingston. The Executioner hadn't become one of the world's most successful warriors without always keeping an eye open and preparing for the next mission, be it ten minutes down the road or on the other side of the world. He kept a mental catalog of potential safehouses and storage facilities to be utilized as bases of operations and resupply depots.

The driver started to get out, but Bolan shook his head. "Thanks for the ride."

"I tell you, this hotel not in business no more," the cabbie said. "At least let me carry your bag."

Bolan picked up the duffel. Despite his recent injuries, he was in phenomenal physical condition, which was why lifting the gear pack seemed effortless, but 150 pounds of weapons, ammunition, communications and other sundries caused him to grunt in exertion. Still, he slung the pack over his shoulder and gave the driver a small salute. He'd already paid the man a handsome amount for delivering him, so there was no reason for him to stick around any longer than necessary. "I've got it. You've got other fares to catch. Money to make."

The cabbie swallowed.

"If anyone asks about where you took me, let them know," he added, handing him another pair of hundreds through the cab window. "I'm expecting visitors, and I don't like being left alone."

"Oh man…this doesn't look good," the driver said.

"No, but you're just someone answering questions about a man with a pack in an abandoned building," Bolan said. "It's sure to garner you more money for your family, and there's no chance of reprisal for you."

The cabbie's brow wrinkled with concern as he balanced his clan's needs, and the basic human decency of not throwing a stranger to the wolves. It wasn't made easier by the very fact that this man was asking to have perdition land on him like a ton of bricks.

"I'll be fine," Bolan said. He put another hundred in the driver's hand. "See to your family's needs."

Bolan knew the look of gratitude and reluctance in the man's face. The soldier had just doubled his income for the entire year. With the cash, he could provide for his family like never before. That kind of gift, at that kind of cost to his fare, was stunning, something the cabbie had never come across.

"Just remember, sir. The Lord loves all of us sinners. There's no reason to look for death."

Bolan smiled. "I'll be fine," he repeated.

With that, he tapped the roof of the cab and the taxi pulled away.

It was time for the Executioner to roll out the welcome mat. He'd have two hours at best, especially since it was already so late in the day. Come sunset, the hostiles would be in full regalia.

As the sky reddened, the last rays of sun spraying the upper atmosphere after disappearing below the horizon, Bolan spotted the first movement. One of the reasons he'd selected this particular building was that it had a fairly open tarmac around it that had served as a combination of parking lot and outdoor lounge. A lone umbrella stand with a naked steel pipe sticking up from it stood about twenty-five yards from the picked-bare remnants of a circular bar, three in five roof slats missing, railing torn off and sold for scrap metal.

When the hotel failed, all of the tables and chairs, except for the lone umbrella and pipe, had been stolen. Outside, it was picked clean, while the interior showed signs of temporary nests for wayward kids to hang out. Empty bottles, used condoms and paint-scrawled walls showed the level of usage the hotel still enjoyed. Bolan wasn't surprised, however, that there were no kids coming in to lodge for the night. It was too early. This place was a refuge for kids crawling out of sight of the rising sun, sleeping until late afternoon.

Jamaican nights were cool and too beautiful to

spend cooped up in garbage-strewn hallways and hotel rooms. Even sexual encounters would start somewhere else and finally end on a mattress in a cleaner part of the hotel, not in the rooms above where he'd holed up.

Just to be certain that his visitors weren't innocent kids, Bolan used his pocket night-vision telescope to confirm. His initial count was correct—four, and they were all armed. Two had shotguns, one had an AK of some form, and the last packed a stubby little MAC-10 knockoff. It was considerable firepower, and proof positive that the Executioner had made an impression on "Fort," the Haitian. Their dreads betrayed that they were local muscle.

Though Bolan could have taken them out—a suppressed Designated Marksman Rifle was part of his war bag—he wanted to avoid throwing rounds away from the abandoned building toward where bystanders might get hit. As it was, he knew that the four gunners weren't the last to show up. He swept the perimeter with his telescope and found three potential hiding spots for reserve gunmen to wait in ambush.

Bolan ignored the initial quartet, leaving them to search aimlessly through the halls for the time being, trading his telescope for the XM-110. This rifle was a version of Reed Knight's SR-25, set up specifically for the U.S. Army's Sniper/Scouts. As such, it had a quick-detachable suppressor at the end of its twenty-inch barrel, a collapsible stock and a folding bipod. Chambered for 7.62-mm NATO rounds, the weapon could take out targets six hundred yards away, but the quick-detach can on the end could be removed for close-quarters battle. The big advantage of the XM-110 was that it operated the same way as the Executioner's preferred assault rifle, the M-16, just with its mechanisms scaled up for the larger rifle cartridge. Though it wasn't capable of fully automatic or 3-round burst fire, the XM-110's 7.62-mm death messengers possessed considerable punch, making up for the lack of "rock and roll."

Bolan's Beretta and Desert Eagle were in their usual places, ready for fighting in tight places, the selector switch on the 93-R set to 3-round burst and the Desert Eagle locked and cocked in quick-draw leather. The tiny PX4 Compact was his backup gun, giving him fourteen more chances to win a fight if all the hundreds of other rounds from the larger weapons failed. Knives and explosive munitions rounded out the Executioner's battle gear, other weapons and ammunition seeded around the hotel for resupply as well as trip alarms and assorted booby traps to give him an edge.

"Fort" had given the soldier only two hours to prepare for an attack. He might as well have given him the rest of the week. Bolan wasn't someone who was afraid of hard work and had been able to turn the abandoned building into a death trap.

The XM-110 had its usual Leupold daylight scope replaced with night optics, a CNVD-T thermal imager to be exact, enabling the soldier to see the figures of opponents even behind foliage and light cover if necessary. The infrared scanner wasn't perfect. Bolan's battle uniform, his blacksuit, had as part of its current configuration a weave of polymers that was capable of masking his heat signature. While he wouldn't be invisible, even in the black of night, he'd still be of sufficiently low profile that he could have an edge against anyone looking for him.

The thermal imager picked up opponents in two of the hidden copses, their bodies yellow-outlined with blobby red cores. The dark shapes of assault rifles were clearly visible in their hands as deep blue stick shapes. Bolan couldn't tell the gear, except for various AK types by their long, curved magazines, but it was still enough firepower to wage a full-blown war against the Executioner. After a quick count, the warrior knew that the odds were twelve to one, but the one thing he wasn't certain of was if these men were sent blindly in, or if there was someone actually overseeing the attack.

Bolan wanted a prisoner to give him more information about what was going on. The Haitians were up to something, a plot that involved mass murder and terror and there was no real clue about what was afoot other than a tenuous link to the Black Alchemists, and by extension, the Tonton Macoute.

Count confirmed, the Executioner put away his rifle. The suppressed Beretta was going to take on the bulk of the deadly business ahead. The time for thunder would have to wait.

## CHAPTER EIGHT

Mack Bolan was in stalking mode, and the four Jamaicans who had advanced on the hotel were his quarry. His position would be untenable in most cases, but the Executioner had turned the abandoned building into his own personal fortress. He'd set up snares, warnings, and developed chokepoints that would allow him to dominate any force that dared to make its move against him. The only thing that was keeping Bolan from completely wiping out the quartet was their backup and the need to know who had hired them so he could work his way up the food chain to the mysterious Haitian Rambeau had called "Fort."

He'd decided to sling his combat rifle across his back and use either the suppressed Beretta 93-R or one of his fighting knives to eliminate foes until he could snare a prisoner. He had reached the lobby only moments before the hired Jamaican gunmen arrived, and they carefully moved through the doorway. One of them had a filtered, hooded flashlight, sweeping for signs of tripwires.

Bolan gave them an A for effort in respect of their preparedness. The flashlight, as the Jamaican had set it up, had a red lens, the better to minimize the spread of the glow to betray their position. There were two other teams out there, eight men total, and they were in overwatch position for their comrades. If Bolan made a mistake and gave away his presence, there was a good chance that they had access to at least night-vision devices, if not thermal imaging scopes like the one on his XM-110. Though the Executioner wore his blacksuit, its Nomex and Kevlar blend combining with a layer of polymers to minimize his heat signature without compromising his ability to move or keep his body cool, his head and hands were exposed and there wasn't greasepaint that could hide his infrared signature. Gloves and a hood would have helped, but the soldier had spent too many years without them. Besides, hoods could shift and limit his peripheral vision while leaving his fingers bare allowed him his full sense of touch, which was vital on night operations.

Four men, two radio headsets among them. If they lost one of their communications men, the other would call for him. Gaining control of one of the units would be a lost cause because they would shift over.

These men either were former military or they had been trained and equipped by the Haitians. Either way, Bolan would have to act quickly. There was a temptation to take them all out with head shots, but if the outside teams lost contact with the whole crew, depending on their weaponry, the hotel could be scoured off of the face of the earth. Besides, he had to determine the capabilities of his opposition and the makeup of this squad. There was a chance that someone in this group could provide information he needed.

He remained perched above the group on a second-floor walkway, his frame obscured by a railing that had slats that allowed him to observe them while remaining hidden. The group trudged toward a set of stairs, moving slowly, carefully, until they stopped cold, two steps in front of where Bolan had put a taut length of fishing wire across the flight. The wire was long enough that a collection of empty tins and cans hung at either end. The men without the communication gear examined the trap.

The Jamaicans weren't taking any chances. They saw the primitive alarm and snipped the line, lowering the metal to the floor without making too much noise.

Bolan made a decision. He knew where the backup teams were, and this squad was moving slowly and surveying the battleground thoroughly. The bunch here would be occupied for as long as it would take for the Executioner to pay their buddies a quick visit. Let them do their thing; Bolan would keep active.

He picked one of the windows he'd chosen for an emergency egress, a broken-out pane on the first floor. With a vault over the rail, he went from the rail to the lip of the walkway, then finally dropped the last two feet, landing in a soundless crouch. The Jamaicans hadn't looked back to the lobby they'd cleared, their one mistake, but Bolan wasn't sitting in the open. He ducked into the shadows, slithered through the office door and out into the Kingston night.

The Executioner had chosen that window thanks to the presence of a rusted fifty-five gallon drum half-full of charred trash. Its bulk was sufficient to hide him, and he brought his rifle with its thermal imager to his shoulder. The backup teams hadn't changed positions from their hiding spots in the foliage planted in the perimeter of the parking lot. Trees, bushes and long grass obscured the two four-man squads. However, the barriers would give way to twenty-first century thermal optics.

There was one problem with the infrared—even its high-tech, supersensitive heat imager couldn't see objects hidden behind truly solid objects, especially at a distance. Bolan counted on that for his protection, but he was also aware of the limitations of his own gear. From his scan with the IR viewer, he could tell that there was no one within range who had hidden within foliage that he wasn't aware of. As it was, the soldier had picked this route not only because of the drum that would camouflage him by the window, but because he had a clear route that would block his infrared signature easily from most directions.

Padding on silent feet, the soldier wove between all manner of trash and discarded artifacts of modern Kingston life, keeping his profile low as he approached the first of the two backup teams. As he closed on them, he heard a soft voice speaking into a radio.

"Any contact?" one of the hired Jamaican guns asked.

"Negative," came the muffled response. "Stay sharp."

Bolan paused, sweeping a perimeter beyond the small group he shadowed. There was a good chance that these four gunmen were simply bait, a taunt to bring him out into the open and into the middle of a cross fire. Bolan was situated now in the shadow of a thick tree trunk, something that would block his infrared profile. He scanned through the scope, "slicing the pie" by revealing only a sliver of himself as he advanced in a circular arc to view the world beyond his cover. By such subtle movement, the soldier minimized his exposure while maximizing his visibility. He paused as he spotted a van parked fifty yards away. He could see two figures through the windshield, one sitting in the driver's seat, the other riding shotgun. The body of the van, however, was able to hide myriad sins, such as opponents who were shielded from view by the bulky vehicle.

With the van situated in his mental map of the battlefield, Bolan paused before taking action against the small crew in the copse ahead of him. He could quickly take out these four, but they had someone looking out for them. This was a further distraction, but the Executioner turned the thermal imager toward the abandoned hotel, sweeping for signs of the enemy. He caught a glimpse of one of the four gunmen through a broken window, but couldn't see any of the others. He checked along his own back trail and around the parking lot, but those places were empty of armed gunmen. Moving slowly and easily, he disengaged from the squad he'd tracked, turning to deal with what had been hidden behind the van. It was easy to flank them as he stayed low to the ground, keeping solid mounds of earth between him and the one figure who had poked his head around. A scan with the IR imager showed that there was a spotlight of illumination that didn't match the shadows that deepened with the encroaching night. Bolan knew that the opposition had night vision, and when he saw the IR spotlight's beam, he froze. He wasn't the only one here who was utilizing high technology. The Jamaicans were well equipped, and they had two layers of backup, just in case Bolan had tried to outflank the men hidden in the treeline.

He had grudging respect for their abilities, but he was under no delusion that these were cold-blooded, heartless murderers. The firepower they had on hand and the way they had nearly killed Carmody, the DEA agent, were only two of countless indicators of their true, lethal nature.

If anything, the men who were on the inner rings of this assault were sacrificial lambs, mercenary gunmen who were hired to flush him out into a position where they could drop fire on him. If the Executioner hadn't been so experienced and anticipating a professional's response to him, he would have missed the sudden glimmer of infrared-only visible illumination and missed the backup squad.

Bolan slithered along the ground, preparing his XM-110 for an attack on this group. The other teams wouldn't be expecting someone to land on their partners by surprise, and just to keep an edge, the soldier kept the powerful marksman's rifle suppressed. He might have the chance to take out the crew by the van without a sound. He might be able to pull off a quiet coup against that group, but he wouldn't count on it. The moment gunfire started booming, the doomsday numbers would fall away, the edge provided by surprise dulling with each sound.

Bolan edged around the corner slowly, avoiding sudden movement that would attract attention. Through the thermal imager, he spotted six men, hunkered down with assault weapons of various sorts. Had he moved in on the other groups, they would have easily wiped him from the face of the earth with the firepower they had on hand. At least two of them had grenade launchers attached to their rifles, and the Executioner had only barely survived near hits from such weapons by luck and the proximity of boulders or steel to deflect the hammering punch of an explosive shock wave. No amount of skill could counter an impact from a 40-mm packet of notch-wire-wrapped plastique. Bolan sighted on one of the grenadiers and triggered the suppressed rifle.

High-velocity copper-jacketed lead impacted in the center of the grenadier's face, smashing in the bridge of his nose and blowing his brains out the back of his skull. The single shot had cored a massive channel through the Jamaican's head, spraying spongy blobs of gray matter against the back of the van. The sudden spasm of their comrade accompanied by the wet splash yanked the hardmen's attention toward the man who had died so fast, his legs hadn't even gotten the message that they weren't attached to a central nervous system.

"Man, what happened?" one of the gunners asked before the grenadier's hollowed skull swiveled toward him, exposing the dusk sky through the cavern blown through it.

Bolan hadn't waited for the Jamaicans to understand what was happening. The second man with a grenade launcher was next, the 7.62-mm NATO round striking lower than the nose, missing the brain entirely but vaporizing the gunner's jaw, bursting it apart in a spray of blood and pulpy muscle tissue. Splinters of bone speared hotly into necks and cheeks, jolting the Jamaicans into a flinch under the destruction of their friend's mandible. Hot gore geysered skyward as the bulk of his neck was torn out by the shot.

With two of their number dead, the enemy gunners were only instants from realizing what was happening to them and where the rain of death was coming from. Bolan sighted on one of the commandos, then held his fire. The man looked as if he were the leader of the group, and the Executioner could see the tumblers fall into place as he mentally unlocked the grim circumstances of their predicament. Bolan switched his aim and put an open tip boattail match round through the upper chest of the gunman beside him. Ribs splintered under the supersonic hammer blow, and the new target staggered backward. The leader of the group whipped around and watched another of his men slam against the doors of the van with a resounding thud.

"Fuck!" the leader of the group bellowed into the night as Bolan whipped his muzzle toward the fourth man in the strike squad. Four shots in the space of two seconds, and only two Jamaicans remained standing, their leader's weapon rising to his shoulder. The fourth of the gangster targets spun, his shoulder disintegrating underneath the high-powered rifle's impact. That spin was an effort to deflect the squad commander. It was a painful, maiming wound, but Bolan had placed the round where the brachial artery would have been severed by the violence of the 7.62-mm bullet. The blow was so sudden, so overwhelming that the mortally wounded man didn't cry out, his limbs flailing like spaghetti. The Jamaican boss's weapon was knocked skyward, bullets ripping into the night sky.

With that racket, the Executioner's presence, the way he'd flanked the whole group, was betrayed. He swiveled to see if the others had noticed. At the moment, they were caught completely off balance. It would take two seconds for them to focus and respond to what had happened. Bolan plucked a flash-bang grenade off his harness and lobbed it underhanded toward the two survivors. He'd need prisoners, which meant that the stun-shock bomb had to buy him time to deal with the sudden, increased response to Bolan's actions.

The two Jamaicans were bowled over by the flash-bang's detonation as the Executioner focused the thermal imager on the closest nest of gunmen. They had scrambled to their feet, and Bolan knocked the biggest of them down with a well-aimed XM-110 round to his center of mass. The Jamaican's heart, torn in two by the force of the impact, floated in a churned caldron of blood and gore. His legs stopped cold, and the three men behind him crashed against the still-standing corpse. He was so big that his body formed a wall between Bolan and the other three. That gave the Executioner the opportunity to tag off three more quick shots, bullets spearing through the stunned ambushers.

Through the imager, he could see their blood spray, the heat of their body temperatures changing subtly, but quickly. Those four targets were dead or dying, and they were no longer moving. They, and the four others farther downrange, weren't going to interfere with the Executioner and his acquisition of prisoners.

Bolan lunged from the shadows, swinging the rifle on its sling so that it was out of his way. he reached out toward the Jamaican gangsters who were still alive. The leader of the strike force lifted his head, his eyes dazed and unfocused. The soldier cupped the side of the Jamaican's head and drove his elbow into the temple on the opposite side. The impact, atop the thunderbolt crash of the stun grenade, was enough to render the lead assassin a limp puddle of twitching muscle and sinew. With that killer out cold, Bolan turned toward the second of the attacking gunmen. He'd managed to recover enough of his senses to pull a pistol to replace his fallen submachine gun. The soldier clamped his hand over the assassin's wrist and snapped his knee into the gangster's elbow.

Bones dislocated at the joint and the gunman's hand opened up. He let out a cry of agony even as his elbow bent in a direction it shouldn't have. Bolan slammed his forearm across the side of the disarmed man's neck like a guillotine. He dropped to his knees, and the big American shoved him to the ground. The Jamaican wouldn't be getting up for several minutes, and even if he did, his combat effectiveness was severely compromised by the badly dislocated elbow.

Gunfire popped in the distance, punctuated by the smack of lead against the van's bodywork. The Executioner stepped out of the line of fire, knowing that he'd finished his task just in time to deal with the second squad of backup gunners rushing to the aid of their partners. Bolan pressed himself against the van, using it as a shield, and took a moment to dump the partially spent magazine from the XM-110, feeding it a full box of twenty 7.62-mm NATO skull busters. The rattle of metal on metal was almost musical, a full-auto drumbeat that Bolan listened to carefully. He noticed that the salvo was homogenous, the four enemy gunmen going at it all at once. The chatter of their weapons ended abruptly.

The flank attack from the rear had taken the ambushers out of their game, and the hit team hadn't staggered their return fire. As such, they'd all run out of ammunition at once. Bolan swung around, shouldering the XM-110. Sure enough, the Jamaicans were reloading, although three of them had scrambled to the cover of a couple of rusted-out automobiles, limiting his shots against them. The Executioner popped the skull of the one loner refilling his assault rifle out in the open, his head bursting like a balloon once it was punctured by a single high-powered bullet. The assassin dropped bonelessly into the street, his concerns evacuated from his head in the trail of brain tissue following the supersonic round.

The other three turned as their comrade fell, distracted by the man's sudden death. One of the gunners leaned his head out into the open to check on the corpse. Bolan took this one behind his ear, placing his shot right into the tangle of dreadlocks that hung down the side of his head and neck. Practically decapitated, this gunman toppled onto what was left of his face after the bullet exited his forehead.

The last two hunkered down behind their cover, knowing that they wouldn't stand a chance if they moved. That was good enough for now. Bolan swept his rifle toward the hotel and saw three men rushing across the parking lot thanks to his thermal scope. Behind them, there was another heat signature, but it was cooling quickly. The Executioner's deadly little maze of traps and tripwires had evened the odds somewhat. As it was, he had enough breathing room to turn back toward the group leader, slipping the nylon cord of a cable tie around his wrists, securing them behind his back and high enough so that the Jamaican couldn't get enough leverage to slip his hands down under his heels.

At that moment, the rear door of the van opened. Bolan drew his Desert Eagle in a heartbeat, but even as he leveled the muzzle of the big handgun at the man at the back, he knew to keep his finger off the trigger. That didn't matter to the slender young man who was looking down the .44-caliber muzzle, something that looked like a cavern from his point of view.

"Don't shoot! Don't shoot!" he called, crossing both empty hands across his face.

Bolan looked at the Jamaican commander lying on the ground, then took his opportunity. With a palm strike, he knocked the unarmed young man back into the van. He stooped and grabbed the unconscious ambush leader by the upper arm, hauling him into the vehicle.

"I ain't armed!" the young Jamaican shouted.

"That's why you're still breathing. Where's the other guy?" Bolan growled.

"He took a chest full of lead," his second prisoner said. "I was trying to get out of the way."

Bolan peered through the windshield, seeing that there were shadows moving in the distance. The enemy gunners hadn't taken any fire for several seconds, and they were beginning to get their act together. He had no doubt that the trio who'd escaped the hotel had joined with the other two survivors. He looked to the youth. "Did you drive this thing?"

The kid nodded.

"Back behind the wheel. I'll give you cover fire," Bolan said.

There was a moment's hesitation on the young man's part, but Bolan pushed him into the driver's seat, then brought up the big Desert Eagle, putting the luminous tritium dot of his front sight in the center of one of the gun-toting shadows. A stroke of the trigger, and a .44 Magnum slug rocketed out of the barrel, the muzzle-flash lighting up the interior of the van. Downrange, the Jamaican gunner he'd targeted jerked violently, staggering off his feet.

"Go!" Bolan ordered.

The engine turned over, and the kid wrenched the gearshift into Reverse. Tires squealed and the rear wheels bumped over the corpses that the Executioner had left behind the vehicle. Bolan continued to fire, but any hope of precision was lost the moment the van peeled out into Reverse. Luckily, the hotel was a good solid backstop that would keep his gunfire from searing hundreds of feet beyond the battlefield to strike an innocent bystander.

"What did I do to deserve this?" the driver asked, hitting the brakes then clutching up through First and Second, not stopping until he hit Third. Bolan saw the rear doors flopping open and closed as the youth accelerated.

"You hung out with the Rastas," Bolan answered.

The Jamaican, this one without the telltale long hair and dreadlocks of a true Rasta, looked at Bolan in shock. "I'm just a driver. I just take them around."

"Find new employment," Bolan replied. "I'm looking for someone to ferry me."

"My name's Hopper," the driver said.

"Stone," Bolan returned. They had left the Jamaican ambush group behind. "Stop here."

"For what?" Hopper asked.

"I don't like leaving loose ends, and I don't want them chasing us into crowded streets," Bolan said.

Hopper took a quick turn, pulling the van out of sight behind a copse of trees. "Your dime."

The Executioner regarded Hopper sternly, then left through the back doors of the van. There would be cars full of gunmen coming along any minute, and Bolan had to return to the hotel to defuse his deadly booby traps. He'd also have a chance to scavenge new arms and ammunition.

It was time for him to counter the enemy's counter-ambush.

# CHAPTER NINE

Once again, the Executioner's instincts were on target. There was a pickup truck—a Toyota by its shape—racing down the road in pursuit of the escaping van. Bolan locked the safety on his Desert Eagle, stuffing it back into its holster as he transitioned to the XM-110. While the .44 Magnum pistol was known for its ability to cut through a windshield, it wasn't truly an antivehicle weapon. The 7.62-mm NATO rounds of the marksman's rifle were better. It wasn't the same as the far more powerful .338 Lapua Magnum round or the .50 BMG, but against a nonmilitary vehicle, the sniper rifle could wreck its engine with well-placed shots.

Bolan sighted on the front grille of the charging pickup and milked out two swift rounds, knowing that he had to cut off the mobility of the enemy truck. The two suppressed shots were answered by the sound of the shattered engine choking as its blown pistons ground to an ugly stop. The gunmen inside the vehicle threw open its doors, AKs shouldered and laying down a withering fire, pouring bullets up the road in an attempt to catch the Executioner.

Bolan had disappeared from where the Jamaican gunsels were aiming, moving as soon as he knew he'd made his hits. Autofire ripped the air far from him as he flanked toward the pickup. There were two gunners in the front, using the doors of the cab as their personal shields, not that it would have done much against the NATO hollowpoint rounds that his rifle utilized. There were two more men sitting in the cab. Bolan was at a right angle to the truck and he shouldered the sniper rifle. One bullet tore through the neck of one of the shooters in the cab, tumbling out of the torn throat of the ambusher and crashing into the left temple of the second man. The pair of them jerked violently under the two-for-one shot. Since the XM-110 had a suppressor on its muzzle, the two gunners in the front hadn't noticed the sound of the Executioner's single shot, just knew that their comrades collapsed, rifles clattering on the metal floor of the pickup bed.

Before the two could even begin to look for where the new round of sniper fire came from, Bolan shot the driver through the ear. His brains jettisoned out of the other side of his skull, filling the interior of the cab with the pulpy mass that used to be his central nervous system. The second guy turned to see the fountain of death that had poured from his partner's head, and he knew that he was in the line of fire. The 7.62-mm NATO round had lost energy, its path deflected by the corpse's skull so the last marauder was free to duck behind the body of the vehicle.

The Executioner grimaced, knowing that he'd have to flank the last man, or make use of another stun-shock grenade. He heard the telltale click and scrape of metal on metal as the Jamaican dumped his spent magazine. Bolan's attention would be occupied for at least a second. With a lunge, he was at the corpse of the driver, scooping up the dead man's submachine gun and hurling it toward the bed of the pickup.

It landed with a loud boom, its metal bulk's touchdown amplified by the echoing box of the truck bed. As soon as it landed, Bolan heard the gunman on the other side curse, struggling to bring his weapon back to operating condition. The Executioner slid across the hood of the pickup, landing in the dirt to see the last of the gangsters fight the bolt of his rifle and open fire.

The Jamaican cut loose on full-auto, bullets slicing through the metal fender, creating more than enough racket to occupy the gunman's senses. Bolan lunged at the distracted Jamaican, snaking his arms around the man's head and neck. The soldier jammed his fist right into the gangster's jugular, a knot of mass choking off the vein that emptied stale blood from the human brain. As the carbon dioxide built up, Bolan's prisoner fell unconscious. The gangster went limp, but the Executioner wasn't going to allow the sudden slackness in his opponent to lull him into a false sense of security. He kept up the pressure for several seconds longer until he heard the release of breath escape from the man in the chokehold.

Bolan left his foe on the ground, quickly field-stripping and disabling the weapons the unconscious gangster had possessed. He wasn't one to murder a helpless man, and just to make certain that an irate thug wouldn't wake and cause mayhem, the nylon cable ties were brought out to bind his wrists and ankles.

Hopper pulled up with the van, looking at the corpses strewed around the pickup. Wide eyes betrayed the feelings of the young Jamaican driver. There, for the sake of being an armed killer, went he. If he'd been aggressive in trying to escape the van, he'd have been as dead as these men. His loyalty to the gunmen who'd hired him to drive them around had disappeared the moment a salvo of full-auto bullets had torn through the windshield and nearly killed him, plucking the life of his escort.

Bolan had seen the corpse of another young man, an employee hired to keep the van safe. Hopper had lost a friend as well as his faith in the gangsters who'd hired him.

"You done here?" Hopper asked.

"Back to the hotel. I have to make sure that no one stumbles in," Bolan said. "I also need to police the scene, see if anyone else is useful to me."

"Then where?" Hopper inquired.

Bolan frowned. "Then we take him—" he indicated the unconscious ambush leader laying on the floor of the van "—to somewhere I can talk to him."

Hopper nodded.

HOPPER HAD INADVERTENTLY run over the other unconscious gangster in his zeal to escape the wild panic fire unleashed by the gunmen. A tire tread across the man's flattened throat, as well as the resultant spray of gore from eyes and nostrils, was more than enough to betray the finality of his death.

Rather than risk cutting through a maze of his own

creation with police on their way, Bolan borrowed one of the assault rifle/grenade launcher combos and targeted the rooms where he'd set up deadly traps rather than simple trip-wire alarms. Five shells from the M-203 underneath the barrel of an M-16 were enough to sanitize the abandoned building of lethal threats. With the resultant explosions, the police would definitely be on the way. Autofire was one thing for the cops to investigate at leisure, waiting until warring gang members had killed each other off or had retreated from the scene of the battle. Explosions, however, would attract the attention of Kingston's elite police.

The Executioner wanted the special teams to come by. They'd be thorough in their investigations, and Stony Man Farm would piggyback their evidence gathering, feeding him related information through their global intelligence network ties. Knowledge of the Jamaican gang involved with the Haitians would grant the soldier even more of a handle by which he could track them down. As it was, Bolan had several threads that he could follow.

There was the Macoute angle, with their subsequent voodoo ties.

Add to it that they were able to assemble a significant force of Jamaican hardmen to come after Bolan, he knew that he'd either have to lay himself out once more as bait, or lean on the unconscious head assassin for further information.

Either way, Bolan had a few hours to wait until Calvin James arrived and ran the prisoner through an

EKG to check for heart problems. If the Jamaican gang leader's heart was strong enough for chemical interrogation, James would break out the Scopolamine, a powerful drug that inhibited resistance to questioning. While nothing was an infallible "truth drug," James and Phoenix Force were skilled at using Scopolamine and thorough questioning to break through the resistance of a prisoner to answering their inquiries. The process would only take another few hours, after which Bolan could rest and plan before moving on to the next leg of this hunt for the Haitian.

That would bring the Executioner to the next evening, once more venturing out into the darkness, himself a shadow hunting shadows, bringing fear to the fearful and terror to the terrorists.

Out there, a madman had proved that he had no qualms about torturing innocent people and transforming them into mindless maniacs, horror-programmed missiles that he'd thrown into crowds of innocents, leaving scores of murdered and wounded in their wake. The Haitian Macoute angle sat like a beacon of dread in the landscape of the conspiracy that Bolan had stumbled upon.

The Tonton Macoute was nothing less than the purest example of "Animal Man." The group had been the chief enforcers of two of the world's worst dictators, Papa Doc and Baby Doc Duvalier. During their reigns, opposition party members disappeared. The lucky ones had been turned into ground meat for pet food. The unlucky had been dosed with the darkest concoctions of the worst voodoo practitioners, stripped of their humanity by toxins and hallucinogens to become "zu-vumbies," slaves to *houngans*. They toiled without respite until even their drugged, unfeeling bodies collapsed under the relentless physical strain of incessant servitude.

In a country that barely had enough money to import food for their starving people, the men of the Macoute had the finest uniforms and weapons, eating high off the hog and taking their pick of women as playthings. The corruption rampant in the administrations of the Duvaliers was legendary, leaving behind a legacy of nightmarish abuse of humanity that the Western world struggled to forget. This black stain on the heart of humankind's conscience was something that only the most despicable of pundits fed upon. Though the original Tonton Macoute had long since disappeared, their descendants adhered to the same principles.

The Macoute descendants were very dangerous human beings who backed up their psychotic religious fanaticism with firearms and deadly toxins that killed or mentally mutated victims so quickly and with such subtlety that the average layperson could not be blamed for assuming that powerful sorceries had been unleashed.

Whatever dark alchemist was at work, he backed his ploy with automatic weapons and mind-wiped berserkers.

The Executioner had only survived his initial encounter with the maniacs by sheer skill, and luck had saved Bolan from being flanked by the hired guns in the enemy's employ.

This conspiracy had only one type of mercy in store for those in its way, the cold respite of the grave.

That was all right with Bolan.

He would warm them up with the purifying fire of his unyielding blitz.

FORTESCUE HAD KNOWN better than to be present to deal with the mysterious Colonel Brandon Stone, but Romy phoned in the results of the attack on the American soldier. Fortescue had made certain that Romy was in nothing more than an observation position, far back from the action so that he wouldn't be caught in the cross fire, but close enough to take in all the happenings.

Romy sounded shaken over the cell phone. "Seventeen men went down in less than five minutes. Seventeen men with assault rifles and grenade launchers."

"Calm down," Fortescue said.

Fortescue could hear Romy's loud gulp as he tried to settle himself. "It's too hard to. I just watched a one-man army in operation. I know we got video of this guy, unarmed, taking down Morrot's crazies, but with firearms, he's even deadlier."

"He's just a man," Fortescue reminded him. "Someone who outthought his opposition, not outfought them. From what you described, he was sneaky and clever enough to catch them off guard, especially utilizing a suppressed weapon. You could have done the exact same thing."

"I wish I'd taken video of this guy in action. As it

is, all I have are blurry shots of him on my digital camera," Romy said.

"Blurry?" Fortescue asked. "We acquired those cameras because they wouldn't take shaky, unfocused photos."

"He's that fast. He's just that fast," Romy said, repeating himself breathlessly.

"Come back, we'll take a look at things here, from a better perspective," Fortescue ordered.

Romy made a guttural sound that was close enough to an affirmative for the Haitian's tastes. The last thing that the Black Avengers needed was to end up in the middle of a full-blown war with a guy who'd scared the living hell out of one of his finest leg-breakers.

Of course, now Fortescue had to break the news about the loss of seventeen gang members to a single man. Javier Orleans had fought his way to the top of his gang and turned the Grim Strokes into a force to be reckoned with in Kingston's scene. The loss of seventeen was going to be a major dent in Orleans's numbers, but he had only lost ten percent of the usual force he could field.

Before he could initiate the call to Orleans, his cell phone rang. It was the Grim Strokes boss.

"It's Fort," he said, taking the call.

"What the fuck just happened?" Orleans asked. "I lost contact with the crew I'd sent to the hotel."

"They're dead."

"All of them? What happened, did this guy have an army?" Orleans asked.

"My man said he was by himself. He was just fast and skillful," Fortescue said.

"Fast and skillful?" Orleans asked. "One man? What's his name?"

"The name we have is Brandon Stone, but it sounds like a cover," Fortescue replied.

There was a dull grumble on the other end. "It probably *is* a cover. Whether it's official or not, we might never know."

"Not official?" Fortescue asked.

"This man you describe, he sounds familiar," Orleans told him.

"So you know the kind of man who'd cut through twenty heavily armed Rastas?" Fortescue asked.

Orleans's tone dropped a few levels. "They say he only looks like a man. He's more like a god of Death."

"What kind of bogeyman are you talking about?" Fortescue was beginning to lose his patience.

"I've been hearing stories from time to time about a man known simply as the Soldier."

Fortescue grimaced. "He's a myth."

"Then how come the story of seventeen dead hardmen is something that fits into that mythology?" Orleans asked.

Fortescue snorted.

"You brought the man down on us. What the fuck were you thinking?" Orleans pressed.

Fortescue could barely contain the growl of frustrated rage in his voice. "Listen, we have someone knocking on our door, and you're involved with me anyway. What the hell was I supposed to do? Sit on my thumb?"

Orleans let out an exasperated sigh. "I knew the ruckus around Long Eddy a few weeks ago seemed familiar."

"Long Eddy," Fortescue repeated. "That wasn't you taking out the competition? There was plenty of corpses, it sounded like the Grim Strokes were taking care of business...."

"No, it was someone else. Now, we have a description matching a myth, and more bodies spilled all over the place. The Soldier is in Kingston. Usually, he doesn't stay long in the same place, but this might have been a return trip based on you."

"We didn't pull anything to attract his attention until the first day we saw him," Fortescue replied.

Orleans grumbled. "So he was relaxing, on vacation after cleaning up Long Eddy. And you, for all your dumb luck, dropped a crisis right in his lap."

"Romy saw that a man was captured. He also took one of your vans," Fortescue said, trying to get away from the blame game.

"It wasn't my van, and it wasn't seventeen of my best, either," Orleans replied. "Any idea who the prisoner was?"

"My man said it looked like the guy who was giving orders," Fortescue added.

"Shit!" Orleans's exclamation was harsh over the cell phone's speaker, and the Haitian winced. "The one good leader I send on my errand, and he's the one taken."

"So what's the plan?" Fortescue asked.

"The plan is for you and me to not be too closely linked for now," Orleans said. "And for me to find my man before he ends up spilling his guts."

"How do I know that you're not going to sell me out?" Fortescue asked. "From what I've heard of the Soldier, I know he's good at turning allies against each other."

"Oh, now you're suddenly a believer?" Orleans asked.

"Considering how things went to shit the two times we got involved with him, I'm going to err on the side of the worst-case scenario, and for now, that worst case means that we are dealing with nothing short of the kings of the underworld showing up and my name being at the top of the bargain menu when they want to chow down."

"Just keep your head, and I'll keep mine," Orleans said, then hung up.

Fortescue looked at his cell. "It's not your head I'm worried about."

JAVIER ORLEANS wasn't happy with the news that he'd been dragged into a shooting war when he should have had his power consolidated. There were opportunities to be had, though keeping the favor of Fortescue, who was en route to becoming one of the most powerful men in Haiti, was still on his priority list. He'd sent men, mostly capable kids who were culled from the street corner gangs looking to rise in the ranks and join with one of the strongest organizations in Kingston.

This was their chance to graduate to the "big leagues" and, thus, they were eager and primed to get the job done right. They were trained and had good equipment, but they were still amateurs.

Orleans was also a man who believed that even an army of deer could be lead to victory by a lion. Orleans had sent one of his truest lions, Corboun, with the group of newcomers. Sure, there was a chance that this was a trap, that was the reason that Orleans had sent in scrubs, not his top players. His caution had proved to be warranted, and his loss was only in the form of potential recruits. They could be replaced as easily as throwing a rock into a crowded street.

But Orleans had lost Corboun.

It wasn't just any kind of loss. A bullet would have been the ideal. The end of Corboun's existence would have left Orleans an anonymous shadow in the background. Corboun had stayed back to be the door slammed shut on Colonel Brandon Stone, not out of cowardice but because he was a certain that he would be right in line to get a first shot at the lone man and whatever backup he'd have.

Corboun was a lion, and now, the great, powerful hunter was caged.

Orleans gathered his lieutenants around.

"I need you to look at every single place the cops would be hiding one of mine," Orleans said.

One of his lieutenants, Riscio, looked doubtful. "Nobody would snatch Corboun. You've been workin' too hard to make your bona fides. Why would they hide him from you? They just process him, then you bring in your lawyers, and it's all good."

"This wasn't an arrest," Orleans replied. "We've got a third party down here. Not another gang, nor the law."

"But he'd use police resources?" Riscio asked.

"He might know where they have safehouses, and use them while no one's looking," Orleans returned.

Riscio frowned. "Someone with that kind of pull or knowledge, why is he so interested in us?"

Orleans sneered. "I did someone the wrong favor."

"Fort," Riscio grumbled.

Orleans regarded the lieutenant. Riscio was someone who'd come up through the recruitment process to reach all the way to near the top of the heap. He was someone whose hunger wasn't sated, and he was always looking for more. As such, that meant he took in every detail that he could. There was little of Orleans's administration of the Grim Strokes that had escaped his attention.

That kind of hunger made Riscio the kind of man who would gladly push Orleans into a meat grinder if he leaned over just a little too far. Then the lieutenant would gladly grill up all that ground gang boss and feast as he turned his attention toward taking over more and more of Kingston's underworld.

Orleans knew the hungry look because he was in the same position. He'd made that hard scrabble up the ladder of importance from being a wet-behind-the-ears teen with a knife all the way to being the man with the $500 suit. He constantly kept in touch with his other businesses, his legitimate covers that washed the dirt out of his illegal money. Orleans was hungry for something bigger and better. That was why he'd kept ties with the outcast Haitian who he'd run and gunned with in his earlier days; that was why he agreed to lend muscle to remove someone who was stepping on his group's plan to turn Haiti back into a place where the Grim Strokes could profit.

Corboun may have been the lion of Orleans's team, but Riscio was a jackal, looking for his chance to take the largest portion. Right now, Orleans realized two mistakes. One was underestimating the target that Fortescue had unleashed him on. The second was showing that he'd underestimated a foe, and now was in a weakened position.

Orleans knew he'd have to eliminate the hungry young savage before he felt Riscio's jaws clamped around his throat. The fortunate thing was that Orleans had the perfect tool for removing the power-hungry gangster. That was no less than the Soldier himself. If Riscio won, then the Soldier was no longer a sword of Damocles hanging over Orleans's head. If the Soldier won, then Orleans didn't have to worry about betrayal from below and behind.

Then the Grim Strokes' might would be focused, one way or another, on one enemy instead of two.

That was the plan, but as Orleans thought about the knife hidden in his forearm sheath, he knew that plans were something you had until you ran into a real problem. Once those hit, all you could count on was yourself and whatever you had up your sleeve. Five inches of razor-sharp steel seemed like just the ticket for that kind of crash.

# CHAPTER TEN

Corboun had looked as if he were in phenomenal physical condition, but there was a reason why Calvin James always put prisoners through physical examinations before injecting Scopolamine. That examination also included a run through a portable EKG machine to look for weaknesses in the heart, something that the dose of "truth serum" would exacerbate into a full-blown heart condition.

"We can't drug answers out of him," James said.

"So much for that plan," Bolan said. "You have any other ideas?"

"There's always water-boarding, but that's a tactic that isn't really reliable," James said. "Without a baseline to work off, we could end up having this dude confess to shooting Abraham Lincoln."

Bolan nodded. "Part of why that's only a last resort."

The Executioner walked over to the rest of James's equipment. There was a polygraph—the so-called "lie detector"—that measured stress responses to questions. By itself, it wasn't as useful, but combined with proper questioning and the inhibitions removed by scopolamine, it would make finding lies and falsehoods much simpler. Alone, it only measured changes in metabolism forced by emotion, something that people could beat if they tried. The prisoner they had was a cold, hardened killer who wouldn't feel nervous about being caught in a lie, the same autonomic response that triggered the monitor.

"Cal, you've been able to pick up readings without your subject having to answer a question, right?" Bolan asked.

"Yeah," James replied. "Sometimes we do word-fishing. We hit something they recognize, they register. It's something that researchers are trying to improve upon. Mind-reading technology, based off of magnetic resonance."

"I know. There's also a system called brain finger-printing. It measures brainwave response to words, phrases or pictures. Right now, it's controversial and hardly usable in a court setting," Bolan said. "There've been rumors of brain-fingerprinting technology being tested by less scrupulous inventors in a smaller package. That's really neither here nor there. Right now, we don't have actual mind-reading skills, but we do have someone here, and we can fish for reactions from him."

James rested his forehead against his palm. "It's not going to be perfect."

"Right now, it's the best we've got," Bolan stated. "We'll do something to make things a little more in our favor."

James lifted an eyebrow. "You're going to do what Schwarz did back when he was at NASA? Make him think we've got brain-fingerprinting devices right here?"

Bolan shrugged. "I really like his ideas sometimes. Besides, it beats 'Dysfunctional Spy Agency Theater.'"

James gave a mock bark of dismay. "That was Stony Man gold! And it got the job done."

"You need Carl to sell it," Bolan told him, referring to the big, brutish ex-cop Carl Lyons, leader of Able Team. Lyons's size and ability to channel his inner caveman had proved just the right flavoring to convince a prisoner that he was in peril of being turned into human stew. James was in the role of conscientious objector to torture while the Able Team commander was in full-on psychotic mode. Their prisoner had buckled in moments.

James shrugged. "All right. One whacky scientist willing to experiment on human brains coming up."

The Phoenix Force medic went to his kit and got out a small diabetic blood-check lancing device. It was shaped like a pen, but it was a simple little machine that could be cocked and made to "fire" a small metal point into skin to draw blood necessary for sugar checks. James smirked as he loaded a lancet into its neck and screwed the tip back on.

"What's that?" Bolan asked.

"Schwarz is a smart guy, but he's more of an improvisational type. Instead of punching a nail into someone's head and risking giving the poor bastard tetanus…" James looked around and scrounged up some USB cords. A little bit of electrical tape to the end of the lancet device, and he had something that looked as if it could plug into a machine. He rolled it out and taped it to the side of the polygraph. "This looks like something a medical specialist would use, not a jury-rigged…"

"Gadget," Bolan concluded for James as he searched for the word.

James chuckled. "Yeah. No offense to Schwarz, but I like my ruses to actually make sense."

"Would you need help with this?" Bolan asked.

"You could sit in and observe, look for something that the polygraph misses, but I've got a digital video recorder to tape this," James told him. "If you have other tasks to perform, you can do them while I take care of all the boring interview work."

"It's not boring," Bolan offered. "At least not to you."

James smiled. "It's still less fun than firing an M-203 into the windshield of an automobile trying to run me down."

"So that's where McCarter's wild streak went," Bolan noted. "Back on topic, what would be useful for the Farm in terms of brain-fingerprinting technology?"

"Honestly, the polygraph we have is good enough. The method invented by Dr. Larry Farwell mainly uses electrodes that we have on the polygraph. That, plus backup methods including TARA—Timed Antagonistic Response Alethiometer—which is the measure of how long it takes a subject to fabricate a falsehood."

"And TARA just needs a laptop, measuring the ability to perform two actions at once," Bolan said.

James nodded. "It's still an experimental format, but initial testing garners an eighty-five percent accuracy rate, while FBI tests of the Farwell method trend higher, though it has the limitations of human memory and individual perception. Right now, I don't have the electrode harness to do the fingerprinting, so I'll be working not from brain waves but nonautonomic functions as I go fishing."

James put his gear together on a rolling table to take into Corboun's room. "What will you be up to?"

Bolan frowned. "The Jamaicans aren't acting in a vacuum. I'll be talking to Hopper again. We already know that this attack was a tryout for the Grim Strokes, the gang that hired Hopper. I'm going to head out to see what's going on at the street level. If anything, it'll hang bait as I do my own form of fishing. I'll also track down Rambeau and see what he knows about the Strokes and the Haitians."

James nodded. "I know we have to keep OPSEC around Hopper, but do you think that you can trust him?"

"I don't believe that he's a risk to the mission. He was unarmed, just a driver. I found a pistol under the seat, but nothing bigger," Bolan said. "His dead friend in the passenger seat wasn't the driver shoved over. His blood was all over the shotgun seat."

"So he's not a shooter, just a wheel man," James said. "I could check him out with some Scope."

Bolan shook his head. "First, he's just going to be my driver and guide. I can keep an eye on him, and he's already physically intimidated by me."

"You're a foot taller than he is," James added. "And you're saying that your gut tells you he's good?"

"Not every young gangbanger is a savage out for

cheap thrills and bloodletting," Bolan answered. "This one is looking for enough money to get by, and he's only doing as much as he has to. He could make more money by shoving a shotgun in someone's face, but he's stayed out of that. He's got none of the telltale marks of regular firearms handling, or hand-to-hand combat."

James looked Bolan over. "How do you get that kind of detail? Really, are you Sherlock Holmes's illegitimate great-grandchild?"

"No," Bolan said. "But I do keep my eyes peeled. Missed details means I might end up taking a hit. And I pay attention to things I *know* are common signs that a person engages in regular violence."

James looked down at his hands, seeing tiny scars and scuffs, both old and new, reminders of battles and training. The most common sign of hand-to-hand battle were fight bites, the inevitable result of punching another man in the mouth. James, a tae kwon do practitioner, didn't have marks on his knuckles, but did have them where the heel of his palm mashed into mouths during "shuto" strikes. He also had signs of recent burns from hot brass striking his wrist during a trip to the range. Some would fade —like the brass burns— but others like the repeated shuto strikes left a callus that could be recognized by the sharp-eyed. "It's been a while since I was a cop. I forgot about 'perp hand.'"

"It helps separating the innocent from the guilty," Bolan said. "Trouble is, I have to use Hopper as bait alongside me. That could end his chances at getting on the right path."

"It's a risk, but he hasn't taken off," James countered. "He wants to stick around and make things right."

"Or he could be afraid of what will happen if I have to chase him down," Bolan noted.

"All right. I'll dig through this guy's memories, making use of what data the Kingston police have on the Grim Strokes. You handle the really tough part," James said. "I'll take boring over morally damning any day."

Bolan sighed. "I knew I could count on you for backup."

The soldier turned and headed to the room they'd reserved for their new ally.

Lonny Hopper was eighteen, and while he'd seen a lot on the back streets of Kingston, he'd never seen a white man as physically large as this Stone guy. Granted, he was a few inches over six feet, and his muscles weren't like those of the body builders who frequented beaches to tan their overly swollen bodies. The size wasn't in just the frame and muscles of the man. He had a presence like a tiger. When he moved, one could see the muscles flow, limbs containing power that were filled with restrained energy. Or maybe it was just the supreme confidence with which he strode among the rest of the world, the aura of unstoppable force that he could direct as easily as one would blow a kiss.

Now, Hopper walked behind Bolan as the pair walked by his old street. The storefronts were strewed with tables full of goods put out onto the sidewalk.

Bolan paused every so often to look over a piece of fruit or a rack of postcards, looking for all the world like a tourist. If Hopper hadn't known better, he would have sworn that the man in front of him had shrunken from a giant to something less, merely another face in the crowd. The lean arms that snaked out of the sleeves of his black T-shirt were relaxed, their movements still smooth and fluid, but they didn't betray the corded muscle beneath.

"How do you do that?" Hopper asked as Bolan spun a display of sunglasses, looking in the lenses at eye level.

"Do what?" Bolan asked.

"Change," Hopper said. "Last night you were a superhero in black. Now..."

"It's the suit," Bolan answered, managing a slight smile. "It just makes me look more impressive than I really am."

"What, it's got fake muscles packed in?" Hopper asked.

Bolan gave the young Jamaican a tap on the side of the head, a gentle cuff that didn't hurt, but it focused his attention. "Mind on business, not me."

"You are my business now," Hopper returned.

"Fair enough," Bolan answered. Hopper was surprised at Stone's vanity as he kept looking at his reflection in the mirror.

"You've got to be his twin brother. The lazy, inane brother," Hopper muttered.

Bolan looked over at Hopper. "Who?"

"Stone. The big bad fucker who grabbed me last

night," Hopper answered. "You're primping and preening like—"

"Quiet," Bolan said, his soft, casual voice disappearing for a moment, replaced with the deep, commanding timbre of the man who had come within inches of killing him the night before. His tone lightened again, and the stern glare that had struck him had melted back into the simple, almost dopey tourist he had transformed into.

The man was a chameleon, Hopper thought, changing tones and moods faster than people could don and doff a hat.

"I'm watching a couple of guys who are giving me the hairy eyeball. They're not sure that I'm the one that they were sent after."

"Because you're acting all soft?" Hopper asked.

Bolan didn't have to answer such an obvious question. He selected a pair of glasses and handed some money to the vendor. Hopper followed him across the street to the next corner. Bolan reached back, hand open. On instinct, Hopper reached forward and took his hand. The grasp was gentle.

"I… I didn't…" Hopper began.

"Didn't think I was gay or interested in you?" Bolan asked.

"N-no," Hopper answered.

"I'm not," Bolan said. "I'm just playing a role to keep them off balance. Does the gang know you're gay?"

"It's hard to hide that in a street gang," Hopper said.

Bolan tugged him closer. "That's why I agreed to drive for the hit against you."

As soon as he mentioned his involvement with the attack, Hopper pulled away from Bolan's arm. "I'm sorry."

"Just stay like that," Bolan said. "For one, it's okay. For two, I need you as my camouflage, and you need it to stay alive."

"Me?" Hopper asked.

"You need some excuse for why you're still alive when everyone else is dead," Bolan told him. "You did the smart thing—you ditched the battle and ran. You picked up a tourist at a resort. You haven't been seen because you've been with him. That's why you're still with him…me."

Hopper rested his head against Bolan, a little tentative, but finding some comfort now that he had the big man's approval. He'd been captivated by the man the minute he'd seen him in full battle regalia. There was something in him that had to have had women falling at his feet, as though he were a dashing hero from a spy movie come to life. A woman in every port, and yet he was so assured, so masculine, that he felt no discomfort whatsoever holding a young gay man close. He gave off no vibe of sexism, no racism, either, as Stone spoke to him as an equal, not a lesser being.

Again, the word magnificent flashed across Hopper's mind. Stone was a man with a big heart, and no urge to ostracize him. Hopper knew he was being used now, but he also realized that the man wasn't going to endanger him. He felt protected, not exploited.

"Heads up," Bolan's gruff voice broke in. "Their curiosity got the better of them."

Hopper's hand tightened with his, a white knuckle grip, though it was like trying to crush the hand of a statue. "What do we do?"

"Answer their questions," Bolan told him. "If something goes bad, you hit the floor right away."

"Hopper! Oy!"

The young driver tensed. He turned to see the two men that Stone had mentioned. He recognized them from the group who'd called in the recruits. He didn't remember their names, but he knew that they were cruel-voiced thugs.

"Hopper, where the hell you been?" one of them said.

Bolan released Hopper's hand, keeping his back to the pair.

"That's right, faggot, don't fuckin' look at us," the other barked at the big American. "Wouldn't want to wreck you, too."

"Leave him alone," Hopper said, his instincts kicking in. He wanted to protect the man, even though he knew that Stone didn't need any defenders.

The thug who'd called out Hopper backhanded him. "Shut up. You're breathing while your mates ain't. Why's that?"

"Because the fuckers took a shot at me through the windshield," Hopper answered, his ire rising. His adrenaline was pumping so much that he didn't notice the sting raised on his cheek. "I'm supposed to stick around when I'm being shot at by the idiots I'm supposed to be working with?"

"So you steal our van?" asked the one who taunted Bolan.

"I'm supposed to run off by myself?" Hopper asked. "They already tried to shoot me, I'm supposed to become an easier target?"

The Taunter—as Hopper had named him—glared at him, then looked back at the motionless Bolan. The Taunter sneered at him, keeping his attention focused. The man didn't want Bolan sticking his nose in this business, while Thug Number One continued to grill Hopper.

"So you don't call in?" Thug Number One asked.

"I'm sorry. I forgot I owed you that. Who are you? My mother?" Hopper asked.

"Listen, can I just go?" Bolan asked in a nasal tone.

Taunter snorted. "No. Stick around. We want you to know all our business."

"O-okay," Bolan replied, tensing up.

"Bob, shoot that fucker if he tries to run away." Thug Number One grunted. He turned back toward Hopper. "You're going to tell us why…"

Hopper heard the rustle of fabric, and then a sickening crunch. Bob wailed in agony, his hand bent at a ninety-degree angle to his forearm. The gun clattered on the sidewalk, and the Jamaican gangster's scream went higher when he saw the snapped ulnar bone sticking through his skin. Hopper took a step back and could barely follow the blur of Stone's hands. Bob's head snapped around for a second, then his torso jerked forward. Thug Number One was frozen at the suddenness of the attack. One moment, Bob had been standing, and now he was flat on his back, blood and spittle flowing from the corner of his mouth. Hopper wondered if Stone had broken the guy's neck.

Hopper finally focused on Stone as he held the second man up against the wall. Thug Number One suddenly appeared taller than before, and Hopper had to look down to see that the thug's feet were dangling two feet off the sidewalk. Even as he looked at the ground, he saw another pistol drop, bouncing away with a metallic clatter.

"It's…" The thug began before his weight choked him against the collar of his shirt.

"It's me," Bolan replied. "Brandon Stone, the guy who killed a hell of a lot of armed men last night."

"You're a fa—"

Bolan hefted the gangster a bit higher, cutting him off. "Clean up your language."

Hopper turned back toward Bob on the ground, who was grasping for breath. The barely conscious man moved his hand up to wipe blood from his lips, but that was about the extent of the strength he retained.

"We're going to talk someplace a little more private," Bolan told him. "Hopper, pick up those guns. I wouldn't want them to fall into the wrong hands."

Hopper did as he was told. Bob's lips moved, his eyes blinking lazily.

"He'll be fine. He just caught an elbow in the mouth," Bolan reassured them.

"Okay," Hopper replied.

Bolan held Thug Number One in a headlock, whispering questions to his prisoner as they were out of sight in a gap between buildings. Hopper stood back, having stuffed both pistols into his waistband. He untucked his shirt and hid them. There was a sudden movement, and the gang member was shoved hard against the wall. Hopper heard the thump of a fist against ribs, and the man collapsed to his knees.

"Let them know what I told you," Bolan growled. "Otherwise I'll be disappointed. And you don't want me to be disappointed, right?"

"Right," the gangster croaked.

Bolan turned to Hopper. "Come on. I have another errand to run."

"Will they know where we're going?" Hopper asked.

Bolan nodded. "I'm hoping so. I'll make sure you're out of the line of fire."

"I'm packin' now," Hopper said.

Bolan shook his head. "You've got a pair of pistols. That's not the same as being able to take care of yourself."

He pointed to Bob, still on the sidewalk. "He had a gun. I didn't. I'm the weapon, guns are just tools. I'll keep you alive, son. You have the chance for a future."

Hopper followed Bolan, remaining silent. The guns in his waistband felt like ugly, useless lumps as the duo returned to the rental car.

# CHAPTER ELEVEN

The Executioner watched as Hopper shoved the confiscated weapons into the glove compartment, remaining quiet and unnerved to be in the middle of this situation. He hated having to have been so gruff with the young man, but he didn't want an untrained civilian to catch a bullet because of false confidence. Bolan had suffered enough friendly dead over the years, recent ones still haunting him like palpable phantoms. Hopper wasn't going to end up being another one.

Hopper pulled the car to a stop on a secluded road. This was an only partially developed area of Kingston, where there were as many trees as there were houses. These weren't planted for beautification, either, they were wild, tangled things that drooped limbs in wide canopies, grasses and shrub exploding around them creating a thick underbrush worthy of some jungles that Bolan had tromped through. This wasn't a place tourists visited, and what few people were here didn't care to do much more than keep themselves alive. Litter mixed in with the grass at the edges of the hard-packed dirt road, a rusty dark brown strip that was only barely smooth, walled in by sporadic wooden slat fences that extended six feet in height. Shacks sat behind those fences and rows of thick growth, as if ashamed to show themselves, huddling under the leafy claws of the untamed trees towering over them.

The stench of trash and waste hung in the air, despite the breezes washing over the semiurban landscape. A group of children who had been kicking around a partially deflated soccer ball stopped, their faces punctuated by wide eyes locked on Bolan's ride. When the soldier stepped into the open, the kids darted into the undergrowth or sought cover behind one of the slat fences. He could tell that they hadn't completely run away, stubby fingertips gripping the edge of one of the slats betraying the position of one young boy who was curious about the newcomer.

Hopper got out of the car, but Bolan waved him off.

"Take this somewhere up the road, out of sight," Bolan told him. "I need the car hidden, and you ready to pull out fast if necessary."

"Like a robbery," Hopper said, not missing a beat. "Got it. Will you know where I went?"

"As long as it's down the road in that direction, yes," Bolan said.

Hopper had driven two circuits around this neighborhood before the soldier had him stop the car to let him out. They both had seen potential hiding places, and it wouldn't take much guessing to figure out where Hopper would secrete the vehicle. "I'll be waiting."

"Be careful," Bolan said. He handed over one of the confiscated weapons from Bob and the other gangster. It was a .38 Special revolver, with only six shots, but it was simple and powerful enough to help Hopper survive any incidental violence.

"I thought you said…" Hopper began.

"This is your last resort. Be smart and survive, don't take the fight to anyone. Your brain is your best defense, this is only a tool," Bolan told him.

He could tell that Hopper's gaze had fallen to the windbreaker Bolan wore. Underneath, the Executioner was outfitted for street combat, wearing his shoulder holster and gunbelt containing the mighty Desert Eagle and Beretta machine pistol he preferred. The two guns accompanied Bolan on nearly every mission he'd undertaken ever since he'd retired his prior signature weapons, an AMT .44 Automag and a 9-mm Beretta Brigadier. As such, his proficiency with them was in an elite class all by itself, enabling him to equal the fighting power of multiple opponents with assault rifles and other long guns in many instances. Bolan hoped that this visit wouldn't come to that kind of mayhem, but just in case, he had six magazines of thunder—ammunition for the .44 Magnum Desert Eagle, and six magazines of whisper—magazines to feed the suppressed Beretta machine pistol.

He had come here in search of links to the darker side of the *Vodou,* the Haitian form of what the rest of the world called voodoo. As such, there was the possibility that even if Bolan had brought an assault rifle with a grenade launcher, he might not be armed well enough. Bolan had contacted a *mambo,* a priestess of the hybrid religion formed between Roman Catholicism and West African *Voudun. Mambos* and *houngans* were priests, spiritual leaders who called upon the *loa* spirits to convey prayers to the supreme being, and thus wouldn't be involved with the wicked witchcraft as performed by the Tonton Macoute to cow the Haitian people. The Duvalier family were either *bokors* themselves, or lorded over them. It was the *bokor,* the dark sorcerer, that had brewed up the mysterious powers that created zombies or cast illness upon their enemies.

That witchcraft had been surprisingly effective biochemistry, the utilization of poisons and hallucinogens that were powerful enough to convince a man that he was a lifeless, soulless drone to do the work for the *bokor.* It wasn't the first time that villains utilized religion to provide the trappings of their power, twisting the faith of followers into fervor to perform atrocities that went totally against the morals and faith of the true religious beliefs.

The danger of the voodoo sorcerer was in the potential for more dangerous weaponry than a gun or a knife. Bolan knew he wasn't immune to the neurotoxins that they utilized, and had even been felled by such poisons before, surviving only by luck or enemy design. He also knew that a zombie—some poor innocent who had been drugged and brainwashed—could ignore multiple rounds to his center of mass and continue to fight even with his heart blown in two, at least until the oxygen in his blood had run out thirty seconds later.

Mambo Glorianna had directed the Executioner to this lonely stretch of unfinished road. Here, children were wary of any movement, disappearing at the sight of any man simply because they knew a dark evil nestled in the shacks somewhere. The curious boy who peered around the fence had noticed that Bolan was a white man, and was alone. He leaned his head out farther.

Bolan walked toward him, his hands open, smiling, showing no signs of hostility. The boy, still wide-eyed, stepped into the open.

"You here for the Gray Man?" the kid asked in a soft, high-pitched voice.

"Is he the *bokor?*" Bolan asked. He already knew, Mambo Glorianna having given him a good description, but only a rough location of the dark sorcerer. He asked the boy, giving him the illusion of power and knowledge, making him more willing to give Bolan information freely.

The child winced at the dark term. "He has strong bad."

Bolan nodded. "And I bring strong good."

The soldier tugged on a shoestring around his neck, showing Mambo Glorianna's charm. While it wouldn't change his blood chemistry to defend against voodoo powder, it was a symbol that was recognized and trusted. No man who wore Glorianna's charm was a bringer of suffering. Apparently, Glorianna's magic was strong enough that the boy's eyes widened with wonder.

"You do," he said. "You do bring good."

The boy raised his hand. Bolan figured out that the child wanted to hold his hand as they approached the Gray Man. He complied, and the kid tugged him along, little feet moving with purpose and determina-

tion. Bolan would have been amused by this, had he
not come here to face off with a *bokor.*

Once they reached a gap in the fencing along the
north side of the dirt road, the boy pulled Bolan into
the underbrush. Luckily, the soldier hadn't released his
hand, otherwise the kid would have slipped after tripping on a root. He scooped up the child and let him ride
on his shoulders. Bolan was sure-footed, even in the
thickest of terrain.

The boy hadn't spoken since acknowledging Glorianna's charm, and probably for good reason. Who
knew what sentries the *bokor* had around his dwell-
ing? The kid steered Bolan, stubby fingers pointing
where to go next. When they had gone far enough, the
boy tapped on Bolan's forehead. He lowered the child
to the ground as they stood in the shadow of a particularly thick tree. Twenty yards ahead, visible through
breaks in the underbrush, was a shack that had to have
been Bolan's target.

The boy opened his arms, and the soldier leaned forward. He had been expecting a whispered admonish-
ment to take care against the Gray Man. Instead, the
child hugged him tightly around the neck.

"Thank you," the kid said. He turned and disappeared into the brush, making his way back to the dirt
road. The boy was at once grateful for Bolan's presence, and terrified of the dark sorcery that festered in
this twisted bramble of dark wood. The Executioner
turned to look at the Gray Man's shack.

It resembled a shrine to bones, pieces of skeletons,
both animal and what could have been human, hang-

ing as wind chimes around the awnings of the dark cabin. As Bolan approached, he could smell the stale stink of rot. Lives, animal or human, had ended here. He paused at twelve yards out, staying low and within the shoulder-high grass. Something was in there with him, moving slowly.

The Executioner's instincts kicked into full gear at the scrape of metal on metal, and he dived to the ground, ducking under the whistle of a machete blade. Bolan rolled onto his back to see a pallid, tall Jamaican recover from his swing. Blank eyes stared down at him, and Bolan kicked out, tagging the "zombie" in the kneecap. With the crunch of bone, the dronelike sentry crashed into the undergrowth. Able to feel pain or not, the dislocation of a knee joint would bring anyone down.

The dead-eyed man twisted and lashed out with the machete again. Bolan rolled inside the swing, his shoulder stopping the zombie's forearm as it dropped. Momentum and leverage dislodged the silent guard's weapon from numbed fingers. The soldier snapped a heel-palm strike into the zombie's jaw, snapping bone and pushing its head back to the ground. With a pounce, Bolan straddled his stunned opponent, then jammed his thumb hard against the man's carotid artery. No amount of hallucinogens or toxins could negate the brain's need for oxygen. The sentry tried to thrash free, but he faded quickly. Bolan waited until the man went limp, then released his grip. The zombie had survived enough brain damage, he didn't need further disability thanks to oxygen deprivation. There was a chance that he could recover from his zombification; others had broken out of the drug-induced spell.

The Executioner got to his feet and knew that there were more barriers between himself and the Gray Man. He had been lucky and prepared, and that alertness had saved his life. The luck he had, hearing the drawing of the machete, had been helpful, but now it was time for Bolan to make his own luck. He charged toward the Gray Man's shack, catching the silhouettes of more of the *bokor*'s unblinking guards out of the corner of his eye, hearing the hiss of blades swatting toward him. But they found only grass and branches to chop.

Bursting into the open, Bolan turned and looked back. The neurotoxins and hallucinogens used by the Gray Man to keep his "zombie horde" numb were also the same that kept them from having reflexes quick enough to tag him with the edge of a tree-chopping blade. Even so, it had been close. He was tempted to draw his Beretta or Desert Eagle, punching rounds through their brains as they emerged from the foliage, but he knew that they were only victims of the *bokor*.

He remembered the savagery of other opponents only a day before, and the violence they had unleashed thanks to powers beyond their control. He'd gone soft on them, and they'd occupied him long enough that innocent people died. Bolan was here alone, however, alone except for the Gray Man who lorded over these shambling guards. He looked at the front door of the shack. It looked weatherworn and flimsy, so he lunged at it, putting all of his strength into a side kick against the door. What should have been disintegrating wood was simply disintegrating veneer and paneling over a crude steel sheet.

Luck helped Bolan again in that he hadn't twisted his ankle trying to knock down the door. Recovering from the kick, he backed up onto both feet. One of the zombies raised his weapon and charged at the Executioner. Bolan saw the movement in his peripheral vision, bent and sprung into the waist of the chopping drone. The tackle knocked the shambler off his feet, a punch into the armpit caused enough neural trauma to make him drop the long blade.

"I'm starting to get sick of machetes," Bolan muttered as he saw two more of the Gray Man's guards emerge from the forest. He scanned the area, reviewing his mental image of the shack's surroundings. There had been a rake four yards to the left of his current position. Two long strides later, the haft of the garden tool was clenched in his hand, ready to meet the blades of the zombies.

When they had a clear sight of their target, the sentries picked up their pace, coming at Bolan with a swiftness that belied their earlier numb shamble. It didn't matter. Bolan dug the metal tines of the rake into the forearm of one of them, slashing the terrain chopper out of his hand and yanking his attacker off balance. In the same twisting movement, the Executioner extended the rounded end of the long handle into the solar plexus of the second man, stopping him cold, and out of the slashing range of that one's machete.

Even zombies had to breathe, and the stunned sentry staggered, trying to suck air into his lungs. With a pivot of the rake, Bolan swept the guard's feet out from under him. Another step closer, and he was able to knock out the drugged man with a powerful kick to the jaw. The other two zombies got up from where Bolan had floored them, bracketing him like grisly bookends. They had been disarmed, but that didn't hinder their willingness to tear out the soldier's throat. They were still capable of killing, either with jagged, broken fingernails or chomping teeth.

He wasn't going to underestimate them. They'd proved capable of short-range quickness, and had been selected as zombies because they were big, strong-limbed men. The one to Bolan's left attacked first, his fingers hooked like talons, ready to rip flesh. Bolan stopped him with a kick to the pelvis, folding the guard over. A quick, hard elbow to the base of the zombie's neck knocked the fight out of him.

While Bolan was dealing with that opponent, the other leaped, crashing down on his shoulders. Nails ripped at the soldier's neck. Instinctively, Bolan snapped his head back hard, and he felt teeth in his scalp just before he dislodged them. He half turned and wrenched his elbow into the zombie's rib cage, feeling bones break under the impact. Completing the turn, Bolan grabbed his stunned foe by the back of his neck and shoved him forehead-first into the metal door. Sure enough, the door was reinforced, but the last zombie collapsed onto the cabin's front deck, groaning as it clutched its split-open hairline.

Bolan saw the hinge of the door, now that he'd kicked the paneling off the front of it. While there appeared to be a doorstop keeping the steel from buckling inward, it was simply nailed into a sturdy wooden jamb. The Desert Eagle came out, and Bolan blasted the wood that anchored the hinges. Huge gouts were driven into the thick lumber, and with their base badly weakened, Bolan fired off another kick.

The steel panel pivoted, twisting on the metal strut as its hinge was ripped out. The lock on the other side of the door snapped, thanks to the leverage Bolan had. He grabbed the door and pushed it aside. In the cabin, he saw the Gray Man, standing like a grim wraith.

The appellation fit the sorcerer. His hair was the color of ash, as was his thick beard and eyebrows. A slate-colored cloak and hood rode his head and shoulders, the garment closed down the front to conceal any other details. The Executioner knew that wasn't good and quickly swung back the steel-armored door. Bullets chattered on the other side of the metal, the twin rip-rip of dual machine pistols pummeling out a counterpoint to the nearly musical sound of their payloads striking Bolan's shield. Once again, his instincts had kicked in even before his conscious mind caught more than a glimmer of warning. He dived out onto the porch, the armored door clanging on the floor inside of the cabin. Bolan drew his Beretta, but held off return fire. He came to ask questions, and even a *bokor* couldn't get answers from a corpse.

"You come here looking for the Gray Man?" came a shout from within the cabin. "You good enough to handle my zombies! But I have strong magic!"

"And a couple of machine pistols," Bolan answered. "I guess your magic isn't that powerful."

Bolan knew the back and forth was simple mental warfare, boasts thrown by the sorcerer to break the will of less experienced opponents. All it would do was give away that the *bokor* was nearing the doorway. The clatter of empty magazines on the floor also informed the Executioner that the man was unarmed for a moment. Bolan was skilled, but he couldn't evade streams of autofire blazing at him from arm's length. This was going to be the best opportunity he would have to take down the Gray Man. He lunged through the doorway, seeing the Gray Man with one pistol jammed under his armpit while trying to push a magazine into the butt of the other.

The soldier grabbed the Gray Man's wrist and wrenched it toward him, preventing the insertion of the fresh magazine and hauling the *bokor* off balance. He whipped his forearm up and under his opponent's jaw, the leverage provided by the Jamaican's own arm turning the impact into an instant knockout.

The Gray Man slithered to the floor bonelessly. Bolan paused and took his pulse. He still lived—the Executioner's chopping forearm hadn't broken the *bokor*'s neck. Though the man seemed aged and frail, up close Bolan could tell that the sorcerer had dyed his hair gray, and under his cloak, he had a lean, powerful body that was under sixty, somewhere between the late forties and early fifties. Bolan restrained his captive's wrists and ankles with nylon cable ties, then gagged him to prevent a possible suicide attempt. The dark voodoo practitioner might have thought that death would be preferable to questioning, or the semblance of death, since the man's biochemical skills were sufficient to make the men outside seem dead enough to have been put in their graves.

Speaking of the men outside, Bolan patrolled the unconscious minions of the *bokor* and applied restraints to them, as well. When they recovered consciousness, their lack of leverage would keep them from bursting free with their maniacal strength. As he finished with the last one, Hopper appeared, revolver in hand, drenched with sweat.

"Stone?" he asked, gasping for breath, looking at Bolan rise from the last of the zombie men.

"I'm fine," Bolan returned.

"I heard gunfire," Hopper said between ragged inhalations. "I—"

"Probably would have gotten hurt if the shooting was still going on," Bolan answered.

Hopper's eyes betrayed his hurt feelings, the gun hanging limply at his thigh.

Bolan smiled. "But you came running without thought for your own safety. I appreciate that courage. Next time, pace yourself."

Hopper's mood lightened with that. "Thanks."

The Executioner needed his allies, and right now, Hopper was the best local on the ground working with him. James was an excellent partner against the monster makers, but nothing gave Bolan an edge like a local. Hopper was brave, and he hadn't needed to come to Bolan's rescue, yet risked his life.

Bolan just wanted to be certain that Hopper didn't end up as another dead man.

# CHAPTER TWELVE

Thanks to Morrot's programming, the berserkers ignored Fortescue and his troops. There were ten of them, each internally seething but remaining still. These were the conversions made from rough-and-ready sailors, the fishermen. While they had lucked out with a couple of athletic young men and women off the yacht, these were tough men who used their muscles on a daily basis. Though some had layers of fat, they all had cores of toil-packed muscle. These creatures were truly dangerous, though even the tiny women from the U.S. had proved lethal.

Fortescue had studied the video footage from their radio-controlled, camera-equipped model plane, and he knew that there was no way that a 90-to-110 pound woman would have been able to last long, even under the drug-induced madness that Morrot had given them. The men, twice the weight of the young women, could take much more damage and continue to fight and kill.

In a nod toward enhanced durability, the ten maniacs with their machetes were clad in primitive armor. This mission was more than just to induce mayhem, and so Morrot wanted to conduct an experiment in optimization. Thus, the berserkers were in bargain body armor, bought through black market sources, and each of them wore hard leather scooter helmets. They'd provide enough protection to keep the brawny fisherman berserkers going, even with a glancing head shot. It wouldn't last forever, but each extra moment that the maniacs were on the loose, Fortescue had the opportunity to complete his mission.

He climbed through a door cut in the trailer, and one of his men helped him out.

"Ready to go?" Fortescue asked. His soldiers nodded in unison, each of them primed for action.

There were a dozen of the Tonton Macoute descendants with him, each with concealed sidearms under their shirts. Also under their loose, linen shirts were belts carrying spare magazines for the assault rifles they'd hidden away. Low profile was the order for the day, at least until the maniacs were unleashed.

Morrot wanted to expand his army, and there was only one surefire way to accomplish that. The plan was nothing short of insidious, and it had taken weeks to bring to fruition. Fortescue had doubted that everything would fall into place cleanly and perfectly, but now that the pieces were in position, he had hopes. If they accomplished at least one of their goals, this day would prove to be an overwhelming success.

Morrot said that there was no way they could fail. Fortescue slid into the shotgun seat of one of the small fleet of pickups they'd brought, hoping that the dark, one-eyed shaman was correct.

"Hit it," he growled. A half dozen engines roared to

life, and the formation headed toward the Adult Holding Center in Kingston, where more than one thousand criminals were held.

PAUL MARTIN FELT in his pockets, hoping to find at least one more cigarette, but all he came up with was a crumpled, plastic-wrapped, empty package. He was tempted to throw the thing down in disgust, but the floor of the overwalk was already a horrendous mess. Janitors weren't too meticulous in most parts of the Adult Holding Center, mainly because the guard staff was far too undermanned. Anything that was left behind after a push-broom was run down the walkway was left there. The waist-high railing of the walkway was rusted, as well, and Martin didn't want to slip or stumble. Having to rely on the flimsy rail to keep him from striking the cafeteria thirty feet below was just too much of a gamble.

Instead, Martin jammed the empty packet back into his pocket, then rested his hand on the receiver of his Vietnam-era M-16. Since the weapon was more than forty years old, and had never been cleaned, Martin was afraid of what would happen if he'd ever have to use the rifle. Sure, the gun had stopping power—that is, if the gunpowder in the cartridges hadn't degraded over time—but would it be reliable? All he'd have would be the 6-shot Smith & Wesson revolver that was even more ancient, but at least it worked. While its finish was pitted and scratched, it operated smoothly.

Below, one of the prisoners buckled and collapsed to the floor of the cafeteria. Martin keyed his radio, sending out a signal about another inmate falling over. This was the thirtieth in four days. Nerves were on edge as the prison population was trading stories about a curse striking from the shadows. Nearly three dozen men were in the infirmary, each nearly comatose from unexplained causes. With the feel of impending riot hanging in the air like ozone after a lightning strike, Martin had one small slice of consolation. None of the guards had gotten sick.

Yet.

"No curse gets me," Martin muttered as he looked at the mass of inmates backing away from their fallen comrade. "But that's not what I'm 'fraid of."

Technically, the faculty was designed to hold 1026 prisoners. However, the Jamaican justice system had too much to handle with gang crimes overwhelming an underequipped, poorly funded Constabulary Force. Martin didn't have a count of how many inmates there were, just orders to let fly with a wall of lead if things got out of hand. Below, prisoners had to barter and beg for more than just a basic meal a day, trading for essentials like soap and toothpaste.

Medical care was likewise negligible. The infirmary set up for the sick prisoners was nothing more than a gymnasium with cots set out. Having passed among the unconscious, Martin felt a tingle of terror tugging at his spine. At least half of them had their eyes open, but they stared glassily at the ceiling of the gym, unblinking even as flies landed between their lashes. No one breathed more than ten times a minute, and even when Martin had placed the muzzle of his rifle against a patient's forehead, the sick man didn't react.

Martin didn't know what kind of disease was on the loose, but he knew that it wasn't natural. Something dark and foreboding haunted the prison. The whole complex stank of fear and rising anger.

Three of Martin's fellow guards rushed onto the cafeteria floor. They were packed in their riot armor, and each man wielded a three-foot-long piece of black wood that looked as if it had been a table leg only moments before. Martin watched, ready to fire lead at anyone who dared approached his mates, but the prisoners were too frightened of what was striking them down to want to get close to yet another victim.

One of the riot guards hooked the sickened inmate under his armpits and dragged him along the floor, getting him away from the nervous crowd. The other two backed off, holding their black clubs like torches to fend off a pack of wolves. Martin sighed as his comrades were safe now, but there was no denying that the next time the "curse" struck, nothing would hold back the horde of frightened prisoners.

This wasn't a high-security prison, and the mixture of violent and nonviolent prisoners was an explosive concoction. The weak were pounced upon, their meager incomes stolen, and they were stripped of anything valuable. This produced resentment. Throw in some strange plague sniping inmates at random, and the volatile population was on a short fuse to a large explosion.

Martin had been through two riots in his time with

the facility. They had proved to be bad, especially since contraband such as firearms and knives were hard to keep out. Bribes flew fast and free as the more organized criminals paid guards, Martin among them, to look the other way as goods were smuggled in. Between hard drugs and weaponry, it might as well have been as if someone had placed a contraband deposit window in the side of the big double-winged prison building.

Martin, knowing how much had been paid to him to let stuff through the cracks, didn't relish the idea of those inmates possessing firepower that was in a lot better condition than a rifle from the previous century. "Shouldn't have come in to work today."

Unable to afford a pack of cigarettes on his usual pay, Martin knew he needed the extra skim of bribe money, especially with everything his supervisor took as a cut not to hurl him into general population with the inmates for being "corrupt." The money that kept him going, day to day, was the same cash that would end his career, if it weren't for the fact that there were few enough guards. Martin sighed and spotted the butt of a cigarette sticking out of a crushed cup. Bending carefully, he pulled on it and found a mashed end. But it was dry and except for bends and wrinkles, it was viable. It didn't even seem to have lost more than a few flakes of tobacco.

"Finally," Martin muttered. He wondered the health of the last person to suck on this cancer stick, and then remembered all of the poisonous chemicals he'd be breathing in. He mouthed the cigarette butt and reached for his lighter.

"Bad luck is better than no luck," he told himself, bringing the flame up to the end of the tube of tobacco.

That's when a violent jolt hurled the Jamaican prison guard against the rail. Arms waving wildly, he lost the M-16, his lighter and cigarette butt, his fingers wrapping tightly around the flimsy pipe that made up the railing. The metal bent under Martin's weight, but much to his surprise, it held him up.

It felt as if a bomb had hit the building, but as far as Martin knew, no one had that kind of firepower among the gangs of Kingston. Still, Martin wouldn't put it past the thugs in Trench Town to try to whip something up. Most of the hardened gangbangers were born and bred in Trench Town, a neighborhood mentioned by name as a place for tourists to avoid if they didn't want to get mixed up in a gun battle or be attacked and raped.

Getting his bearings, Martin pulled from the railing while looking down. Something had buckled the wall of the cafeteria, cinder blocks strewed across the floor. Prisoners had been caught in the landslide of collapsing wall, but most of them had rushed to the other side of the cafeteria. As Martin's vision focused, he saw the back end of a semitruck's trailer, the twin doors still closed but hanging awkwardly on their hinges after having been driven through the wall. Outside, alarm sirens wailed their belated warning, telling of a breach of the facility's campus. Martin scrambled for his revolver, knowing that at least he was far from the inmates and their ability to attack him. There was no way for them to get up into this overwalk, so he was good.

At least until he saw the M-16 rifle lying on the concrete below.

"Of course. It'd probably jam on me, but for one of those rots, it'll work perfectly," Martin cursed. He prepared to gun down the first man heading toward the rifle when the doors on the trailer exploded open, figures bursting onto the floor.

They moved too quickly for Martin to do more than identify them as vague humanoids, but there was a combined guttural snarl from the men escaping the truck. If Martin hadn't known any better, he'd have thought that the big eighteen-wheeler had dropped off a new load of prisoners, but terrified and agonized cries rose from the inmates below him. Blood sprayed and body parts now littered the floor as the newcomers swung their chopping blades with power and speed. The prisoners below screamed as they tried to climb over one another to escape the berserker horde that had descended upon them. Meanwhile, the trailer grunted, metal grating on stone as the truck outside tried to drag itself free. Martin was torn between getting off the overwalk or trying to protect the inmates below.

The guard decided that it was his job to keep people from escaping, and there was no way that anyone was getting off the prison grounds, not with the mayhem going on right now. He turned and raced toward the end of the catwalk and pushed through the door.

"All guards! We have gunfire emanating from the infirmary!" A voice blared from Martin's radio. He recognized Hotchkins's voice, and there was a fear in it that he'd never heard before. "We need help here!"

Either static or autofire ripped over the airwaves, because suddenly Hotchkins was cut off. Martin didn't know what was going on, but it involved psychopaths with long blades carving apart inmates while automatic weapons discharged in a far part of the facility. Mayhem had just struck the facility, and Martin was alone.

THE SEMITRUCK HAD made short work of the front gate of the facility, the cowcatcher on the grille of the big vehicle spearing through the wrought-iron bars and chain link, folding the two doors inward as if they were made of paper. The driver hit the brakes, and eighteen wheels squealed, kicking up dust. Fortescue watched the truck pivot, and it was as if he were watching a movie. The whole length of the cab and trailer whirled, enabling the driver to grind the transmission into Reverse.

Fortescue, in the pickup directly behind the eighteen-wheeler, gripped his assault rifle tightly. His ride, as well as the other five SUVs, peeled off toward where their contact had told them the prison infirmary was situated. "Come on, come on."

"We're on schedule," his driver, Bertrand, told him.

Fortescue saw several guards running out of the doors of buildings, four of them leaving the gymnasium in response to the racket. Those guards hadn't even had their hands on the grips of their pistols, which made them easy targets as Fortescue shouldered his Brazilian copy of the Tavor TAR-21 Israeli assault rifle and squeezed off five rapid bursts. Valleys of 5.56-mm rounds, guided by the holographic sight mounted on the sleek little bullpup weapon, ripped through the Jamaican constables who'd exited the makeshift infirmary. Two men were shredded by bullets shrieking along at 3200 feet per second. The other two guards froze, one of them clutching a torn shoulder, looking at the row of pickups in shock as more door gunners cut loose with their high-tech rifles. The two that Fortescue had missed screamed and were burned down by multiple streams of autofire.

Bertrand stomped the brakes of his pickup, pulling the SUV up almost at the infirmary's door. Fortescue hadn't even waited for the vehicle to stop before he leaped out of the cab, charging through the doorway. The others were going to be on his tail.

Four men had left the infirmary, which meant that there would only be one constable left, as well as doctors, nurses and orderlies. The last of the facility's guards was fifteen feet down the hall, his eyes wide at the sudden chatter of automatic gunfire. That man had the opportunity to have his sidearm in hand, but the shock of seeing an armed commando burst through the door made the constable jerk the trigger, sending his shot high above Fortescue's head.

The Haitian commander grit his teeth, milking the Tavor's trigger, emptying six 5.56-mm slugs into the upper chest of the last of the armed guards. The Jamaican let out a dull grunt before he toppled to the ground, pulling the trigger a second time, blowing a hole uselessly in the ceiling with his dying reflex. Fortescue fired again at the fallen man, making sure he was anchored down as a corpse. He leaped over the carcass on the floor, landing deftly, seeing the medical staff making a beeline toward the other end of the gymnasium.

Fortescue dumped the partially spent magazine in his rifle, feeding it another 30-round box before focusing on the unarmed men and women. The goal of this mission was to sow terror as much as any other task. That meant corpses and the "needless" spilling of blood. Fortescue wanted to tell himself that this wasn't why he'd picked his role as a fighting man, but these weren't Haitians, just mere Jamaicans, the servants of the English who remained on their knees while Haiti stood proud and independent. Putting bullets into sniveling slaves was a pleasure.

The Tavor barked out its deadly messages, bodies tumbling amid the screams of dying humans and roaring guns. Romy was at Fortescue's side, adding his own firepower to the carnage, 800-round-per-minute bursts smashing open chests.

"All right!" Fortescue shouted. "Let's get these fuckers loaded onto the truck."

"Need help here!" a voice called from a doorway. The Haitian soldier turned at the sound, bringing his autorifle to bear on the sound of the plea. He held down the Tavor's trigger, its bullets striking the plasterboard wall at 2854 feet per second, each bullet carrying 1250 foot pounds of kinetic energy. The velocity turned the slender 5.56-mm NATO bullets into meat-rupturing hammers, made all the more messy by the deformation of the rounds as they were mashed by the plasterboard. On the other side, the constable on the radio had his rib cage churned into a gory slop that frothed from entrance and exit wounds, escaping air from his lungs blowing bubbles in the freed blood.

The guard plopped to the ground, gushing his internals through the horrendous wounds Fortescue had ripped into him.

"The semi's stuck!" Bertrand called from the entrance.

Fortescue sneered. "I knew things were going too well."

"SCARVES! SCARVES NOW!" Louis Montego shouted to his fellow Grim Strokes inmates. They had been waiting in jail, some sitting and awaiting trial for three months. Montego had been assigned by Orleans as the leader of the imprisoned Strokes, and the previous week, he'd been warned to make certain all of his people were to have red scarves handy, and to cover their noses and mouths when they received a signal.

Montego had asked what that signal was, but Orleans had been evasive, as if, perhaps, he hadn't known what the cue to wear the masks would be either. For some reason, the scarves had to be bright red and cover the lower faces of each of the men who wanted their freedom. They'd also been informed that gathering their own weapons would be necessary, as well. The impact of a truck against the prison felt as if a bomb had struck the building. For all Montego knew, it *had* been a bomb. Orleans had promised that the inmates awaiting trial would be given their chance at freedom, if only they followed his directions.

There was a cacophony of terrified screams rolling down the hall from the cafeteria following the thunderous crash. Montego saw guards racing down the hall, distracted by the noise. He turned to the men in his cell. "Do it!"

Normally, the racket of three strong men driving a smuggled, handmade hooligan tool into the concrete holding the hinge of the jail-cell door would have been more than enough to bring dozens of guards along. However, the facility was under attack. Alarm Klaxons filled the air, and mayhem had broken out in all corners of the facility, seemingly. Montego and his two partners surged with all of their might, the pry bar digging the hinge hardware out of its concrete anchor.

The tip had been blunted on the first stab, but that is why they had sharpened both ends. With another surge and the strength of the trio, they had wedged the tip of the other end between stone and metal. Five hundred pounds of muscle shoved on the leverage of the steel shaft, twisting the second hinge out of place. There was a third hinge, and the bolt between the lock and the other side of the doorjamb, but Montego and his allies knew they wouldn't have to deal with that. All three men braced themselves on the floor and each kicked the bottom of the door with everything that they had. Two, three, four stomps of their unified might was more than enough to twist the door, pivoting on the central hinge, and the lock bolt out of shape. Montego crawled through the improvised hatch first, scurrying into the open with a foot-long knife that he'd made out of rigid plastic.

Others had breached their cell doors, as well, and drawn their weaponry, looking for nearby guards.

Gunfire cracked at the far end of one corridor, meager pistol shots ringing out, stopping after only a few moments as death screams echoed the horrors coming from the cafeteria.

Within a few moments some of Montego's fellow Grim Strokes showed up, each man brandishing an old Browning Hi-Power or a Smith & Wesson revolver. Between the group who'd managed to squirm to freedom, five of the thirty men had managed to get pistols. It wasn't much, but the rest still were in possession of their knives.

"How many down?" Montego asked.

"Four," came the answer from an automatic-toting gangbanger. He held out the pistol, butt-first, to the Grim Stroke commander.

"Thank you," Montego said as he accepted the weapon. He indicated his knife. "You need?"

"No," the other man said. He slid a length of sharpened steel from his waistband. It was spattered with smeared, fresh blood. "I prefer closer work."

Montego grinned under his scarf. "Let's move."

The gang members worked their way along the corridor, those who'd confiscated keys popping every lock they passed, except for those of cells that they knew housed direct rivals to the Strokes. The Kingston Royales were blood enemies of the Strokes, and there would be no compromise between the two clans, even if it meant that their combined forces could only increase the chances of success at an escape. Montego had seen too many of the Royale jackals pounce upon fellow Strokes members, using superior odds and treachery to ensure that they killed his comrades.

Montego paused at one door, seeing two Royales glaring at him through the bars of their cell door.

"What you think you doing?" one of the gangsters called. Montego recognized these two all too well. They had nearly killed him when he'd just arrived at the facility, only the presence of four of his fellows arriving at the last moment driving them off. Montego felt the fissure of fused flesh where the medic had stitched his forehead and cheek back together.

"Let us out, asshole," the other Royale said. "Or you too scared?"

Montego lifted his Browning and fired into the face of the one who doubted the Strokes member's courage. The single 9-mm bullet punched through the bridge of the Royale's nose, and his head whipped backward as he dropped away from the cell door. The other gangster reached through the bars to try to deflect Montego's aim, but he pulled the trigger twice, two slugs slicing into the man's armpit, severing the brachial artery and flooding his lungs with hot blood.

Montego wanted to stay to watch the one man bleed to death, but a racket sounded at the doors to the cafeteria. Two seething figures, both wielding machetes, stood in the doorway, their eyes wild and unfocused.

Montego could see the gore dripping from their blades, and he paused. The berserkers regarded the group of Strokes, all of whom had covered their faces, even as their cell doors were opened. A man who wasn't part of the Strokes stood along side Montego, and the two maniacs charged. Montego pressed himself to the wall, but both of the killers ignored him, bringing their blades down on the poor soul who didn't wear a red scarf to mask his features.

One looked up, snorting through his nose, blood beaded on his dark features. There was a low growl from the blade-wielding madman, but he turned his attention away, scanning faces ahead for a lack of a scarf. Montego didn't know that Morrot had programmed his minions to strike down everyone whose face wasn't concealed beneath a red bandanna. The crazies rushed down the hallway, leaping upon anyone who didn't have Morrot's color across their face.

Already, Montego's group had doubled in number, and more were freed from their cells on the northwest block of the prison.

The overcrowded facility was going to empty out quickly, between the escaping Strokes and the maniacal rampage of Morrot's zombie berserkers.

Montego didn't care. He ran through the shattered cafeteria wall, taking in sunlight and free air.

# CHAPTER THIRTEEN

Calvin James left the broken and exhausted Corboun to sleep on the cot, ankle and wrist handcuffed to the metal frame of the lightweight bed. There was no mistaking now that Corboun worked for Javier Orleans, a former lieutenant of the Grim Strokes. Stony Man Farm had developed a file on the man.

Orleans had staged a coup over the Kingston gang, putting down the previous administration in a mostly bloodless week. The Farm said it was mostly bloodless simply because the only people who'd died during the change of regime were a select few members of the group's leadership, with two dozen others disappearing. Usually, during such a rise to power, battles waged among lower level gang members allied with one faction or the other. As well, thanks to the relatively violent and careless combat tactics of the gangsters, bystanders usually ended up being gunned down in the streets, caught in cross fires or in the spillover shrapnel of car bombs and thrown grenades.

Such a quick and clean regime change indicated something particularly scary, especially in the wake of Bolan's debriefing on his knowledge of the Kingston underground. Long Eddy had only thin ties to the group, instead allying more with the Kingston Royales, a group that was diametrically opposed to the Strokes. As such, the Executioner hadn't visited them, and the gang had remained untouched in the wake of Long Eddy's fall.

James asked Corboun about the Haitians, and registering the man's reactions, he knew about their presence. Through careful and thorough questioning, he'd been able to map out the captive gangster's autonomic responses to the interrogation. It was a slightly more drawn-out process than the FBI's take on brain fingerprinting, but James's intimate knowledge of interrogation techniques and behavioral sciences were without peer, which was why David McCarter and Phoenix Force had counted on the African American's expertise at prying answers loose. There had been times when James had been forced to utilize all manner of techniques, including one extreme case where waterboarding had been the only option available in the timetable to prevent a disaster. It was distasteful, but James had gotten the information necessary, allowing Bolan and him to take out a threat that would have ended countless lives. Still, James was a soldier and a healer. Causing pain, even with the noblest of intentions, wasn't James's favorite tack. The brain fingerprinting he'd put Corboun through was a success, and along with a map of what the prisoner knew, James had also graphed out the current organization of the Strokes.

If knowledge was power, James had accumulated the equivalent of a tank brigade's firepower. It had taken several hours, but things had fallen into place.

He was about to call Bolan on his cell phone when he saw an alert on its screen. Calling up the message, he saw a breaking news report about a violent prison riot and breakout near Trench Town in Kingston.

James grimaced. The Farm had a news filter set up on one of its search engines, programmed to send out potentially pertinent data to the men in the field based on their current locations. As such, the filter had given Bolan and him the heads-up about the holding facility going to hell. James ran through the article, then opened up related photographs. The prison complex was huge, designed to hold a thousand inmates. Of course, thanks to the overwhelming amount of crime and corruption in Jamaica, the place was overcrowded and undermanned.

Photographs of the building showed fires had been started all around the facility, with a massive hole torn through the perimeter gate and the section of the complex connecting the two cell blocks sported a huge scar where a truck had crashed into it.

James hit the speed dial for the Farm. Barbara Price answered even before he could hear the line connect.

"Cal, you got the news?" Price asked.

"Just now. What's the deal?" James asked.

"We're monitoring Jamaican Constabulary Force radio chatter, and according to reports, somewhere between four and ten vehicles broke through the gates of the prison," Price told him. "At least one of them was an eighteen-wheeler, while the rest appeared to be SUVs."

"Any word on how many escaped?" James asked.

"The place is a madhouse, but they do know that all of the vehicles that had intruded escaped," Price replied.

"What are we looking at?" James continued.

Price's sigh was disheartening. "At least two hundred men."

James frowned. "Two hundred? All from the same gang, I'd bet."

"I don't want to lose money on that," Price said. "The JCF is still sending units to hold things down, but the inmates have gotten control of plenty of firepower."

"Is there any live video on the scene?" James asked.

"Are you looking to deal yourself into that fight?" Price countered.

James paused, but before he could answer, Price spoke up. "Don't. We can't afford it. According to the chatter, the prison is in full mayhem. They say that people are attacking each other, and one Constable unit on the scene had to empty fifty rounds into an assailant wielding a machete."

James's ears perked at the sound of that. "Fifty rounds into one man?"

"This is Jamaica, so it's just possible that the cops could have gone overboard," Price returned. "Hell, at one point, government troops turned on each other when we tried to bring in a 'suspected' drug dealer back in May of 2010. That doesn't even take into account tons of Amnesty International accusations of human rights abuses where police have set up execution squads or tortured prisoners."

"It also sounds like what happens when regular cops

run into someone who is hopped up on a cocktail like crystal meth, PCP, or our friends at the resort and the surf camp with all manner of voodoo drugs in their veins," James said.

Price groaned. "Six of one, half a dozen of the other. If it's the berserkers, then they just turned two miles of road into a war zone. If it's the Kingston law cracking down, then whoever turned the berserkers loose the other day has got the JCF jumpy enough to resort to martial law and fully lethal rules of engagement, meaning that they succeeded in pushing the government and the people around."

"Is there a win-win situation in that mix?" James asked. "Because I can't see any happy endings there."

"The only positive is that the monster-makers have used up all of their ready-made zombie slaves," Price said.

"If we've gotten that lucky," James began, "then I will run through Haight-Ashbury wearing nothing but ballet slippers and a pink tutu."

That got a chuckle from Price, but her voice remained grim. "It'd be a pretty sight, but I don't see anything lacy or frilly in your future. Striker did some calculations, and according to what happened at the resort and the surf camp, the enemy appears to be frugal and efficient in their use of the berserkers. Twelve were released at nearly the same time the day Striker was drawn into this, and we're looking at a group of thirty missing who could have been transformed."

"Even if they let twelve loose at the prison, there's going to be five left, not counting other kidnappings we're not aware of," James concluded. "Missing fishing boat crew rosters might not be too accurate, given underage sailors looking to get a job, and captains underreporting their numbers so as to avoid having to pay the kids full pay and not get in trouble for child labor."

"I was looking at Striker's best-case scenario on the numbers. His calculations also gave us the underreported numbers of missing based on the situation you mentioned, and we can see the numbers between forty and fifty," Price said.

James was glad that Price couldn't see the dread come over his features during the cell phone conversation. To say that he was disheartened was an understatement. Who knew what kind of mayhem was being unleashed at the prison? Was the enemy adding to its conventional forces, or were they harvesting unwitting subjects to create even more of the monstrosities that left even the Executioner bloodied and battered?

Either way, the neighborhood of Trench Town was going to become even more dangerous with an influx of new criminals, raising the mayhem and terror levels in Kingston even higher. James looked toward his gear, eyeing the M-4 with its attached grenade launcher, wishing that he could do something, anything.

"Barb, I'm sending over the information I have," James said. "This is what I've got from the Grim Strokes organization and their perceived ties to an outside Haitian contingent. I'll toss it to you over the Tactical Pad."

Never to be outdone by any electronics company, Hermann "Gadgets" Schwarz of Able Team, Stony

Man Farm's other dedicated strike force, developed a new combat information unit for use by the teams. While he had developed the Combat PDA, it was of limited use for performing with graphics-intensive interfaces. The screen was large enough to handle most applications, but Schwarz and James' partner Gary Manning were brilliant scientists and were prone to extensive note-taking and architectural design work. The Tactical Pad was a bit too large to be carried in an infiltration operation, but it was only ten inches by seven inches and about an inch thick. Roughly the same size as the popular wireless internet–capable device that had been released a couple of years back, its internals were a marvel of miniaturization. The outer shell and touch screen were composed of alloys and polymers that made it capable of absorbing the shock of a .308 Winchester bullet without losing data from its hard drive, while the interactive display surface could suck up the impact from a 9-mm Parabellum round and still retain its interface capabilities. With four processor cores and a 2-tetrabyte storage capacity, it was as powerful as a graphics-intensive gaming desktop unit, complete with high-definition capability. With the extra room, the Tactical Pad had an antenna and wireless modem that was powerful enough to transmit and receive directly to communication satellites even in the more isolated and forsaken locations on the planet. Each had hacking programs capable of busting through tough encryptions on mainframes and cloning and listening in on cellular conversations. The hacking applications were set up by Schwarz and the Stony

Man cyberteam crew to be intuitive enough for even a noncomputer user like Carl Lyons to be able to operate them. With that kind of electronic muscle, Able Team and Phoenix Force had personal surveillance technology capable of fitting into a tiny package.

James had kept the Tactical Pad open, and using a graphics program designed for mapping out organizational rankings and membership, he'd been able to sketch out the Grim Strokes regime with ease, as if he were finger painting it on a dry-erase board. When he cursively wrote a name, the handwriting recognition software converted the names into digital characters, and with a flick of the finger, James was able to place them on the chart and draw connections between them. He called up the information and hit Send. The transmitter modem inside the Tactical Pad launched several megabytes of file in a squirt of electronic data. The stream of information rocketed at the speed of light, reaching the communications satellite hooking him to the Farm in less than a quarter second.

It took less time than it took for James to tap the screen for the jet of encrypted code to reach the Computer Room, and now, the vital information he'd gathered was in better hands. He had been able to free himself for more vigorous activity.

Just then, his call waiting blipped on his cell.

"Hang on, Barb. It's Striker," James said.

"He's plugging into us for a conference call," Price added.

James switched the cell to speaker, set it on the table, then went toward his combat gear.

Bolan's voice cut over the speakerphone. "Cal, stand down."

James paused as he reached for the carbine and grenade launcher combination. Mack Bolan's knowledge of his comrades in Phoenix Force often bordered on a psychic link.

"I don't know what you're talking about, Striker," James said.

"That's bull. I've got a situation here at the Gray Man's," Bolan told him. "And I know that you want to try to help the JCF, but frankly, there's not enough you could do."

"I'm one of the ten most badass mothers in North America, Striker," James said, even though he was turning away from the M-4/M-203. "And I've got a grenade launcher."

"You also don't have a cover that allows you to come swooping in to the rescue," Bolan said. "I don't need you trading fire with Jamaican constables just because they think you're a part of the gang breaking everyone out of prison."

"Right as usual, Striker. What do you need me for?"

"For one, I'm in Trench Town, and I've secured a new prisoner, but he has victims," Bolan said. "Five zombified guards."

"Still alive?" James asked.

"Still alive, and we have the Gray Man's laboratory setup to work backward from," Bolan told him. "Which do you think will be more help? A grenade launcher, or a possible easy way to neutralize the drugged?"

"Are there any left worth saving?" James asked.

"At least a dozen underage fishermen," Bolan said. "You read my estimations. Those kids haven't been tapped yet, which makes me wonder if they're still being held in reserve."

James grimaced. "You know how to push my buttons."

"Letting a prison break go on unabated doesn't do much for me, either, Cal, but you have to know that we have priorities, and the JCF will do everything they can to keep the prisoners in check," Bolan said.

"All right," James said. "What's your location?"

"I'm sending a map with directions from my cell," Bolan told him. "Get over here now."

"I'm on my way," James replied.

"Bring along something heavier than pistols," Bolan added, "just in case the berserkers run wild throughout Trench Town. We'll need the firepower to hold them off."

"On it," James answered.

"Anything else for us?" Price asked.

"I'm uploading video taken of the Gray Man's lab for identification of ingredients," Bolan said, "to see if we can get something from the Farm's assembled knowledge."

"Our best man is right there, Striker," Price replied. "Anyone else on the scene here would only be kvetching his evaluations, unless you want us to feed this information to the CDC."

"Maybe," James said, stuffing a pair of Heckler & Koch MP-7 submachine pistols into a briefcase along with spare magazines. "I'd like someone to confirm my observations. Before I forget, find an irregular who'd come and take watch of Corboun. I don't want him to starve, but I also don't want him to escape."

"I've got a couple of Marines on call. They'll be there within five minutes," Price said. "Would that be too long?"

James also packed away the Tactical Pad, knowing that its high-definition camera and modem would provide even better data to transmit to the CDC if necessary. "No. Corboun's out cold right now, and I doubt he'll be in any physical condition to sit up within that time period. I just don't want to give him an hour alone."

"Acknowledged," Price replied.

"Cal, just be careful getting here," Bolan warned. "Things are hot in less than two miles from my current location."

James wondered if Bolan could sense the smile crawl across his face. No doubt the savvy, alert warrior did so. "Striker, I was born for hot."

The Phoenix Force pro took off to his rental SUV.

THE GRAY MAN opened his eyes and saw that he was upside down, hanging in his cabin by his feet. He saw the big American who had attacked him after fighting his way past five aggressive zombie guards. His eyes were full of crust, and the blood that rushed to his head gave him a massive ache behind his forehead. He wanted to speak, but it was difficult. His jaw was sore and stiff, as was his neck.

"Who…?" he mumbled, managing one word.

"My name is unimportant. It's a fake anyway, not that I'd need to hide my true name from a charlatan such as you," the Executioner told him, squatting to meet the upside down *bokor* eye to eye. "The Gray Man, or should I just call you Reginald Watson?"

Watson blanched at the mention of his birth name. Though not as superstitious as his victims, the *bokor* was frightened at how this American knew his name, not feeling the patina of powder on his fingertips that had been used to gather his prints. There had been no record of Reginald Watson returning to Jamaica after his many run-ins with the law in New York City twenty years earlier, but his arrest record was one that was easily traced. An amateur chemist who had picked up jobs mixing amphetamines and other recreational drugs, Watson had garnered enough heat that he was forced to sneak back to Jamaica. Rival gangs back in Manhattan were hot for his head, and Watson disappeared.

In anonymity, he was able to build himself up, studying under his uncle to become a sorcerer as formidable and respected as the Gray Man eventually became. Until now, only the hardiest of opponents had dared to assail him, and those who did were either killed outright, or had ended up as zombified grunts, guarding his cabin.

Then came the American.

"Reggie, wake up," Bolan said, patting his cheek.

Watson was able to see the charm dangling from Bolan's neck. It was the mark of Mambo Glorianna, that bitch who dared to try to make the Gray Man seem less important than he'd made himself. Watson had turned his biochemistry skills into the cornerstone that had several gangs paying him for support, be it curses against those who were untouchable by assassins, or blessings. The Gray Man's curses were simply skin contact poisons that struck down targets easily, while the blessings were concoctions that galvanized the more cautious of gang members, instilling in them hallucinogen-charged courage and endorphin rushes of euphoria. This shot of immortality had turned many a second-stringer into a top rate enforcer for the gangs.

"Awake," Watson was able to rasp. He cleared his throat with a cough and glared at the white man. "You know my name. Big deal."

"The true name of a *bokor* is akin to grabbing him by the sack and leading him around with it," Bolan returned. "I know the sorcery that you engage in, and you are nothing but a weakling. Me, however, I'm full of magic."

Watson narrowed his eyes, but then he remembered how this big wraith, clad in black, had been able to avoid two streams of full-auto gunfire at a range of less than ten feet. He wasn't certain how Bolan had taken him down. His last moments of consciousness blanked out after he'd started to reload his emptied weapons. All he knew was that he had been out cold for a time.

And during that time, this man had learned his birth name.

"It's a long way from Manhattan and Little Jamaica,

isn't it?" Bolan asked. "But you're still peddling the same dreams made of powder and lies."

"The hell with you, white man," Watson growled.

"I've been there," Bolan said, locking Watson's eyes with a cold, icy blue stare.

The *bokor* wanted to look away, but the force of the Executioner's will was just too much. Maybe he did possess magic....

Watson looked past the white man to see his zombies, each man sitting up, his head drooping and jaw slack. None displayed any aggression, even though they seemed to have recovered consciousness. "Wake up!"

One of his minions lifted his head, his dull eyes glazed over in response to the shouted order.

"You want them to fight for you?" Bolan asked. "They're mine now."

Watson felt a wave of nausea rush through his stomach. "How..."

"Magic," Bolan replied. "You're a pretender, Reggie. Someone who dyed his hair to look ancient, and who skulked around pouring dust on the stoops of unsuspecting idiots."

In truth, had Watson been aware of what happened while he was unconscious, he would have known that Bolan had utilized a gentle sedative given to him by Mambo Glorianna, made from similar natural chemicals that the *bokor* utilized, except in amounts that proved to be truly medicinal. Bolan had been ordered to rub the dust on the lips of any of the zombies he encountered, and sure enough, the taste of the powder had pacified the five guards.

"No…" Watson sputtered.

"The Haitian," Bolan said.

"You know about him?" Watson asked.

"I know. I also know that you gave him the supplies for his own magic," Bolan announced. "The very stuff he needs to bring back the days of Duvalier and the primacy of the dark *loa* over the country."

Watson grimaced. He knew that somehow, the white man had noticed that the cabin sat atop a larger set of cellars with plenty of storage, and could have surmised the loading of toxins and other chemicals into trucks, which had ground ruts into the dirt behind the shack. Though he hadn't kept much in writing, there was still enough to put clues together. Almost enough to even make it not much of a leap to figure out his connection to the Haitian. Watson had impressed the local gang-bangers with similar clever tricks and misdirection.

But there was still the frightening swiftness, as if the warrior were a ghost.

That's when the Executioner reached out and cupped Watson's cheek with a hand that felt as chilled as a grave. Watson's eyes widened at the icy touch.

"Your men are pale copies of what I am," Bolan said. "I have died many times over the years. I died in Philadelphia, again in New York. Another of my corpses lays somewhere in a burnt-out villa in Russia. I'm a dead man. I'm he who has returned from the grave more times than you could ever imagine. Look at me, and know that your world, your charade, is over."

Watson's whole body tingled. The man's hand was as cold as ice, partially thanks to a secluded cooling packet that Bolan had tucked away. If the tamed zombies and the knowledge of Watson's true name hadn't been enough to break the *bokor*'s spirit, then the frozen touch of a walking corpse was the nuclear option. Bolan hadn't lied about his prior deaths, the times when he had been close to the end, or had abandoned his cover persona. In fact, Bolan had always known that he was a dead man walking from the very moment he'd fired the four shots against the loan sharks who had destroyed his family. Four dead mobsters had signaled the end of an American soldier's life and career and the beginning of a crusade against the forces of darkness around the world. Now he was facing down one of those savages, a man who bartered in human life as if it were a profitable commodity.

"What do you want to know?" Watson asked in a weak, helpless voice.

"The Haitian, tell me all you know about him."

The chemist from Manhattan gave up all that he knew, his breathless information focusing on Dr. Killian Morrot and Pierre Fortescue.

# CHAPTER FOURTEEN

While Calvin James worked in Reginald Watson's laboratory, Hopper stood watch in the doorway. He patted his pockets, looking for a cigarette. Like a ghost, Bolan appeared, holding one out for him.

"You can kill a man by poppin' up on him quiet like that," Hopper admitted, taking the cigarette between trembling fingers.

"That's generally what I do," Bolan said.

Hopper pulled out his lighter, hoping the rush of nicotine would cool his frazzled nerves. It didn't have that effect, but he disguised his sigh in an exhalation of tobacco smoke.

"Is it calming down out there?" Hopper asked.

"If you mean that the holding facility riots are contained, yeah, more or less," Bolan told him. "The army moved in."

"That's what all that racket was?" Hopper inquired.

Bolan nodded. "Not before Boys Town went up, too."

"Boys Town" was the juvenile version of the holding facility, where accused youth were kept away from the older predators in the large prison. It was a stopgap to prevent the slide of Jamaican kids into further violence, but the judicial system let them rot there for months at a time, stretches where some became apex predators of the enclosed microcosm of street life. The strong gathered their might and lorded over the weaker. Hopper had spent time there, and because of his preferences, he had to keep his back to the wall. Gay inmates in juvie or regular prison wouldn't last long if they were "outed."

"Think that had anything to do with the troubles at the adult facility?" Hopper asked, genuine worry in his voice.

Bolan frowned, picking up on his concerns. "No armed forces attacked Boys Town, but two or three of the berserkers showed up."

Hopper's mood darkened. "By design or accident?"

"Design," Bolan said. "Our enemy is looking to make Kingston even more unstable."

"You'd have thought that the troubles a few years back would have been more than enough," Hopper said. "This place is supposed to be—"

"Quiet," Bolan rasped.

James moved up, drawing his Beretta from its waistband holster. The black Chicagoan took Hopper by the upper arm and pulled him into the laboratory while Bolan stalked toward the front door, his sleek MP-7 machine pistol at low ready.

Then Hopper could hear it—the sound of someone crashing through long grass as fast as he or she could navigate. It was nearly sunset, and though things had seemed quiet after the rumble and grunts of military vehicles earlier, Hopper imagined that the prison riots weren't quite finished.

Who knew how many had escaped through the holes ripped in the jail?

As he was thinking, clutching his own revolver in a white-knuckle grip, he saw that Stone had disappeared. The warrior was on the stalk, now, and no one would see him if he didn't want them to.

THE EXECUTIONER WAS back in the long grass where he'd first encountered the obscenity that was the Gray Man's zombies. With the sun crawling down from the sky after looming brightly over the troubled island of Jamaica, the shadows were long and thick, making it easy for people to lose themselves in the thick foliage. Bolan was used to this kind of tangle, having originally earning his first battle scars in intense jungle combat, and having revisited the deep, tropical forest many times since then.

The MP-7 was a part of his hand as he kept his ears peeled, picking up the path of a runner crashing through the shoulder-high blades of grass. Since the MP-7 combined the familiar controls of the Heckler & Koch MP-5 and the overall balance of his preferred Uzi or Ingram MAC-10 submachine guns, it felt natural to the soldier, usable as either an oversize pistol or as a longer range encounter weapon with its collapsing stock fully extended and its forward pistol grip snapped down. Though its 4.6-mm size might have seemed anemic, it sat upon a powder charge that was midway between pistol and rifle, making it formidable at close quarters and capable of punching through a GI helmet or body armor at out to a hundred meters.

With a blunt suppressor threaded onto its barrel, the HK MP-7 would do the job as long as Bolan's aim remained true.

Even though he kept his finger off the trigger as he navigated the treacherous, uneven ground, Bolan still kept the ambidextrous safety locked on. He hadn't survived as long as he had without a belt and suspenders approach to everything, including firearms discipline.

Bolan heard the intruder, and his estimate of the newcomer's path was correct. A figure burst through the grass, and the Executioner immediately sized the man up. He was young, slender and covered in bruises and cuts. There was no anger or malice in his coal-black features, only fear. Bolan let the MP-7 drop on its sling and grabbed him, a hand clamped over his mouth and a chinlock to hold him still. Despite his skinny build, the young man was a fighter and would have been able to struggle free from a lesser combatant.

"Shh," Bolan hissed in his ear. "I'm not going to hurt you. Take it easy."

Fingers locked around Bolan's wrist, and the man's brown eyes darted back and forth.

"What are you running from?" Bolan asked, loosening his hold over the youth's mouth, but still keeping the chinlock in a relaxed level of strength.

"The other inmates," came a tiny, frightened voice from his lips. "They're after me."

"Why?" Bolan asked.

"I snitched," he answered. "I got their weapons taken away from them."

Bolan quickly frisked the young man and found that

he was unarmed. "There's a cabin in that direction. Move quietly, and show the man at the door the palms of your hands."

The former inmate looked at Bolan, confusion ruling his expression.

"I'll take care of the others," Bolan said. "You're harmless, and hurting."

With that, the frightened youth took off straight toward the cabin, balancing speed and stealth just right. Bolan didn't know the numbers of the inmates escaping, but there wouldn't be much use in asking the kid for details. He was frightened, and the only real intel he could give would be the direction he was being chased in.

Cutting through the long grass like a panther, silent and quick, Bolan heard the others stomp to a halt at the edge of the field. He weighed his options. Even a suppressed machine pistol made noise and could attract the attention of law enforcement. The last thing he needed was a bunch of JCF stomping through this area, finding Bolan and James keeping six captives and a laboratory full of weird biotoxins and a mass production facility.

Certainly, the two Stony Man operatives would be given a pass by the Farm and Hal Brognola's connections, but the red tape would grow so thick and tangled that Bolan might never get free in time to intercept Morrot's plans, whatever they were. Watson had been loose and fast with what he knew, but what he had known about the Haitian wasn't much more than a name and the supplies he'd desired.

The *bokor* had given Morrot enough ingredients to transform hundreds of people into zombies.

Bolan didn't have time to deal with inmates, but the thought of not acting while gruff, violent men were on the loose in a besieged neighborhood stuck in the Executioner's craw. Besides, if the escaped prisoners did commit more violence, it would only enhance the level of distraction that Morrot had staged this breakout for in the first place.

"Where you at, boy?" came a booming voice. Bolan had shifted to a position where he could see the inmates. They averaged six feet tall, and none of them was shorter than five-ten. Each man had taken advantage of exercise facilities, judging by the thickness of their bare arms and their rippling chests and abdomens seen through the tatters of their uniform tops. Big muscles and size were part of a good soldier's repertoire, but without skill and experience, they wouldn't be that formidable.

Still, the Executioner wasn't going to assume this would be a cakewalk. The five men were armed with clubs and screwdrivers, or saws that had been honed into prison-yard fighting knives. Bolan cinched the MP-7 and took out his own weapon, the Atomics Aquatics titanium dive knife he'd worn while surfing. Its grip would be firm, and the blade was more than sufficient to carve human flesh as if it were pudding.

"Spread out. Get that little bastard," the leader growled.

"Why are we wasting time here?" one of his men asked.

Bolan could see the fresh, livid scar under a set of stitches. "Because that fucker got my face wrecked. He *owes* me. If I'd had my shiv…"

"Fine," his subordinate replied. "We'll get your pay-back."

Scarface's grin was a grisly grimace. Bolan knew that such a violent thug was an apex predator when it came to neighborhoods. That meant these killers had to be taken down quickly and quietly.

Scarface was too far for Bolan to take down in-stantly, not out in the open. The others would be on him, slashing him to ribbons and puncturing organs with their crude but no-less-deadly weapons. He let the group enter the long grass.

"I can't see a thing in here!" someone complained.

"Shut up," Scarface boomed. "Just feel around for the little bugger."

Bolan slid silently behind one of the closest inmates, the one who complained about not being able to see. For the Executioner, it was simply a matter of using his ears to locate a target. The guy was a little more than six feet tall, and close to 250 pounds. What pleased Bolan most about his appearance were the long tails of dreadlocks flowing off the back of his head. When given a handle, the soldier always chose to use it to make things easier.

Almost simultaneously, Bolan took a thick rope of the inmate's hair and yanked back hard while spearing the tip of his foot behind the man's knee. The inmate's leg folded and he easily toppled back to the ground with a crash, Bolan's hold on the stalker's hair giving him enough leverage and strength to slam his head violently against the dirt. A dull grunt accompanied his crash into the depths of the long grass, and that drew a call of concern.

"Bando! Where are you?" Scarface called.

Bolan did his best to duplicate his victim's tone of voice, adding the grunt and rasp of injury and embarrassment. "Tripped in this shit."

Even as he spoke, Bolan had one hand clamped over his target's nose and mouth, the titanium dive knife thrust in the hollow of his jaw. There was some struggling as the five-and-a-half-inch blade sank in, but it speared through the roof of the inmate's mouth and into his lower brain. A powerful twist snapped bone and shredded core neural pathways, ending the thrashing and the pressure of Bando's attempt to breathe.

One down, four to go.

"Well, get your ass up and keep moving," Scarface snarled.

Bolan rasped out a few curses, pulling his blade from the dead man's throat, wiping slick blood on the corpse's tattered vest.

"You sassin' me, Bando?"

Bolan only grunted as a form of answer.

"Better not!" Scarface warned.

The crunch of stalks alerted Bolan to the approach of another man.

"Bando, you idiot," began the inmate's whisper before he parted a curtain of grass blades to look for his friend. "Let's get out—"

Bolan had been anticipating the shocked millisecond of recognition on the part of the other man. With a classic fencing lunge, the Executioner drove his knife deep into the bridge of the Jamaican's nose. A wicked shiv, honed from a broken saw blade, toppled from the killer's hand as the head strike slashed through his brain through the thin section of bone. Bolan used the handle of his knife to keep the guy from crashing to the ground, attracting more attention. He twisted his dive blade out of the corpse's face, letting him rest behind Bando.

Now was the time to go after Scarface.

"I don't hear you fuckers moving around there!" the leader of the escaped inmates bellowed. "If that little snot gets away..."

In every operation, good luck and bad luck were factors. So it was at that moment. Scarface was too aware of his surroundings, turning just in time to see the dark wraithlike form of the Executioner charging toward him, knife ready to chop down.

Scarface had been the largest of the five, his arms long and knotted with thick muscle. As fast as Bolan had been, the big Jamaican lifted his fist and snapped it toward his attacker's face. Bolan tucked his head down and danced away from the punch, even though it deflected his path. Out of position to grab and stab the hulking escapee, all the soldier could do was ram his shoulder into Scarface's ribs. The impact knocked the inmate off balance, but a swift elbow cuffed the back of Bolan's head, sending him staggering to the ground.

"Stuck your nose in the wrong business, fucker!" Scarface boomed, bringing up his weapon, a piece of steel bar with its bottom taped up. The square shaft didn't have any traditional cutting edges, but Bolan knew that if it struck flesh, the corners would peel apart skin and flesh easily. The weight and stiffness of the bar would also break bones, especially with a titanic bruiser like the Jamaican behind it.

Bolan knew he didn't even have time to roll out of the way of the descending weapon, so he kicked his heel hard into Scarface's knee. There was the crack of bone to reward Bolan, and the flesh-rending impact was turned into a glancing blow. The Jamaican's assault was deflected just as the soldier's ambush had been. Losing his footing, the big escapee struggled to remain upright, a tentative balancing act that gave the Executioner time to get to all fours and spring upward.

The Jamaican watched Bolan rise, and he tried to stand, but he lost his balance, staggering a step forward. He tightened his grip on the iron bar and shrugged to stand erect, but gravity had taken hold of Bolan once again, and the Executioner's elbow crashed into the side of Scarface's head like an ax. The blow was so powerful, the escapee's ear was shorn from the side of his head, dangling on a thin ribbon of skin.

As soon as Bolan's feet touched the ground, he jammed a hard fist into the Jamaican's solar plexus, knocking the wind out of him. In a fluid motion, Bolan slid his hand down the length of the inmate's arm, seized the man's wrist and broke the limb across the elbow that had torn his ear off.

Scarface, mutilated and unable to breathe, couldn't scream. The punch to his xyphoid process had paralyzed his lungs momentarily. Bolan released the mangled arm and brought his knee up into the big man's groin. That folded the Jamaican giant forward, giving the Executioner all the leverage he needed to seize the guy's head and break his neck with another pinpoint-placed elbow strike.

Unfortunately the flurry of combat and activity had caught the attention of the other two escapees, and they lurched into view even as Scarface collapsed in a bloody mess at his feet. Bolan had the opportunity to pick up the dead man's iron bar, matted with skin, blood and hair from other victims. He regarded the two newcomers with cold eyes.

"The one you're looking for owed this corpse for his time and pain. Do you have a legitimate beef?" Bolan asked.

The two men looked at each other, paused by the Executioner's bluff. That gave him enough time to see the bloody leftovers on their weapons. Like Bando, Scarface and the other prisoner, they had fresh gore on their clubs and blades. These were killers, so letting them free wasn't going to be an option.

Their hesitation didn't last long. As they raised their weapons, Bolan lunged forward. The iron bar swung up under the jaw of one of the escaped murderers, the mandible bone pulverized into splinters by the meeting of skeleton and heavy metal. With that inmate toppling backward helplessly, the soldier diverted the path of the iron bar, lashing its blackened length across the neck of the other man. Sure enough, the five-pound length of iron with its sharp corners opened up a twelve-inch gash in the man's neck, even as his clavicle folded under the impact. Bolan further anchored the escapee with a stomp to the side of his knee, bending it at a ninety-degree angle until the man was on the ground.

He took a step back, drew his suppressed Beretta and planted a mercy round into each of the inmates' heads. A fast draw wouldn't have been quick enough to take both men, but once he'd incapacitated them, the sleek 9-mm rounds' quiet coughs punctuated the end of their freedom from prison. Bolan reloaded and reholstered his piece.

James was standing on the porch of the cabin, his own machine pistol hanging at low ready. "I heard a couple of shots. Anything?"

"Took a knock to the head," Bolan answered. "Nothing too bad."

"The two shots?" James asked.

"Murderers who'd cut their way out of prison with shivs and shanks," Bolan told him.

James nodded. "Our newest foundling is just inside. Hopper's talking to him."

"Get a fingerprint?" Bolan asked.

James grinned and held up a glass.

"Gave him some water, got the prints. Photographed and transmitted back to the Farm," James said. "And if he's a murderer, too?"

"We'll leave him cuffed for the police," Bolan said. "However, I don't think he is a killer. He was prey in prison, not predator."

"So relatively minor offenses," James concluded.

"Hope so," Bolan said. "Anything on Watson's little den of iniquity?"

"Sucker's got a pantry stocked with all the best biotoxins around, from puffer fish to man-o'-war and sea snake venom," James said. "He's basically the central clearing house for lethal substances for Kingston. No wonder Morrot came to him for enough *juju* to build an army."

"A legitimate army," Bolan mused. "What about the hallucinogens? And why the berserkers I took down died after only being knocked unconscious?"

"I hate to say it, but I think that Morrot's too good at programming. The tox screens finally came in over the Tactical Pad from the blood you'd collected, and it turned out that they had 'suicide' pills," James said.

Bolan grimaced. Innocent young men and women, barely at the beginning of their adult lives, had been pushed into committing suicide because they had recovered consciousness and realized that they were prisoners. "What was the pill made of?"

"Powdered cyanide," James answered. "It worked in the cold war, and human anatomy and biochemistry hasn't changed since then."

Bolan looked toward the prison. "If any of the berserkers survive, the police won't know to look in their mouths for a poison capsule. More victims of Morrot are going to be lost."

"Barb and the team are trying to get through to the JCF with information about the cyanide, but I doubt that the constables had the same kind of patience you do. They'd just shoot someone who'd hacked apart a dozen prisoners and guard staff," James said.

Bolan's eyes narrowed, his jaw setting firmly.

Calvin James saw the seething fury uncoiling within the Executioner's frame.

Morrot's death warrant had been signed days ago, but Bolan wasn't going to rest until the zombie maker was in a shallow grave.

## CHAPTER FIFTEEN

Hal Brognola pushed the off button on his remote, chewing grimly on his unlit cigar. The situation in Jamaica was spiraling out of control, despite having two of his best people on the scene in Kingston. The carnage at the holding facility was horrific, dozens dead, hundreds wounded, and dozens missing from the prison's infirmary. With the prison thrown into riot, other facilities had raged out of control, whether it was by design or by happenstance.

The big Fed didn't mind if murderers killed one another in the course of their petty fits, but prison staff and civilians had been caught in the cross fire. As the prisoners waged war on everyone in sight, innocent people were killed. Especially disturbing was the news that armed commandos had raided the infirmary and made off with fifty comatose prisoners. Given the information that James had sent to the Farm, those fifty missing inmates were going to be put to grim, deadly use.

As it was, according to Bolan's observation of the kidnappings of vacationing teenagers and missing fishing boats, there were still innocents who were caught up in the clutches of the madman Morrot. Even now, Brognola received information over his personal data assistant, the file on the chemist who had been in the Tonton Macoute's employ for his whole life. Haiti had learned to fear the man's name, as he was the right hand of the Duvalier regimes, dispensing agony and insanity at his leisure. According to Amnesty International, Killian Morrot had been responsible for the torture and disappearance of thousands during the Duvalier reign.

"Killian Morrot," Brognola read.

"Dr. Kill More?" said a familiar voice. Brognola looked up to see the President, ready to meet with him for a debriefing about the Jamaican crisis.

"It's a sick joke if that's why he picked the name," Brognola said. "I doubt that fate was twisted enough to provide a maniac like him with the perfect moniker."

"You've already got people on the ground, so I want to know what's going on," the President said. "I thought the attacks the day before yesterday were an isolated incident. At least, that's what the head of the JCF told me."

"Would you spread the word that there were people who felt no pain on a rampage?" Brognola asked.

"They feel no pain, but they'd still die," the man responded.

"Only with a central nervous system hit," Brognola said. He handed over the file folder. "My expert looked at this. Even if you'd completely destroyed their hearts, an unlikely task even with a fully automatic rifle, there'd still be enough oxygen in their system to continue fighting and killing for up to thirty seconds."

"You've got to shoot zombies in the head," the

President said, looking over Calvin James's notes. He looked up. "I was joking."

"You saw the passage about the 'zombie' drugs used to make these berserkers," Brognola said.

"Fast, tool-using zombies," the President said. "It's amazing that all of this crap has to happen on my watch. Environmental disasters, riots around the globe, and now we've got the zombpocalypse in Jamaica."

"Technically, before you took office, there was another zombpocalypse in Kenya," Brognola mentioned.

The President's upper lip curled at that thought. "Right. Al Ghul."

The Man rubbed his forehead, putting the file folder on the table. "What's going to happen if you're not around to stop these things? I mean, loose nuclear weapons and other weapons of mass destruction are one thing, but *this?*"

"This isn't a fundraising drive," Brognola said. "We do well enough on our own that we scarcely need any funding from official channels. I'm just here because I have prior knowledge of what you're going to be dealing with."

"Whatever happened to the good old sixties' ghouls that shuffled their feet?" the President asked.

"Dr. Morrot didn't think that they were that effective, probably," Brognola said. "Otherwise, we'd be seeing shamblers, not runners. We're just lucky that he hasn't done even more to play to the fears of the general public in Jamaica."

"Like what?"

"Zombie makeup. War paint. Who knows?" Brognola asked.

"And the new information is that the berserkers who were let loose into the prison were wearing armor?" the President asked.

"Cheap stuff, but more than enough to make it sixty bullets to the torso rather than a mere thirty rounds," Brognola explained. "More than forty constables died emptying their weapons into the maniacs. Even rifles and shotguns needed dead-center hits to put them down."

"Forty for ten to twelve of them," the President mused.

He walked to the window, looking out over the spray of lights that made up the Washington, D.C. skyline. It looked as if someone had thrown a handful of diamonds onto black velvet, a beautiful sight that normally made him think that there was something better in the world.

Video footage of the berserker rampages in Jamaica, another beautiful place, flashed in his mind. He wondered what would happen if they had been released in America, the kind of nightmare that would blot out those gleaming lights, replacing them with the fires of destruction and carnage.

He turned back to Brognola. "Your best man is down there? Striker?"

"He's been on this since the first of the maniacs attacked," Brognola told him. "He's garnered more intel on this than the JCF and the Justice Department agents dispatched to Kingston combined."

"So we can assemble an army and drop in on Morrot, right?" the President asked.

Brognola shook his head.

"What is his take on this?"

"His take is that there are still people worth rescuing from Morrot," Brognola said. "He hasn't used up the initial kidnapees yet, even though he arranged for even more."

"Fifty comatose patients," the President stated. "According to your man's report, the comatose conditions could be caused by the toxins and hallucinogens necessary for the creation of new...berserkers?"

"It's a less outré description than zombies," Brognola told him. "Just in case we have to tap other agencies for assistance...."

"Describing a zombie outbreak to them would make them think that the administration just went bonkers," the President concluded. "What kind of support could we give Striker if things get out of hand?"

"There's an aircraft carrier an hour out by helicopter. Jet support could move in sooner, but only on your say-so," Brognola offered.

"Striker and your teams have been there to keep the planet from going to hell plenty of times. You've got permission to sheep-dip any force you need," the President said.

Brognola nodded. "Not as if Striker will actually call on this for himself."

"He's stubborn that way," the President acknowledged. "But I suppose if there's a chance he can save anyone..."

"He'll take the shot, even if he has to pole vault naked over a lava flow," Brognola finished.

"Give him my best," the President said. "Because he's never given America anything less than his best."

Leaving the Oval Office, Brognola silently agreed. But in the face of a Haitian madman and his zombie horde, would even the best of the Executioner be enough?

THE WAREHOUSE WAS full, bustling with activity. Morrot, his one good eye sweeping the crowd from above, smiled. Fortescue made his way onto the catwalk with him. Morrot watched the younger Haitian, his whole body brimming with energy.

"You had fun at the prison?" Morrot asked.

Fortescue nodded. "How did you know we'd accomplish this? How did we pull off this crazy stunt?"

Morrot smiled. "Because I planned it that way. I set it up, I thought through every angle a million times before I took the first step. Poor young soldier, you are brilliant for a regular person, but my mind is an exploding cascade of brilliance."

"Something's up between those ears," Fortescue admitted. "How else can you break and program people in only a few days?"

Morrot smiled. "That is my power."

"You sound like something out of a comic book sometimes. If it weren't for the fact that you actually build real zombies, I'd think you were crazy," Fortescue said. "Instead, you just creep the hell out of me."

Morrot's grin remained undiminished. "All part

of my plan. Because if you weren't intimidated, you might think you didn't need me."

Fortescue nodded. Morrot took note that the Haitian, a man who'd weathered many battles in the service of the Jamaican drug gangs, never stood close to him, always keeping a few feet back at minimum. Morrot couldn't even remember a time when the young Black Avenger even accepted his extended handshake. That kind of fear was something that Morrot fed upon like a bear wallowing in honey.

"So now do you feel that my next plan will succeed?" Morrot asked.

"Seventy or so berserkers, backed by hundreds of gang soldiers?" Fortescue asked.

"And the Black Avengers," Morrot added.

"And my group," Fortescue replied. "We have U.S. armed forces in the area working on humanitarian relief. What's to keep them from arming up to stop our coup?"

Morrot's smile grew. "I have prepared for their intervention. There will be no doubt that they will be preoccupied."

"Really?" Fortescue asked. "What's going to keep the U.S. military busy?"

"In 2010, one oil rig failed dramatically, creating an oil slick catastrophe that was one of the greatest environmental disasters in history. The United States Navy sent every possible resource into the Gulf of Mexico to aid in its containment," Morrot replied.

"Who's going to hit an oil rig for us?" Fortescue

asked. "And just who would be crazy enough to launch an assault on a rig like that?"

"I've imported some help," Morrot said. "Once I let the word out in the Middle Eastern nations, there were plenty of people who would love to have Christianity lose an entire island, as well as strike another brutal blow against the American people."

Fortescue took another step back. "You're having a suicide Islamic fundamentalist group help us out? I know that they want to make another big stink, but just what convinced them that you were going to turn Jamaica Muslim?"

"I simply told them that I would," Morrot said. "But the *loa* know the truth in my heart. They know I am lying to the deluded subjects of a false god. The *loa* were here long before Yahweh and Allah. They will still be here long after those fads have faded."

Fortescue's face blanked. Morrot could tell that it was a defense mechanism, a means of keeping the old *bokor* from looking into his feelings, but just the fact that the blast shields went down to hide his emotions was enough to betray the truth. The younger Haitian was stunned at the faith in voodoo the old man projected. The shield buckled, a wave of relief pouring over him.

"I was afraid that you were simply using the trappings of our religion," Fortescue said.

Morrot felt the genuine thrust of that statement, but didn't betray his surprise. He knew that the Black Avengers were practitioners of the darker aspects of the religion. He'd seen Fortescue praying in front of a small shrine he'd produced, and heard him discussing the vengeance of the gods against France and Haiti. For someone of Morrot's intellect, it was a simple matter of manipulation. So far, he had met every single one of Fortescue's expectations, which allowed him to continue drawing out the young soldier's faith in him. The declaration of his devout observation of ritualistic trickery was the final nail that would inspire Fortescue to charge the very battlements of hell under Morrot's command.

Indeed, the invasion of Haiti would be akin to such an assault. Certainly, there would be forces withdrawn from the Caribbean in the event of a terrorist attack in the Gulf, but the Navy would not be so naive as to pull all of the Marines and Navy ground units from Haiti.

The Marines would fight hard, their ferocity formidable, even for body-armor-clad berserkers. Still, Morrot had anticipated losses. He'd counted on hundreds of sacrifices, especially among the Black Avengers themselves.

The invasion was a prelude to the real change of regime. A wild, all-out attack on Haiti would provide the grounds for members of the old government to sweep their plans into the forefront. Martial law would be declared, and at that point, control of the impoverished nation would fall back into strong, steady hands. As kingmaker, Morrot was willing to toss five hundred souls into a sacrificial bonfire to forge a government as firm and stalwart as that of the Duvaliers. As the power behind the throne, Morrot was going to be satisfied with the rewards he reaped.

Morrot was a man who worshipped a powerful god that was neither Jewish, Christian nor Muslim. That god was the almighty dollar, and greed was what had carried him through decades of life, engaging in intrigues that turned gangster against gangster, bandit against bandit, revolutionary against revolutionary. Morrot had made his bones from the Bermuda Triangle to the steamy depths of the Amazon River Basin, to the Philippines, where Communists and Islamic radicals fought each other and their government, causing chaos to earn the money necessary to live in the style to which he was accustomed.

"The carcass that Haiti has become will crumble once you set foot on the beach, Fortescue," Morrot said, not lying to the boy for the first time in his life. "You will arrive, and the ashes will collapse, sloughing off the skin of a brilliant phoenix that will rise from its prison, refreshed and renewed."

Fortescue nodded, eating it all up. Already, the images of taking over in the name of the Duvaliers, and more importantly, the *loa,* danced behind his eyes, a glimmer that Morrot picked up on as if Fortescue's face was a brightly lit stage.

And Morrot would build a new kingdom, several of them in fact. All because he knew that the United States of America was more interested in petroleum product than the starving, Third World masses rotting in Haiti.

AKIRA TOKAIDO WAS multitasking, his fingers flying over the keyboard in an effort to keep up with his thoughts even as he was running simulations on the kind of damage that more than fifty well-armored berserkers could do if unleashed on a city. The numbers weren't looking good, with thousands dead before the last of the maniacs was put down by gunfire.

"Of course the zombies always win," Tokaido said. "Happy endings for this shit simply aren't possible."

Price leaned over him and popped the earbud that had been pumping thrash metal into his skull. "They're not zombies. They're victims of brainwashing."

"Technically, they're more zombies than the living dead critters in the movies," Tokaido said. "They're produced by the real-world process, which inspired the mythology of the *zuvumbie*."

"So stop calling them zombies," Price ordered. "Bad enough that we've dealt with enough similar crap that we're no longer fazed by the concept. I don't want to be jaded about an apocalyptic scenario, no matter how outlandish."

"We have more to worry about from the synthetic life-forms created over the past couple of years," Tokaido said. "And there's always the chance that the entire computer network that humanity's set up will become complicated enough to turn sentient."

Price glared at Tokaido. "You forgot about the AI that nearly wiped out Stony Man and the American defense network?"

"Oh, yeah," Tokaido said. "No, I was thinking more along the lines of all machinekind being animated as a single hive organism to exterminate the organics mucking up its works."

"Don't ever try to cheer me up, Akira," Price murmured. "Ever."

"No problem there."

Tokaido was distracted by an alert on his screen. He pulled it up to full-size. "Barb, we've got a new development. Someone just uploaded a video to a Jordanian website claiming responsibility for the destruction of an oil rig."

Price looked down. "We haven't gotten any word from the Middle East."

"No, according to the autotranslate I set up, it's supposed to happen in the Gulf of Mexico," Tokaido stated.

"Are you certain?" Price asked, looking at the screen.

Tokaido turned up the volume, rewound and hit Play.

There was no mistaking the word Mexico among the spoken Arabic.

"Some days it just doesn't pay to get out of bed," Price murmured. "Did he give a clue as to where he was going to strike?"

Tokaido looked through the autotranslator's transcript as it ran up the side of the screen. "No."

"So that just narrows it down to thirty-five hundred," Price said. "Great."

"Thing is, this video file wasn't supposed to be noticed," Tokaido said. "It's being kept in reserve on the news site's mainframe until the actual incident happens. And Jordan hasn't given our country a heads-up."

"It could be a newsman trying to keep the lid on a scoop," Price mused.

Tokaido's brow wrinkled as he looked at the code accompanying the video. "Or it just could be a really good al Qaeda hacker who left this inside of the mainframe. See that section of code?"

Price glared at Tokaido. "See it? Yes. Understand raw binary? No."

"I swear, Barb. You speak more than one language. How hard is learning more than one numeric system?" Tokaido asked.

"Because," Price said.

"Because what?"

Price gave Tokaido a slight slap to the back of his head. "Because this conversation's wasting time!"

Tokaido winced at the playful cuff. "It's a timer for when to make this video available to anyone who doesn't have God-level IT access, and even then, it's pretty tightly wound to stay out of their sight."

"You're telling me that you have more power than an Information Technology God?" Price asked.

Tokaido dropped his voice a few octaves. "God? Such an appellation holds no meaning for the Devourer of Worlds."

"Akira, I swear..." Price began.

"It also helps that I have a 'herald program' inside each of these Arab television news networks," Tokaido said.

"A built-in monitor?" Price asked. "Wouldn't their IT notice it?"

"If it stood still," Tokaido said. "It's not a tap, but a

small artificial intelligence program I developed. It can 'move' in order to stay out of the sight of anyone looking for a glitch in their system. It surfs their network."

"A little surfer herald?" Price asked. "Which is why you call yourself…"

Tokaido's voice dropped again. "My name is unspeakable, earth-woman."

Price gave Tokaido's shoulder a squeeze. "I might not have a big, stony brute to get you to behave, but I do have Ironman."

Tokaido's eyes widened. "So according to the timer, we've got less than ten hours to find out exactly what oil rig is going to be hit. If we know the target, we can do something about it."

"Who's in the area?" Price asked.

"Rafe and Gary are in the Florida Keys," Tokaido said, referring to Rafael Encizo and Gary Manning, two members of Phoenix Force. "They just arrived last night, returning from an underwater salvage operation they took in their off time," Tokaido said.

"So they were out of touch when Jamaica went down," Price said. "I hope that digging through sunken ships rested them, because they won't even have time for a nap."

"Calvin is on deck in Jamaica, but I don't think you want to pull him off support for Striker," Tokaido mentioned.

Price bit her upper lip. "As much as I'd like to keep Cal on support for Mack, he's a SEAL and one of the two best divers Stony Man has. Plus, he and Rafael are designated team leaders for oil rig operations."

"We could always call in Force Recon," Tokaido mentioned.

"We could, but then there's unit integration to take into consideration," Price said, almost as much to herself as to the young hacker. "Have Cal on stand by, in case Rafael and Gary do have to move."

"Right," Tokaido answered.

"I'll get back in touch with Striker and Cal," Price said. She walked to her station quickly, a tap of her touch pad bringing up her communication board. There were times when she felt more like a cyberage switchboard operator than a mission controller. The link to James's Tactical Pad fired up, and a beep sounded to alert its owner of an incoming call. The small web camera built into the device became active, and she could see right up James's nostrils before the pad was turned around and set upright on its flat kickstand to survey both Bolan and James.

"We've got bad news," Price stated without preamble.

Bolan nodded. "There's going to be some kind of distraction. I've narrowed the options down to a massive explosion at Kennedy Space Center or an attack on an oil rig in the Gulf of Mexico."

Price managed a smile, despite the grimness of the situation. If there was one thing about Mack Bolan, it was that he knew his enemies well and could anticipate their needs. Even an army of hundreds wouldn't be enough to change the situation in Haiti without something to pull the attention of the United States away.

"The second. Since you're so smart about the kind

of diversion that Morrot would use, can you pinpoint which rig?"

"No," Bolan said. "I was hoping you'd do that. Right now, I'm suggesting that you have someone run a check on chartered boats here in Kingston."

"Any particular kind?" Price asked.

"A cigarette boat would be the ideal platform," Bolan replied. "It could get to the Gulf within hours, and be quick and small enough to slip past any patrols unnoticed."

"Naturally. That's why cocaine smugglers love them," Price added. "The Coast Guard needs better and better radar and infrared technology just to catch up to them."

"Striker also said that you'd want me on hand, just in case it was an oil rig attack." James spoke up. "But right now, I might do a little better on the ground than out in the Gulf."

"How so?" Price asked.

"While you've got the potential to pick up on a rental, Cal here has some old contacts inside the Jamaican Constabulary Force. Correction, had. Now they're retired," Bolan said.

"Not enough to get me a pass if I'd ended up going full SWAT on a prison by myself, but they can hear things, and investigate others themselves," James said. "As soon as Striker figured that Morrot would be looking for a diversion, he had me call up my old chums."

Price nodded. "Nip the show in the bud before it gets out to the oil rig."

"We're hoping," Bolan said. "If anyone has information about off-the-record speed boats in Kingston, it'll be Cal's contacts."

"In the meantime, who's going to help you deal with the berserkers?" Price asked.

"Once again, thinking outside of the box helped us immensely," James said. "Striker was given a sedative by a local Mambo. A cure isn't going to work with the hallucinogens, but the powder that she gave to the five sample zombies belonging to Reggie Watson still hasn't worn off after several hours."

"That would give us the time to examine them for cyanide capsules," Bolan said. "We can save the last of his innocent hostages and the inmates that had been rendered comatose by him."

Price noticed something about the relative lack of urgency on the Executioner's part. "You don't sound as if you're in a rush to come down on Morrot just yet."

"I have time. From what we learned from Reginald Watson, ten hours from now, Morrot is going to have allies make an attack on a Gulf oil rig. He'll need a few more hours to make certain that the Navy is well on its way at full steam even before he begins to send his army to Haiti. Once the Navy is past the point of no return, even for its fighter contingent, then he'll move in," Bolan explained.

"You've got the timetable already?"

Bolan nodded. "I'm sure the math is off by a few minutes, but Morrot has been operating three steps ahead of me all this time. He's smart, logical and experienced. With all of that combined, it's easy to anticipate his course of action."

"I hope so," Price said. "Otherwise, we won't only have Jamaica and Haiti in flames, but we'll have a gigantic oil slick that'll hammer the Gulf Coast all over again."

James's cell phone rang, and he pulled it from his pocket. "Yeah?"

"Is that…" Price began.

Bolan nodded. "The ex-constables coming through."

"It sounds like you're sending him alone," Price noted.

Bolan's features grew grim and dark. "Cal has his task. I have unfinished business to take care of. A mess I'd inadvertently caused when Long Eddy became shark food."

"Javier Orleans and the Grim Strokes," Price said.

Bolan touched his nose to indicate that she had gotten it right. "For Orleans, it's judgment day."

## CHAPTER SIXTEEN

The weight of the armored, load-bearing vest felt good on Calvin James's shoulders and back as he approached the darkened boathouse. The skiff was guarded by a half dozen Rasta gangsters, and they were alert. Two men watched the water while the other four took turns patrolling. None of them bunched up, but they rarely passed out of sight of at least one other man, ensuring that no one would sneak up on them. He could tell that the men weren't protecting anything good by the fact that each was equipped with a Fabrique Nationale P-90 Personal Defense Weapon.

The P-90 was an item that James had used before, and it was a good, reliable weapon. Holding a 50-round magazine full of cut-down versions of the U.S. Military's 5.56-mm NATO round, with a powder charge optimized for the SMG's eight-inch barrel, it provided the same armor-piercing capabilities and manstopping punch at close range without the rifle cartridge's propensity to produce face-roasting fireballs out of such a compact, stubby weapon. James's MP-7 operated on the exact same principle as the Belgian-made weapon, only the caliber changing, the overall weight remaining the same. The P-90 was a step ahead of the MP-7, as its regular 50-round box was a no-snag design that rested atop the weapon's receiver, enabling a flat, low profile. A 40-round magazine extended from the butt of the MP-7, a curved banana clip that would be hard to conceal under a trench coat, necessitating the flush fitting 20-shot box.

That the Jamaicans were armed with such high-tech gear and were coordinated to almost military discipline levels added up to bad news happening within the boathouse. Calling it a "house" was a misnomer, as it was more along the lines of an aircraft hangar in shape and size. It was befitting the craft inside, as James knew that cigarette boats were the fastest things on the water, owing to their powerboat racing heritage. An average specimen was capable of ninety miles per hour over calm water, slowing only to a mere thirty miles per hour in choppy seas. Another nickname for the sleek boats was "Go-fast," a term originating from the military, most especially the Navy SEALs who utilized the craft for rapid insertions and emergency extractions.

For the most part, the cigarette boats carried only five people, or two pilots and cargo, making them ideal for high-speed smuggling across the Caribbean. The Navy, however, had been able to up the crew to a full SEAL platoon of twelve men.

All of this ran through James's mind and he had to tell himself that there was the possibility that the Jamaicans, if they could afford armor-piercing PDWs, probably had even more impressive engines and hull designs, giving them greater velocity, necessitating the use of helicopters with snipers to intercept them.

Though the official record was only in the 280-mile-per-hour range, there were those who died at speeds as fast as 300 miles per hour. James doubted that the Jamaicans could make their boat go that fast. One mistake, one impact on a swell, and it was akin to tripping on a concrete berm and smashing your head into a solid steel wall at more than 250 miles per hour.

Still, 180 miles per hour was an achievable velocity for the smugglers, expert boat pilots who were used to evading surface and air pursuit.

"Glad I came early to this party," James whispered to himself as he lowered into the water. Even as he submerged to his neck, he heard the unmistakable growl of a quartet of 350-horsepower engines, the power plants that put the "fast" in Go-fast. The ex-SEAL snarled, pulling himself out of the water, cursing all the way. The cigarette boat had pushed out of its hangar, gliding on the surface out into the open.

James shouldered his MP-7, wishing that he'd had the foresight to lead with the grenade launcher, another Heckler & Koch model called the M-320. Against the fiberglass hull of a boat twenty yards away, James didn't like the chances his little 4.6-mm rounds doing anything. These were craft that required a .50-caliber weapon to stop, but he fired anyway. The suppressed weapon made little noise over the snarl of the Go-fast, but the boat's pilot ducked as bullets splashed against the cockpit.

That got their attention, and maybe it was just enough to keep them from tearing out at two 200 miles per hour. James's heart sunk as the cigarette boat's engines roared even louder, spitting up rooster tails of foam before it rocketed off.

"Damn!" James cursed.

Already, the Jamaicans on guard had turned their attention to the shadowy figure that was scrambling up the steps to the pier. James wouldn't have a lot of time, but if he could get into another of the Go-fasts, he might have the chance to catch up to them. All he had to do was to hammer his way through six armed guards, each capable of opening up their fight at 850 rounds per minute from 50-shot magazines. The weight of the load-bearing vest was made even more cumbersome now, as opposed to the comfort he'd had before. The armor wouldn't do much to stop a 5.8-mm penetrator from punching deep into his internal organs.

James brought up the MP-7, peered through its holographic red-dot scope, and triggered off two 3-round bursts that chopped into one Jamaican who had knelt to provide a stable platform to shoot from. The 4.6-mm slugs struck the Jamaican in the hand and face, betraying the tunnel vision that had locked onto the weapon his opponent wielded. Two 4.6-mm channels were drilled through the guard's skull, and then whipped his brains into a frothy foam, dropping him dead, his P-90 spitting into the night sky without coming anywhere close to the Phoenix Force pro.

James hit the ground, skidding on his rear end behind the cover of a forklift as more enemy fire lanced toward him. The steel of the loading vehicle gave the former SEAL a reprieve long enough for him to tear the M-320 grenade launcher out of its plastic packaging. He had planned to infiltrate the boathouse under water, but the departure of the terrorists and their cigarette boat had shot all of that to hell. Now, James was left to find a way to catch up.

Part of that meant upgrading from 4.6 mm to 40 mm, a charge of high explosives burping out of the muzzle of the grenade launcher and sailing toward one of the enemy guards who had holed up near the double doors of the boathouse. The plastique payload detonated, the blast shredding the doors and the shrapnel core flying out in a sheet of murder that lacerated the sentry James had intended to take out. The bloody guard remains staggered to the edge of the boardwalk, then dived headfirst into the water.

James had been on the move the moment he'd triggered the M-320, knowing that the 40-mm blooper round would buy him sufficient distraction to close with the smugglers' sentries. While one of the Jamaican gunmen was still gawking at the raining chunks of the boathouse striking the water, James stiff-armed his MP-7 and fired it at contact range to the Jamaican's head. The bullets designed to punch through body armor at a hundred yards had little trouble shattering the guard's skull and spewing his brains onto the ground.

That was the extent of the free shots he'd get at the smugglers' protectors, as the others whirled at the flash of movement.

James hit the corner of the warehouse just as enemy bullets sought his flesh. The Phoenix Force commando reloaded the MP-7, feeding it another forty rounds before he reloaded the M-320. This time, he had inserted one of his favorite combat tools, the 40-mm buckshot round. Turning the grenade launcher into a double-size shotgun, the shell was capable of generating a cone of high-velocity death, just the ticket that the ex-SEAL needed to get into a Go-fast and take off after the other craft.

He fired a "Hail Mary" shot around the corner where the remaining Jamaicans tried to advance on his position. The M-320 kicked like a mule, and it had taken everything James had to hold on to the grenade launcher. However, for all the ache he suffered in his wrist, elbow and shoulder, he was rewarded with a lull in the PDW fire that raked at the corner he'd hidden behind. James peeked out into the open and saw that one of the guards was only ten feet away. His body had literally been cut in two, from a spot just below his clavicle to a point on his sternum. The hundreds of shotgun pellets loaded into the buckshot grenade had torn the man apart. Behind him, another gunman rolled on the ground, screaming as he clutched his bloody face.

James transitioned to the MP-7, raking the mutilated survivor with a mercy burst before he looked for the last of the three Jamaicans. He didn't see anything, which meant either the guard had gone into the water or he'd retreated to flank James from behind. Either way, this was the time he had to take the inside of the boathouse and search for a way to pursue the other craft.

He charged between the shattered double doors, and saw a man wearing coveralls laying on the skiff next to a boat. The man was unarmed and bleeding, holding a wounded shoulder where he'd caught some shrapnel. There had been a pair of guards inside, but the leftovers of their corpses were strewed across the inside of the hangar, having been at ground zero when the grenade blew the doors to hell.

"Is that Go-fast working?" James asked.

"Loaded," the mechanic said with a cough. "Fueled up."

James peered over his shoulder, anticipating the approach of the last of the sentries. "Hang on, I'll tend to your wound."

"Don't do me no favors," the injured Jamaican growled.

That's when James heard the stomp of fast-running feet on the boards just outside. The Chicago badass whirled, bringing up the stock of his machine pistol. It was a perfectly timed stroke, the steel buttcap crushing the guard's jaw with a single blow as he whirled through the doorway. The sentry landed on his back, out cold.

James turned to regard the injured mechanic after making certain the last of the guards was down. All he could see was the glare of hatred from him, but no effort to go for a weapon.

"I'll help you," James offered.

The mechanic winced. "Help yourself, fucker."

With a shrug, James cast off the mooring ropes as swiftly as he could. The next thing was to engage the Tactical Pad he'd tucked away in a pocket of his lead-bearing vest. "Phoenix Four to Roost. Phoenix Four to Roost."

"We read you, Cal," came the response over his wireless earpiece. "It looks as if you lost track of the Go-fast according to the DLIR satellite you had us maneuver there."

James settled into the driver's "couch," an ergonomic seat that surrounded the pilot in a cradle of protective roll cage armor. There was a familiar scent and he glanced over his shoulder to see bales of weed tucked into the passenger cabin.

"Barb, I can do without the running commentary. I saw the bastards get away."

"We know. We were watching you," Price said over his earpiece.

James checked the startup. This boat was nothing less than a jet fighter that skimmed the water, so the prelaunch program was going to take a few moments. He didn't want to have the combined 1300-horsepower engines explode while he was throttling along at well over 100 miles per hour. "What's their heading?"

"They're running parallel to the Palisadoes," Price said, referring to the thin finger of sand that formed a natural enclosure to Kingston Harbour. "But they're doing an easy one-fifty."

James was about to key the throttle when a shadow loomed over him. He looked up in time to see the mechanic swinging a wrench at him. If he hadn't put the helmet on, James's brains would have been decorating the interior of the cockpit, but even so, he was stunned by the ferocity of the attack. The mechanic was about to pull back to take another shot at James, but the Chicagoan grabbed the man's wrist, pinning it down.

"You're dead! Dead, asshole! Dead!" the mechanic bellowed, trying to free his trapped hand.

James didn't answer. He was still stunned and scrambled, his free hand trying to reach across his body to grab the handle of his Beretta. There was no way, not without freeing the wrench and risking another head shot. Rather than stretch out the fight, James yanked on the nylon cord around his neck, drawing his Woo neck knife. The flat blade, worn like a necklace or a concealed badge, had been a backup of James's for a few years. Now, he needed it and he gripped the blunt-shaped blade's handle. Out came a razor-edged, square length of steel, only two and a half inches long, but with a half-inch spine that provided axlike strength.

James whipped the neck knife across the mechanic's forearm, parting clothing, skin and muscle before sticking in the Jamaican's ulna. The would-be killer wailed in agony, his wrench falling from numbed hands. James flicked the knife upward, lashing it across the center of his opponent's face, splitting the skin from chin to forehead.

"I'm not dead, motherfucker, and I'm sure as hell prettier than you!" James yelled back as the man fell away from the cockpit. With a tease of the throttle, the cigarette boat was out of the gate.

"Cal?" Price asked. "What was that?"

"Some idiot who refused medical aid, then tried to smack my skull open," James answered, panting as the boat accelerated, turning along the way toward the tombolo that formed the southern border of Kingston Harbour. "Now he needs even more medical attention, but I've got places to be."

"Remind me never to insult your bedside manner, Cal," Price said.

The quartet of 300-horsepower Crusader propulsors attached to the back of the boat pushed against James hard enough to feel like the one time he'd actually been on a rocket ship breaking from Earth's atmosphere, albeit on a lighter scale. The thrust of the water pump jets was more than sufficient to throw his speed up to nearly a hundred miles an hour in the space of a few seconds. James was familiar with the kind of "oomph" that could be gotten from a Go-fast, but this smuggler boat was a beast. Any more throttle and there was the chance that he could stand the craft on its end before tumbling in a cartwheel that would end in splinters and his shattered corpse.

"Oh, momma," James whispered as he concentrated on keeping the nose down and avoiding swells that would act like stunt ramps, shooting him into the sky like a rocket. He needed to move faster than the other ship before it could swing around the south of the island and proceed to the Gulf of Mexico.

"Cal, were there any terrorists on hand in the boathouse?" Price asked.

"No," James answered. "Why?"

"We're reading only one live heat signature on the craft, in the cockpit," Price told him. "I thought that this was going to be an attack on an oil rig. Did you stumble on a regular smuggling operation?"

James throttled up past 125 miles an hour, keeping the bow of the ship steady as he tore across the surface of Kingston Harbour. "Maybe he's going to pick someone up? No. They would have been at the launch beforehand."

James fell silent as he aimed the speeder like a torpedo. As soon as his mind locked on the term torpedo, he looked back toward the packets of marijuana loaded in the passenger compartment. "Oh, fucking hell."

"It's not a raid team," Price said, coming to the same conclusion James had. "It's a guided missile."

"How much can that thing hold?" James asked, not daring to deviate from the course that had been beamed to his Tactical Pad, now resting on the armrest of his cockpit. The satellite infrared surveillance had tagged and enhanced both his and the enemy's watercraft.

"Crew of five men, call it a thousand pounds of high explosives," Price said. "Basically, given modern formulas, enough to tear a drilling rig in two like it was made of tissue paper, rupturing whatever pipelines are below."

James grimaced, resisting the urge to put every ounce of horsepower into closing with the other vessel, now less than five miles ahead of him. "You know, if my heart weren't already in my throat, I'd be throwing up right now."

"I've got the aircraft carrier on the line," Price said. "You don't have anything that can stop that boat."

"If you can get a couple of F-18s over here, go for it," James said. "But until then, I'm going to have to get creative."

"What do you mean?"

"I'm going to try to throw him off with the wake from my own boat, if I can catch him," James answered. "If he hits the swell put off by my boat, it'll be like driving a Corvette into a concrete divider."

"And what if he tries to do the same thing to you?" Price asked.

James remained silent for a moment. He looked at the infrared blip sitting on the Tactical Pad ahead of him. There was a steady but slow countdown of the distance separating them.

"Going all out? If I'm not lucky, I'll run on water for a few hundred feet before my legs are ripped off."

"And if you are?"

James grimaced under his helmet. "The lobes of my brains will pick an eye socket to exit through, and make the inside of this faceplate really messy. The good part is, I won't feel a thing."

James could hear Price's whispered f-bomb on the other end of the call. "I hope the F-18s get there before you do."

The powerboat skipped over a small wave, airborne for a full second before it touched down, splashing and continuing its forward charge. James had his opponent's course, and already the sailor in him was charting courses of interception. He tried to anticipate the directions that the enemy pilot would make, realizing that he was operating on the knowledge that he was pushing a bomb at over a 150 miles per hour.

That's what the satellite image and Aaron Kurtzman's calculations had given for the enemy Go-fast. While James's boat was laden with bales of Jamaican grass, the terrorist ahead of him had to steer his craft carefully, avoiding too many bounces that could turn his bomb into a premature explosion. Even with that caution, James had to cut corners.

The cigarette boat had low-scale radar, capable of looking ahead of the ship to sight waves that would otherwise be invisible to the pilot. Once more, James thought of the men who only hit minor bumps at 300 miles an hour, the history of water-speed record challengers killing themselves in spectacular fashion as incompressible fluid was as solid as steel when struck at such velocity. In the other craft's cockpit, there would be a similar radar, scanning for dangerous turbulence necessitating a slow down.

The other craft veered toward placid waters to the north as a section of rough chop popped up ahead. James aimed right at the very edge of the rising waves while the other pilot, less experienced, kept himself well aside any danger, skimming over safe and open sea. The keel of the boat shuddered beneath James as the craft shoved him through minor swells like a knife through wrinkled skin. It wasn't pretty, and James's stomach was doing backflips, but he'd closed the distance. The countdown was in terms of thousands of feet, not miles.

Hitting the enemy cigarette boat with his wake

would be a tricky option, but the only other tactic would be for James to pop open the canopy on his cockpit, take aim one-handed with his grenade launcher and punch out a 40-mm shell. The wind shear off the bow alone would rip the weapon from James's hand, probably even shattering his forearm and wrist in the process. There was a third option, but that would entail crashing into the other craft.

James would die in the resultant explosion, but even then, steering and hitting the target at such speeds would be nearly impossible. The swells kicked up by the powerful Crusader engines at the back of his boat weren't only the easiest solution to the threat of a speedboat packed with high explosives, but also the safest.

If only James could catch him.

According to the GPS on his console, they were nearing the hooklike peninsula of Portland Blight, right where the enemy would begin his northward trek to reach the Gulf of Mexico. James adjusted his course, anticipating the man's upcoming turn. That would trim even more distance between the two, and maybe put James in the lead. Once that happened, he'd be able to make the flat ocean a hell of waves and foam.

The other pilot had to have seen James, as now he turned, as well, maintaining a parallel path. The enemy throttled up, the Tactical Pad telling the Phoenix Force commando that he was closing in on 180 miles an hour. There was a surge forward, but James slammed the hammer down. This was going to be an all or nothing effort.

The other pilot, sensing his lead, adjusted his course north, preparing to sweep across James's path and make him strike his wake. So the enemy knew what would happen at these speeds. James's quadruple propulsors strained as he egged on the throttle, pointing at a spot where their paths would intersect.

"Two out of three results on this dice roll end up with him beaten," James grumbled under his breath.

"Cal, two out of three also mean you end up dead!" Price spoke up.

James ignored the voice coming over his earphone. The keel of his boat burst above the surface, riding a wave as if it were a jump ramp. He came down hard, feeling as if he'd jumped a full story onto concrete in an inner tube. Only the raw, corded muscle in his arms and his skill at piloting boats kept him from swerving his course, the cigarette boat spearing straight ahead. The other boat was closing, growing in size so that he could see it through the coming dusk. It, like James's boat, was painted a dull gray, which helped it disappear amid the ocean waves.

With a powerful punch, James revved the last few grunts of horsepower out of the engines. Their parallel course was going to converge within a couple of hundred yards, and there was no way that James was going to allow a mass murderer to turn the Gulf of Mexico into a sea of oil and pollution once more.

That final wrench of the throttle skipped James's boat along, and he shot ahead of the other craft, steering hard to the south to box in the enemy boat. The high-G turn made it feel as if an infant had grabbed hold of the corner of his mouth and started swinging from it. The blood sloshed around in James's brain even as the other boat ran into the churning wake of the rocketing Go-fast.

The Stony Man warrior felt the shockwave of a thousand pounds of high-efficiency explosives go up. Somewhere in the back of his mind, James remembered that the god Neptune was not only the lord of the seas, but the master of the earthquake. The very air around the SEAL and his boat shuddered, and James pulled back on the throttle. Luckily he was outside of the blast radius, but if a wave struck him at this speed, he was dead.

The cigarette boat bounced violently, but in the end, it was simply the keel rebounding off a dish of water that had been pounded flat by the megablast behind him. With its throttle killed, the Go-fast decelerated immediately, skipping over the few waves that popped up like a stone on a lake. The jostling made James glad for the padded collar under his helmet, and he rested his head against the helm of his boat, breathless.

"Cal? Cal, say something!" Price called.

James pushed up his visor, lifting his head with an effort, but grinning.

"Boom goes the dynamite."

The sigh on the other end of the earpiece was one James would echo once his heart rate returned to normal.

# CHAPTER SEVENTEEN

Javier Orleans was not a happy man. Not when he knew that there was a one-man army out there who had been made aware of his existence. If this was the same monster who had crippled the Royales and ended Long Eddy's life and career, then Orleans and his soldiers were going to be in for the fight of their lives.

He'd assembled seventy of his best men, arming all of them to the teeth and readying them for a manhunt that would scour Kingston for Brandon Stone. It was a fake name, no doubt, just like Orleans's own moniker.

Montego and the other escapees were over in Holland Bay on the eastern end of the island. That was where Morrot had placed the staging area where the former inmates would set up as an army, board their freighters and take off for Haiti. Orleans had been doubtful about the success of such an operation, at least until Morrot had pulled off an unbelievable coup in emptying his people out of the prison in west Trench Town. As a reward, Orleans gave him the failures, men who had been so incompetent that they couldn't evade or bribe the Jamaican constables.

The important people had been brought to Orleans, men who had been pinched on tips and under the bribes of the remnants of the Kingston Royales. These were brains that Orleans needed, not the common street punks who had proved unable to fight their way out of an arrest. Let Morrot whip that group into an army. To Orleans, leading those failures on a successful invasion would be akin to herding kittens through a field of catnip.

Or maybe that was what Morrot wanted—a physically impressive-looking force, strapped to the gills, but all flash, no substance. Orleans suppressed an internal chuckle, finally figuring out just how Morrot intended his invasion to succeed. There, success wasn't going to be based on military conquest, it was dependent on forces within the Haitian government. With a massive threat breaching their island's defenses, opportunists could rally an entire country to accede to martial law and unlimited executive power.

"You're a real damned sorcerer, Morrot," Orleans mused out loud.

"What?" Riscio asked.

Orleans kept his features inscrutable. "Just complimenting our ally."

Riscio grimaced. "Complimenting him? You just gave him a few hundred of our people."

Orleans tried to suppress his glee. Most of those who were going to Haiti as sacrificial lambs were grunts who Riscio had counted as his personal cadre. Not only was Orleans pruning the useless, he was also removing those who would threaten his power. It was a win-win situation for Orleans, especially when he served Riscio up as the mastermind of the entire operation.

The authorities in Haiti, the other Caribbean nations and the U.S. would be looking for blood, and rather than take the blame for sending hundreds of gun-toting marauders into a sovereign nation, Orleans would give up the man that most of the corpses owed loyalty to—Riscio. Whether he was alive or dead, it didn't really matter. In fact, dead would be preferable.

"And now, we're going to throw even more manpower away?" Riscio continued.

Orleans glared at his hungry lieutenant. "Throw them away?"

Riscio rolled his eyes. "Stone chewed through the Royales and decapitated the group. He took out the recruit squad of twenty in the space of a few minutes, and snagged your boy Corboun."

Orleans frowned. "I'm not going to leave that maniac Stone out there to do to me what he did to Long Eddy. If you'd rather end up a corpse, go right ahead. I'm going down swinging."

"Oh, you will be going down," Riscio replied. "You think Long Eddy sat back and let this guy walk all over him? You don't remember all the carnage from a few weeks back?"

"I do. And I can see the mistakes that bastard made," Orleans said. "He didn't think big enough. We're going out in an armored convoy. Look at that."

Riscio glanced at the fleet of trucks and SUVs set up—dozens of men, all of them packing the best weapons that Orleans could afford, riding in vehicles that were being up-armored with telephone books and discarded newspapers packed into the cavities under the hulls. The newspaper and phone books would cushion most of the impact of bullets even after the outer skin was penetrated, and steel plates had sandwiched things. The vehicles were about as bulletproof as possible, though the windows were still a weak point. Improvised plastic riot shields would be carried by the window gunners, the thick polymer much stronger than the glass.

"You'd need antitank rockets to get at the passengers, and with the fenders and hoods reinforced, nobody is going to punch through those cars unless they have a dead-on shot at the grille or the windshield," Orleans said. "What kind of firepower is going to keep him from being run over, or flanked? He'd beaten Long Eddy, and Corboun, by shooting more and shooting first. We catch him on the defensive and overwhelm him."

"You might think that," Riscio replied. "We've only noticed him on the offensive, even when we thought he was in a purely defensive situation. But then, he had still set up enough booby traps to catch one of the strike team off guard. I'd tend to think he might be pretty good on the defense."

"Maybe, but he set that up as an aggressive defense. He was looking to be found, just so he could open up and catch someone, cutting the rest down," Orleans said.

"Yeah, and he succeeded, ending up with your boy as his prisoner," Riscio replied. "We're not going to have much luck if he can anticipate our going after him."

"We'll rain hell on him. He's a man. He's not bullet-proof," Orleans grumbled. "I'll surround him, outgun him and bring him down."

Riscio shook his head. "Do what you want. I'll be here to pick up the pieces."

Orleans grabbed Riscio by his shirt. "You listen to me, coward—"

The click of a knife opening sounded in Orleans's ears. He felt a point pressing against his belly. "G'wan, rude boy. Give me the excuse to gut you like a fish."

Orleans looked down to see Riscio's switchblade held at his stomach. "You won't make it far. There are others who wouldn't bat an eye if you tried to kill me. They'd take you down in a heartbeat."

"You'd still be dead, brah," Riscio said. "And I'd be alive, and in charge, for a few moments longer than you."

Orleans let go of his lieutenant's shirt. "Mutually assured destruction isn't your style."

"Nor yours," Riscio returned. "We'll have this out if you return from your fool's hunt."

"We will," Orleans admitted.

The Grim Strokes leader wanted to maintain his staredown, the dark glare meant to let Riscio know who was still in charge. He was interrupted as one of his armored vehicles erupted in a greasy ball of flame, the whole of Orleans's warehouse shaking under the thunderous impact.

Riscio's chuckle was audible over the screams and crackle of flames. "You wanted to go looking for him, but he found you, dumb ass. Corboun sold you out!"

Orleans snarled and brought out his pistol, ready to burn down his lieutenant, but the man disappeared as a gout of smoke wafted over the catwalk they stood upon.

Now the Jamaican gang boss had two enemies in his midst, both of them out for his blood.

FROM HIS STANDPOINT looking through the skylight of Orleans's warehouse, the Executioner not only had a bird's-eye view of the army assembled to hunt him down, but the argument ensuing between the Grim Strokes leader and his second in command. After a little bit of observation, Bolan had confirmed Corboun's views on the leadership at the top of the gang. Things were volatile, and if Riscio had been left in charge, unchecked, he would turn out to become as great a threat as Long Eddy or Javier Orleans himself. Bolan would have kept Riscio around as a weakened, gelded kingpin of the Kingston crime scene, but his hunger and drive, clashing with the new prince as soon as he was crowned, made him a dangerous threat. Someone with that kind of ambition had only one final destination in his criminal career—the grave.

Luckily, the Executioner had arrived here with everything he needed to take down Orleans's army. Thanks to a quick conference, Rambeau had told him that the Grim Strokes were circling their wagons in preparation for a wild hunt for Brandon Stone. Of course, Bolan had pieced together Orleans's location from information he'd gleaned from both the Gray

Man, Reginald Watson and Corboun, Orleans's chief enforcer.

This time, Bolan's head weapon of war was an old favorite, the M-4/M-203 combination assault rifle and grenade launcher. The M-4 was a compact version of his old favorite M-16, having a collapsing stock and a fourteen-inch barrel. Bolan made up for the lack of barrel length by loading the carbine with 72-grain boattailed hollowpoint rounds, highly effective ammunition that had the weight to penetrate a human body and shatter bones easily. What the carbine didn't have in terms of sheer firepower, the Executioner had in a 40-mm grenade launcher. The weapon was capable of spiking a fat, destructive charge of high explosives through an automobile and destroying it.

To start the ball rolling against the Grim Strokes, Bolan took aim at an SUV that was being loaded with rifles and ammunition for the hunt. The M-203 chugged violently, the stock jabbing Bolan's shoulder as he launched a 40-mm shell in a direct line to his target. He had considered taking out the engine, but the SUV wasn't running, so there would be no fuel coursing through it, insufficiently destructive for his opening salvo. Rather, he aimed at the back of the vehicle, striking the gas tank and the pile of ammunition stored there.

The detonation was spectacular, the sport truck's back end peeling open like a blossom, a rolling ball of fire washing over the half dozen men who had been working behind it. The front of the vehicle flipped forward, split in two by the violence of the explosion, mashing a seventh of Orleans's group under its roof. A thick, choking cloud of smoke rose from the warehouse floor, and Bolan was able to use it as a smoke screen, even as Orleans and Riscio had their argument. Landing on the catwalk in a crouch, Bolan somersaulted to bleed off the impact of his twenty-foot fall.

Orleans was up and running, sidearm out and obviously on the hunt for his rebellious lieutenant. Bolan's grenade had interrupted a spat that would have resulted in one man gutting the other, so the Executioner had actually saved the Jamaican crime boss's life, if only for a few extra minutes. Bolan's goal was a complete rout of the Grim Strokes, a salting of the earth so that the crooks who would support a murderous Haitian coup wouldn't rise again.

Bolan's smoke screen was dissipating quickly, but he was already at the top of the steps leading to the killing ground below. Among the trucks and gang soldiers, there were few who had the presence of mind to look upward to see the warrior descending into their midst. This gave Bolan the chance to feed another grenade into the breech of his launcher and pop off a second deadly missile into a pickup near an exit on the far side of the warehouse. The spinning bolt of thunder split the truck in two, steel flapping like leathery wings under the shock wave and heat of a twenty-gallon tank igniting. Searing heat washed across the floor, men screaming in pain and horror as a new inferno belched hellfire at them.

Gangsters scrambled for their lives, only one in ten gripping an assault rifle as if it were a safety blanket.

Bolan fired off a short burst into one of the riflemen, a trio of 5.56-mm bullets smashing through his clavicle and drilling deep into his rib cage. Heart and lungs shredded by the passage of the supersonic slugs, the gunner flopped lifelessly to the concrete, blood oozing slowly from his deadly wound.

"It's Stone!" someone bellowed amid the smoke and panic. "He's here!"

That declaration was intended to steel the assembled street soldiers, but as the warehouse had been rocked by two devastating blasts, the remaining Jamaicans split into two factions. At least twenty of the group smashed at a bank of windows with the butts of their pistols, prying at the steel grating that was intended to keep thieves out. That security measure was also sufficient to prevent a mass exodus from the Grim Strokes's ranks. A group of four men whipped around to follow Orleans' directions, but black clouds and cries of pain and dismay continued to provide their distractions.

Bolan had his M-4's selector switch set to full-auto, and he swept the squad with a long burst that slashed through their ranks.

The Executioner was a skilled marksman, but first and foremost, he was a trickster. By means of misdirection and intimidation, he was able to slice through seventy-to-one odds. Right now, confusion and terror ruled the warehouse, and Bolan was in the role of supreme terrorist, frightening his enemy beyond the capacity to think clearly. Unable to focus, the army assembled for the wild hunt was now a panicked mob without coordination. The soldier ditched his emptied magazine, giving it a fresh load even as he reached the floor of the warehouse.

At this point, handguns and rifles were barking even though visibility was nearly zero. Every shadow, every movement, drew gunfire. The Jamaicans were doing half of Bolan's grunt work for him, gunning one another down as they sought to protect themselves from the mysterious wraith that Orleans told them had slaughtered twenty of their own a few nights before.

A Rasta gangster stumbled toward Bolan, choking and grinding the stinging smoke from his eyes. As the man, despite his near seven-foot height, was helpless, Bolan swept his feet from beneath him with a kick. A stroke of the steel-tube stock of his rifle and the Jamaican big man was out cold. On the floor, he would be safe from smoke inhalation, and in this stretch of the warehouse, there was little flammable that could draw a fire to him. This man would survive to tell stories of the lone American who had come to Kingston and destroyed the Grim Strokes. The name Stone would eventually be lost, but the basic truth would remain, spread to the underworld.

There was someone out there that shattered armies of criminals by himself. There was a hunter in the shadows and smoke who left behind corpses by the score. In the old days, in his wars with American organized crime and with enemy intelligence agencies, Bolan had relied as much upon his reputation as his actual accomplishments to sow uncertainty and fear among his enemies. So scrambled, they would always be looking over their shoulders, wondering if the bogeyman was real, if the mysterious vigilante was poised, ready to unleash a rain of high explosives and sheets of flame.

The Executioner couldn't be everywhere in the world, but the nightmares he caused would linger.

A growl sounded off to Bolan's left, and he whirled in time to see one of the gangsters, bloody and singed, pull a machete from his belt. The M-4's muzzle whipped around and spoke its brutal message of death before the blade-wielding attacker could take another step. He'd seen enough crazed opponents raise a long knife to hack him to pieces over the past few days to last a lifetime. A full-auto burst stitched the blade man from crotch to throat, dumping his corpse across the hood of an SUV. The thump of a body striking the vehicle drew attention, and two gunmen opened fire blindly, their bullets zipping through the air near Bolan. The soldier threw himself behind the rear fender of the SUV while the pair fired where they'd last heard the blast of his carbine. Bolan poked the carbine under the chassis and targeted the legs of the two feisty gangsters. A snarl of 5.56-mm lead smashed apart ankles and shins, turning bone to splinters and rendering legs as rubbery, floppy sticks that were useless for supporting a human body. As the two gunmen landed on the cold concrete, Bolan abbreviated their suffering with another spray of rounds into their torsos.

The grating covering the windows had been finally torn away, frightened street soldiers leaping to freedom and abandoning the charnel house. Orleans's minions were dispersed or dead, but there were still targets that needed the Executioner's finishing touches. There had been too many times when a surviving, ambitious gang leader had stepped up in the wake of a Bolan blitz to take the reins and continue preying upon innocents. If Riscio was still kicking, he'd rebuild and make a move on the Royale territory, meaning that there was going to be another gang war where bystanders would suffer. If Orleans escaped, he'd lick his wounds and come back, smarter and more cautious.

Out of the corner of his eye Bolan spotted the movement, and he whirled, tracking the M-4 at the approaching target. He fired a burst, but it wasn't a man lunging at him. A volley of 5.56-mm bullets was great for ripping human opponents asunder, but against a falling crate, they only made tiny holes. Bolan lunged backward, but the heavy box slammed into his hip and upper thigh. Sandwiched between the crate and the concrete floor, the soldier looked at the carbine that had skidded from his grasp. He twisted, jamming his free foot against the crate, even as he clawed for the Beretta in its shoulder holster. A figure leaped on the crate, and suddenly the pressure on Bolan's leg increased exponentially.

Through the searing pain of crushing force on his leg, Bolan recognized Riscio, a man with a face that was lean and fierce like a Doberman pinscher's. The ambitious lieutenant had his handgun in hand, leveled at the fallen American.

"This was none of your business, Stone!" Riscio snapped. "It was between me and Orleans!"

Because the crate wasn't flat on a surface, Bolan's

leg making the gangster's balance precarious, Riscio's first shot went wide as the crate wobbled. While Riscio flailed to maintain his balance and high ground over his prey, the Executioner pushed with his other leg. The crate jerked violently and Riscio lost his pistol, crashing to the concrete floor.

Bolan's shove on the crate had also moved most of the box's weight off him and he was able to slide out from under it. He did a quick self-examination, and found that the leg moved, even though his hip, knee and ankle were overextended, twisted almost to dislocation by Riscio's assault. There was no feeling of broken bones, only stressed ligaments. He'd be able to move without risking more damage to his joints.

Just as Bolan was halfway to his feet, Orleans tackled him, driving the big American back against the box that had slammed his left leg. A gleaming talon of steel flashed in the smoky air, but the Executioner's reflexes were enough to bring up his forearm to block the downward swipe of the hooked knife. He straightened his arm, snapping the heel of his palm across Orleans's cheek, mashing his blunt nose to one side with a sickening crunch.

The Strokes boss stumbled away from Bolan, his hand clenched to his blood-spurting nostrils. The Beretta had been knocked away somewhere between the crate's impact against him and the tackle by Orleans, but that was why the soldier carried two handguns. The Desert Eagle cleared leather in a fast draw, but Bolan's acute senses warned him of movement from behind.

He twisted, dropping prone even as Riscio ripped

off four shots in rapid-fire. Orleans grunted as a bullet creased his shoulder. Bolan knew he had an opening and leveled the front sight of the Desert Eagle in the center of Riscio's face. The gangster's eyes went wide with the realization that his rise to power was over. Instants later, the impact of a single .44 Magnum hollowpoint round shattered his face, the force of the slug bursting the orbs from their sockets.

Orleans was on one knee, still holding his knife as Bolan continued his roll, putting distance between himself and the Jamaican crime boss.

"You not man enough to take a wounded man with a knife?" Orleans taunted.

Bolan sighed, sitting up.

Orleans smirked, thinking that his ploy had given him another chance at life. Bolan slipped the Desert Eagle back home on his right hip, then waved for Orleans to take his shot.

"Damn fool," Orleans boasted. "I've sliced up a hundred motherfuckers."

"Then make it a hundred and one and shut up," Bolan replied.

The lunge was a good one, as swift as lightning despite the Jamaican's injuries. It was precise, as well, the hooked point of the blade whistling through the smoke in an arc that would have opened Bolan up from shoulder to groin. Too bad for Orleans that he was dealing with a man who'd been on the receiving end of knife attacks hundreds of times before. A swift slap to Orleans's wrist deflected the path of the blade so that it cut only cloudy air. As the Jamaican's momentum brought him closer to him, the Executioner grabbed Orleans's elbow and drove a bone-shattering punch into his shoulder.

Orleans howled and dropped his knife as the joint was destroyed, his arm now flopping uselessly as it was dislocated out of a ruptured socket. Bolan followed up with a second punch, this one right to the crime boss's kidney. Orleans dropped to his knees, gagging as agony ripped up from his side. He wasn't even able to scream, just watch in wide-eyed horror as Bolan's hands cupped under his chin.

One thrust of Bolan's knee to the crease between Orleans's shoulder blades, and the gangster's trapped head stayed locked in the Executioner's hands while his neck and spinal cord were wrenched from the base of his skull. Orleans's head flopped crazily between his shoulders as he toppled to the ground. Riscio's corpse lay only five feet away, a hideous canyon carved through the center of his face, the dome of his skull nowhere to be seen.

With the Grim Strokes leaderless, Bolan spent a few moments recovering his Beretta and the M-4. While there were dozens of other violent gangs plaguing Kingston, the Grim Strokes had joined their counterparts, Long Eddy's Royales, in extinction.

The soldier favored his sore left leg, reminding himself that he still had a voodoo sorcerer's army to deal with, and drug-maddened young fishermen to rescue.

# CHAPTER EIGHTEEN

Before Stony Man Farm and Barbara Price had contacted the Executioner and Calvin James in the cabin of the Gray Man, Bolan was evaluating the prisoner, Skyler, who he'd helped escape a brutal gang of fellow inmates post prison riot.

Skyler had been in jail for theft, stealing food to be exact, and had come across the ire of the group of imprisoned Royales by betraying their possession of improvised shanks and shivs. As he had been in fear of the Royales, naturally, he had picked up on their quarrel with the Grim Strokes.

"The Strokes weren't going to let me get too close to them," Skyler said. "I'm gay, and in a Jamaican jail, that's the mark of Cain, or a sign hanging around your neck reading 'plague carrier.'"

Hopper, Bolan's tagalong since the battle of the abandoned hotel, rested a comforting hand on Skyler's shoulder. "No one's going to judge you here, Sky."

Skyler glanced toward Bolan and James, who showed genuine concern for the young man's suffering. "If that's the case, this'd be the first time in my life."

Bolan turned to Skyler. "You told us that the berserkers weren't attacking the Strokes, nor you."

Skyler felt around his neck, but his scarf was gone, only the purplish raw skin where the rag had been yanked, burning his throat, by Scarface. "The red scarves. Montego handed them out, saying something about needing them that day, around lunchtime."

"Not being dim, you picked one up," Bolan offered.

"I had my own," Skyler said. "It belonged to my mother, and she gave it to me in a care package, while I was waiting for trial. It was the only thing not stolen from the box except for crumbs."

Bolan grimaced at the Jamaican prison system that was nothing more than a jungle where the greediest, most brutal carnivores preyed upon the weak and gentle. The soldier still had questions to ask, however, about things more urgent than the condition of a broken justice system. "Was it a specific way to wear the scarf?"

"Over the nose," Skyler said.

Hopper handed the ex-prisoner a rag, and Skyler demonstrated the look, something akin to how outlaws wore them in the Old West or how people wore them to filter out choking smoke or dust storms. "It had to be red, though a little bit of white mixed in didn't seem to matter as long as they were predominantly red."

Bolan nodded, then looked at James. "Again, we're looking at Morrot being a pretty savvy programmer of the human mind. He picked something that was unobtrusive, but easily distributed."

"I doubt that the berserkers would have lost any of their color vision, and nobody would be standing around to ask just how the hell some prisoners escaped while others were chopped to pieces," James said.

"You had an encounter with one of the berserkers," Bolan prompted Skyler.

He nodded. "He didn't blink, and even though his face was twisted into a monster mask, he didn't show anything in his eyes. He snorted, looked me over, then moved on, cutting a man apart who was right next to me."

"You've earned your pardon, Skyler," Bolan said. "There won't be a warrant for your arrest for breaking out, and your record will be expunged."

"Why?" Skyler asked.

"Because you just made it possible for us to pull off something that would have been impossible," James said. "Of course, we are going to need a lot more of Mambo Glorianna's magic dust."

"I'm sure she'd provide it for the cause," Bolan replied. "Hopper, can you and Sky go and pick that stuff up? I don't want you sitting around here much longer."

"What about the Gray Man and his zombies?" Hopper asked.

"We'll alert the police. Watson's victims are still sedated, so there won't be much of a fuss," Bolan told him. "However, if the cops find Skyler in his prison clothes, and you with that pistol, things will end up pretty ugly."

Hopper looked at the revolver stuffed into his waistband. "Never was much of a gun-totin' cowboy before."

"I'm not saying to give it up. Just remember, it's for

your protection, and the protection of your loved ones," Bolan said. "And you'll need it, especially if people are still looking for you."

Hopper nodded in agreement with that statement. "What about you two? You're stepping out?"

"Things to see," James answered, jerking his thumb toward the sleeping zombies in the cabin. He then formed an imaginary gun with his index finger. "People to do."

"You remember where you took me to see Glorianna, right?" Bolan asked.

"Yeah," Hopper answered.

"Then all you need to do is pick up the stuff and meet us back at our old safehouse," Bolan said. "We'll be back to get the mambo's sedative, and then you can go home."

"Or wherever you can stay," James added. He pulled out a wad of folded bills. "Hopefully, this can get you some comfortable digs until you two end up getting a good job."

"Just take care of yourselves, okay?" James asked. "Because if you end up on the wrong side of the law, and we come back to Jamaica…"

Hopper shook his head. "I'll stay on the straight from now on."

Bolan gave Hopper a friendly clap on the shoulder.

James looked at his partner. "You know that even if we do wear the red scarves and bring the sedatives with us, we first have to sneak into whatever holding cell the berserkers are in and knock out something along the lines of a hundred people."

"All without Morrot and Fortescue's people hearing us, and before he sets sail for Haiti," Bolan added. "But we have a way to rescue the last of the tourists and fishermen without hurting them."

"Does that apply to the inmates, too?" James inquired.

"We'll cross that bridge when we get to it," Bolan said.

HOPPER TOOK another sip of his bottle of water, trying to hold in his fidgets as he waited for Stone to arrive. Sitting in the van he'd borrowed from the American operative, it had been an hour past the time when he was supposed to meet the two Stony Man warriors.

"Don't jump," Bolan said from behind Hopper, but he still flinched and let out a yelp of startled surprise. "I asked you not to jump."

Hopper could smell the stench of smoke on the big man, his face smeared with dried blood and grease. He also seemed to be leaning more on his right leg, as if to favor the left.

"You look like hell."

"Better to look like the product I'm delivering," Bolan quipped. "Makes it a more believable sale. You okay?"

"I'm good, and I'm glad I didn't wet the driver's seat," Hopper replied. "Mambo had what you needed. She said to be careful, too."

Bolan nodded.

"Where is Cal?" Hopper asked.

"He'll be picking me up in the harbor," Bolan returned. "We've got a cool new ride. A cigarette boat."

Hopper sighed. "Sounds like it'd be a fun trip. Well, at least until you got to that army of mercenaries, gangsters and zombie things."

"Yeah. That's why you're sitting the rest of this out," Bolan told him.

Hopper got out of the driver's seat, handing the keys to the man who'd spared his life and gave him a second chance. The soldier offered his hand again, but Hopper pulled him close, hugging him tightly. Bolan patted his back, showing no sign of discomfort.

Hopper's voice was cracking as he spoke. "What can I tell someone who I know hasn't spent a careful day in his life?"

Bolan smiled. "Live large has always worked for me."

Hopper returned the smile. "Then live large, Colonel Stone."

The Executioner slid behind the wheel of his van and drove off on the next leg of his quest.

BOLAN HANDED James another packet of "zombie sedative" to put into the back of the powerboat. All the while, James listened to the status of their former charges.

"My covert operations team went to Jamaica and all I got was a speedboat loaded with ganja," James grumbled.

With the cockpit's storage area filled, it was a tight squeeze for the two tall men, but everything fit. James had been gassing up the Go-fast before Bolan had arrived with Mambo Glorianna's sedatives, so the craft was ready for its trek to Port Holland, where the confluence of Reginald Watson's shipment tracking, Corboun's recollections of weapons deliveries, and Stony Man's infrared satellite eyes had picked up the location of a camp, an improvised dock and a nonregistered steamer.

The two Stony Man warriors looked at the Tactical Pad and a blow-up of the deck of the lone ship anchored in the isolated harbor. There wasn't a major road for miles from the beach, and there was only one hot spot of habitation on the crescent shapes. James was especially interested in the freighter, just in case it was an improvised Q-ship.

Q-ships were an age-old bluff wherein a ship that appeared unarmed was secretly bristling with weaponry, either to engage in espionage or ambush of enemy harbors, or to appear as a helpless merchantman vessel to bait pirates. Downward-looking infrared cameras, as well as conventional high-magnification lenses had scoured the decks. Sure enough, the powerful surveillance technology available to Stony Man Farm had come through again, showing off concealed nests for .50-caliber Browning machine guns and pintle-mounted 40-mm belt-fed grenade launchers. There were strange-looking cabinets hidden in the main structure, and judging from the fire shielding skirting the unknown obelisks, they were some manner of small rocket launchers. Of course, that went along with the information that Corboun had given up about a lot of money changing hands and secret shipments of truckloads of weaponry. While the gang lieutenant didn't know *what* had been delivered, he had seen ammunition crates for heavy machine gun, cannon and even rocket rounds.

"The only thing these guys don't have packed on board are deck guns," James said.

"With the missile launchers, they wouldn't need them," Bolan said. "Besides, they just need covering fire against conventional harbor defenses in Haiti, not the kind of bombardment necessary for an amphibious assault."

"Morrot's been pretty sharp so far, right?" James asked.

Bolan looked out the windscreen, seeing the bow outlined, its nose a black point swooping up and defined the bioluminescent plankton in the sea foam that sprayed over it. Right now, James was operating more by the high-speed craft's radar than by sight. The instruments were as good as any, and the forward-looking radar on the cigarette boat was better at detecting surface or subsurface obstructions that would turn their hull into a flying cloud of splinters. Much like the Executioner himself, the Go-fast utilized more than just sight to make its way through treacherous waters, and was constantly sweeping everything around it for details that would mean the difference between a full-velocity charge across the Caribbean and a keel-snapping impact that would turn its passengers into sacks of crushed pulp.

Bolan prided himself on paying attention to details.

And right now, he had been looking at one detail in particular that had made no sense. Morrot was a brilliant tactician who had left nothing to chance, stacking odds in his favor to the point that he was changing the minds of innocent victims into savage maniacs and hurling the island nation of Jamaica into a panic.

"Striker?" James asked.

"You're wondering how a few hundred men could take over an entire country," Bolan said.

"Yeah. I mean, I'm assuming that there are going to be people in Haiti who will be allied with the invaders, right?" James asked.

"Even if there were, you'd need entire sections of the civilian police force to be a party for anything to succeed," Bolan said. "Aristide disbanded the army in 1994, and the U.S. had escorted any of the remaining military leaders out of the country.

"Sure, there is dissatisfaction with the current government in Haiti, the revolution and the UN military intervention of 2004 proved that. But it's hard to believe that there's anyone left on the island that thought the reign of the Duvaliers and the Tonton Macoute was a good thing."

James adjusted course, remaining steady on the throttle. "It'd be doomed to failure. As weak as they are, the Haitians would fight relentlessly to keep those bogeymen from coming back. So how the hell could that work?"

"It can't," Bolan said. "I've run every possible military and political scenario in my head, and in all of them, Morrot ends up with a target on his back, either from the Haitians themselves, or from the rest of the world. The UN and the U.S. both have troops in the region, and we're not going to tolerate another mass-murdering dictator on that island."

"So all the weapons, all the gangbangers, all the zombies," James counted off. "They're...what?"

"In the novel *1984,* the people of Oceania tolerated the presence of the Thought Police because the Ministry of Truth told them that not only were they at war, but there were terrorists among them. If people disappeared, it was for good reason, for the protection of society," Bolan said. "Regularly, bombs would strike New London, the signs of a war that seemed to wage fiercely, endlessly."

"But it was all a show, a sham," James agreed.

"Apparently, Morrot is even smarter than we thought. He's taken the kind of conspiracy that idiots consider 9/11 an inside job, and turned it into a real bid to cement absolute power and martial law in Haiti."

James's eyes narrowed into a squint. "Everything's just a sacrifice, not that it's going to do any good for the thousands of people killed or injured by Fortescue's invasion."

"And in the meantime, Morrot can fake his death, disappear and live off the reward he earned for handing over an entire nation to a handful of despots," Bolan concluded. "Hit it, Cal. We can't even let them off the beach."

James cranked up the throttle, 1300 horsepower screaming as the quartet of propulsors pushed the cigarette boat closer to 200 miles an hour.

FORTESCUE KNELT at his shrine, lighting his candles and beginning his appeal to the *loa* for their favor in the coming days. He and the Black Avengers, the sons of the Tonton Macoute, were going to engage in a world-shaping excursion that would forever warn other nations of the folly of resisting the will of their *bokor* and his entreaty to the dark servants of supreme Bondye. Humankind was merely a plaything for cosmic forces that few comprehended, few save for those strong enough to realize that humanity was a joke, an aberration in the universe of untold cruelty and the whimsy of deities.

Fortescue had thirty scions of the Duvaliers' secret police with him, warriors who had hardened themselves in countless battles in the Jamaican drug scene. Each of them had scars, each of them knew the truth of the world and its transient nature. Their existence was one of service to those who demanded blood and souls, and Fortescue had offered up many.

His reward was the mentor Morrot, the one-eyed sorcerer who had been the right hand of the dictators that he'd worshipped. The gift handed to him was the chance and the power to put things right, to return Haiti to its original roots, the island nation that had made its pact with those that the ignorant called devils, gathering the strength to throw off the fetters of one of the world's great powers when no other French colony had succeeded in rebellion. The *loa,* in their might, had brought down the hammer of destiny on the Europeans, gelding them in wars that had turned their army into a joke, and stripping its enlightenment and society down to the point where its contribution to Western society was its brothels.

France had bet against the lords of darkest voodoo and had crashed from their place in history. Where once the nation had gripped the entire globe, rebellion had crippled its interests as bloodbaths in Africa and in Vietnam had shown. Even today, hundreds of years after the pact that unshackled Haiti, Paris still suffered inferno-sprouting riots as immigrants strove to usurp their religion and supplant it with Islam.

"Marinette, slayer of the black pig and liberator of our people, grant me the steady hand I require," Fortescue whispered in prayer.

"Ogoun, mighty ironworker and warrior inspiration of our war in 1804, fill me with the strength to smite down all who deny thy will.

"Ezili Dantor, single mother with the knife, look upon the son raised by one of your own with mercy and grant me succor when I feel faint.

"And finally, Kalfou, loiterer at the crossroads between life and death, relish in those who I send on the journey past you, and be kind should I pass thee in the days ahead.

"Let none stand before me without feeling the backs of thy hands. Fill me with the fury and the power needed to strike down Stone lest he interfere with thy will."

Something stirred in the back of his mind.

Morrot's sorcery, his brilliant planning and the ability to twist the minds of men to be his weapons, was strong, and yet it hadn't done the one thing that was most important to the conquest and liberation of Haiti from Christianity. Morrot's appeal to the *loa* had not done anything to bring Brandon Stone to heel, even though he had proved to be the one man who could derail any part of the great plan.

Fortescue stood from his spot in front of his shrine.

Why would Morrot allow the continued existence of a man who was actively hunting them down? What purpose could such mercy provide if it were not in the interests of the *Petro Loa?*

"The warrior Ogoun whispers to me," Fortescue said softly. "He has planted the seed of truth in my mind. Stone is not the only enemy stalking the darkness around me."

The Black Avenger commander blew out the candles in his shrine, extinguishing the incense and cigar that burned to satisfy his *loa*. He had dire warnings to share.

# CHAPTER NINETEEN

Calvin James had remained behind in the powerboat, letting the quiet electric motors silently idle in case a rapid departure were necessary. On the sea, the cigarette boat's low profile rendering it invisible on the night-black waters, the Phoenix Force sailor would be a great assist. James was ready in the cockpit, armed with the XM-110 sharpshooter rifle, its twenty-inch barrel and 7.62-mm NATO chambering giving the Chicago hardcase command of everything he saw out to 800 yards. If he needed more, he would also have the benefit of a Navy SEAL-provided Mk 48 Mod 0 light machine gun, in the same caliber and possessing the same range as the sniper rifle, but capable of hammering out its 200-round belt payload at 800 shots per minute.

If even that weren't enough, there was the HK M-320 grenade launcher, as well, but if things had gotten that bad, Bolan gave James the go-ahead to call in Navy F-18A strike fighters. Once things got to the point of high explosives being launched, there would be no turning back, and it would be likely that no one could be saved.

Naturally, the Executioner intended to keep the situation from degenerating that badly, but there was no doubting that he had his work cut out for him. In a lifetime devoted to combating monsters on their own turf, Bolan had faced the consequences of failure every time he acted. Occasionally, too often for the perfectionist soldier, he had lost, hostages dying because he was too late, or too slow, or he had underestimated the cruelty and ruthlessness of his opponents. While his victories in saving lives far outweighed his failures, the friendly dead continued to haunt him.

According to his estimations and the crew registries of the fishing boats and missing tourists, he still had between ten and twenty-five souls counting on him. If he didn't find them, or if they were already among the dead, then Bolan would switch to a new plan—utter devastation. He would resort to the cold and calculating killing machine, a warrior fueled by an icy desire for justice that would push him past pain and numb all of his emotions until every last one of the murderers he hunted were dead at his feet.

He closed with the corral, a roofless structure that was made up of twelve-foot walls that stretched a tarpaulin over them to shelter the nearly seventy warm bodies within. Bolan slithered through the shadows with serpentine grace and silence, keeping out of the sight of sentries. Despite their nervousness and jittery reflexes, their fields of view were easy to circumvent in the darkness. The Jamaican gunmen who served on guard duty scanned the night at eye level while Bolan crawled through the undergrowth, below their line of sight and hidden by a three-foot canopy of grass and bushes. Years of jungle survival enabled Bolan to avoid making any more sound than the native nocturnal fauna. The city boys were unused to the forest and were totally unprepared, expecting an intruder to move along in a crouch, not smearing his body through the mud and dirt.

Seeing the actual training and preparedness of the freed inmates, Bolan was certain now that Morrot meant for them to fail. Sure, the assault rifles they carried, Brazilian SAFs, were fairly current production and capable of hammering out 5.56-mm NATO rounds at a rate of 880 rpm, but firepower was one thing. In the face of determined opposition, the superior marksmanship, cover use and determination of U.S. Marines or infantry would tear them to pieces. This group was meant to cause terror among civilians and the Haitian national police, spurring the government to crack down to prevent further terrorist incursions.

The manipulation was an old one, and Bolan had defused similar plots in all corners of the globe, all the way to conspirators trying to do the same to the U.S. government. It was a sadistic, murderous tactic, the refuge of men who didn't believe in dirtying their hands while spilling the blood of citizens.

Morrot was going to give up the names of his co-conspirators, and this would be one instance where Bolan wouldn't have qualms about "enhanced interrogation techniques." The *bokor*'s paymasters weren't going to walk away from this failed invasion, not with the blood of hundreds already on their hands.

The corral was made up of wooden slats that were reinforced by chain-link fence. The slats were placed too closely together for anyone to see in, which also meant that the brainwashed drones inside were also unable to see out. It was a safety measure that was designed to keep the berserkers from being provoked. The entrance was unmanned, but securely chained and lit only by the harsh red glow of a lamp, the long wavelength of light hard to see in darkness and also the "safe" color that Morrot had programmed into the drugged army. Bolan wasn't a man to go in the front door anyway, and trying to deal with the chained gates would cause too much of a racket.

Instead of the direct route, Bolan found a stretch of the fencing that faced the forest. It was dark here, and sentries were loathe to venture too far out into the woods even with flashlights, which were contraindicated by the very menace they were guarding anyway.

He emerged from the underbrush, slipping his scarf over his nose and mouth. For a moment, hiding in the shadows, Bolan had the mental image of another man, similarly disguised, fighting in the darkness. It may have been a misremembered pulp magazine from the soldier's youth, or it might have been a vision of another life, another trip around the cycle of death and rebirth. Either way, Bolan drew his rubber-coated wire cutters, snipping through the chain deftly and swiftly. The nocturnal creatures created enough chirps and creaks that Bolan was able to disguise the slight noise produced by the clippers amid their racket. Once the chain link was parted enough for him to slip through with his war kit, the soldier wrapped two of the wooden slats with duct tape strips that he slid between the gaps.

Bolan applied force to the spot where he'd wrapped the slats, using his hand as a fulcrum and pulled on the bottom of each plank. The duct tape dampened the crack of wood, the inch-thick slats meant more for obfuscation than durability. The chain link was meant to do most of the work of restraint, and the wood was pulled from its tape and tossed into the bushes.

With his entrance made, Bolan slid into the corral and found himself genuinely surprised by what he found. A quick head count put the number of inhabitants of the pen at close to eighty, but all were sitting placidly in patio-furniture-style recliners. Their eyes were open, and each person watched small color televisions that continued to replay loops of video imagery. By the illumination of the personal monitors, Bolan was able to see that each wore headphones.

The setup was identical, if the pieces of technology weren't uniform. Bolan recognized both name brand and knockoff electronics among the TVs and the headphones, while cables ran all the way back to a cage filled with computer terminals and a mainframe server.

Bolan approached one of the prisoners, taking a moment to slip on a latex glove to prevent skin contact with Mambo Glorianna's knockout dust. He spread a fingertip full of the stuff across the lips of the drugged young man before removing his headphones and turning his monitor slightly. Bolan listened in and found himself listening to a squeal of white noise, static that would have given him a headache if he paid attention to it for more than fifteen seconds. Even with his brief exposure to the racket, he could make out subliminal tones in the static.

Once again, the Executioner marveled at the combination of ancient voodoo medicine and twenty-first-century electronics. Deadened by narcotics, the human mind would be left in a hypnotic state where the subconscious would be far more susceptible to subliminal messages disguised by the sonic assault. The flickering screen was a mixture of terrifying and violent imagery, but Bolan saw odd flickers in the video stream. There would be words and concepts interspersed to further influence the drugged minds of Morrot's victims.

Bolan took a moment to check the trapped "zombie's" pulse, then examined his features. This had been one of the prisoners from the holding facility, something readily apparent from his orange coveralls and the identification band around his wrist. A quick check showed that this man had lived a hard, violent life, as well, but Bolan couldn't bring himself to do any harm to an unconscious prisoner. The law would show up to deal with his kind, and he had brought sufficient powder to deal with the whole of the group.

"Striker, it looks like there's some activity around the barracks," Calvin James's voice came over his hands-free headset. "A man matching Fortescue's description is calling a couple of others over to talk. He's agitated."

Bolan grimaced, moving from prisoner to prisoner, painting a trail of dust across each one's lips. Though Glorianna promised him that it would be difficult to affect someone with an overdose of the gentle narcotic she'd mixed, Bolan didn't want to test the limits of the zombies' physical resilience to the drug. There was a good chance that Morrot, looking to even the odds, made certain to disguise the innocent from the guilty. He'd gone through a dozen of the semiconscious drones, and hadn't found anyone who wasn't wearing prison jumpsuits. When he finally came upon a young black woman, she, too, had been stuffed clumsily into a coverall signifying that she'd been an inmate, but Bolan had memorized the faces of the American tourists who were still missing. She was one of them, albeit a little more emaciated than she'd been in the file photo.

Bolan clucked his tongue four times, the signal that he had discovered Morrot's hostages, and that they had been mixed in among the inmates so as to be indistinguishable from the others.

"Read you and confirm. We have a can of mixed nuts," James replied. Bolan knew that if he were inside the corral, he wouldn't have been able to speak out loud, lest he awaken the prisoners. There was always the possibility that the programming wouldn't have taken with all of the berserkers, and the scarf across his mouth wouldn't have been effective.

Even unarmed, they would be extremely dangerous. Bolan still nursed lacerations and a wicked bite wound from his first encounter with them. His leg and head also ached from the conflicts of the prior days, though those injuries weren't indicative of more severe trauma. The soldier had come on a mission of mercy, and with the bumps and cuts accumulated over this operation, he knew that each tinge of pain could slow him just by a thousandth of second.

Bolan continued his task, Glorianna's sedative applied to each set of lips as he moved along quickly, but thoroughly. Once he had drugged each of Morrot's legion into unconsciousness, he'd turn his attention outside the corral, beginning the systematic dismantling of the Haitian's army. The Jamaican gangsters would be an easy rout, if his prior conflict with Orleans's men was any indication, but they were amateurs and as such, he wouldn't take them for granted.

Fortescue's personal cadre was highly trained, and while that meant that Bolan could anticipate their response to a threat, it also meant that they were smart and adaptable. One zag where Bolan expected a zig, and the fight would be over with the American gushing his lifeblood in the dirt. Surprise was the order of the day, and the Executioner would have to act quickly. There was only so much that he could do in silence with a knife or his bare hands, and while his Beretta and the MP-7 were suppressed, they still made noise that would reverberate in the darkness. They might not be recognized as gunshots thanks to the sonic alteration properties of the suppressors' internal baffles, but they would attract attention.

There were four more of the captives left, and Bolan was pleased to note that he still had half of a bottle of the sedative remaining when he heard James's rasped whisper in his ear once more. "Striker, Fortescue is coming right for the corral. And he looks pissed."

Any other man would have spared a moment to utter a foul phrase or two, but Bolan hurried himself, completing the goal of incapacitating the army of berserkers before they could be used or spurred into suicide. He hadn't had the luxury to dig around in their mouths for cyanide tablets, so he didn't even know if they had them or not. With the zombies tamed by the Mambo's concoction, Bolan would have all the time in the world to check them later, especially after he dealt with the gunmen in the improvised army camp.

Bolan had also counted. There were seventy-nine of the would-be berserkers, and three empty couches.

He slipped into one of them, pulling off his scarf and scooping mud and debris from his boots and soiled blacksuit to smear onto his face. He understood the implications of the empty couches—there were berserkers elsewhere in the area, but they didn't need programming. For all he knew, Morrot had each of them on a leash, serving as his personal bodyguard. Maybe they weren't even mindless.

He'd deal with that mystery when he came to it. Right now, he sloughed his vest and tucked it under his seat, settling in just as the chains on the gate rattled. There was dissent outside, hushed whispers tossed back and forth, but ultimately Fortescue's voice cut through the quiet argument.

"I have business inside!"

Whatever was going on, the Haitian rebel wasn't afraid of stirring an army of crazed killers with his bellow. He entered the corral followed by two of his men, walking toward the cage inside. They didn't pay any attention to the blank-faced captives whose faces were illuminated by the small monitors beaming madness into their minds.

"PIERRE, HAVE YOU taken leave of your senses?" Bertrand asked as Fortescue opened the AV cage inside the corral.

He pinned his lieutenant with a hard, smoldering glade. "I have heard the warnings of the *loa*. They have bidden me to take action before our endeavors are wasted."

"What does that mean?" Romy inquired.

"It means that Morrot has been lying to us," Bertrand stated.

"You got this from sniffing the incense in your shrine?" Romy asked.

Fortescue reached out, grabbing Romy by the jaw, pulling his face in close. "Do you doubt my faith, or the words of the *Petro Loa?*"

Romy couldn't talk, his lips mashed together between Fortescue's fingers, but he shook his head, getting a slurred "no" out of his pinched mouth.

"Neither?" Fortescue asked.

Romy nodded in affirmation.

"Ogoun planted the seed of knowledge in my mind. Ogoun is no liar, he is a warrior, direct and fierce, the spirit of our revolution and the strength of its swords," Fortescue continued. "He told me that the man who has been investigating us has not been touched, and for good reason."

He released Romy so that the man could ask why.

Fortescue noted with impatience that Romy turned his attention toward the raptly hypnotized creations of the one-eyed *bokor*. Fortescue slapped him lightly on the cheek to focus him.

"Why hasn't Stone been taken down by Morrot?" Romy asked hesitantly, his eyes still flicking toward the captives.

"He wants a trail of our invasion to be known," Fortescue replied. "That is why the Jamaican thugs we've been dealing with have been tasked with destroying Stone."

Bertrand shook his head in disbelief. "That's... Surely if the truth about our coup came out, Morrot would find himself hounded across the globe. There would be no place for him to hide."

"Except among our corpses," Fortescue returned.

Romy and Bertrand were now focused on him intently. That had gotten their attention.

"Our corpses?" Romy asked.

"Did I stutter?" Fortescue countered.

"He's going to kill us?" Bertrand exclaimed in disbelief. "So what are we doing *here?*"

"We're going to fuck him over before we end up fucked," Fortescue said.

Romy looked at the comatose army of zombified minions. "With what? Them?"

Fortescue regarded the group, which looked more like a bored movie theater audience than a horde of berserkers. "Their programming isn't finished yet. They're useless."

"Then what?" Romy asked as Fortescue finally got

the AV cage open. The Black Avenger commander grabbed a fistful of wires coming from the back of a central hub and ripped them out to a shower of sparks. Suddenly the sea of illuminated faces disappeared, no longer lit by the monitors that they watched.

"I'm evening the odds here, and looking in Morrot's 'drug' cabinet," Fortescue answered. "These things haven't been hit with the real cocktail that makes them dangerous. In fact, he says never to dose them until just before it's time to act."

Bertrand watched as Fortescue withdrew a vial of glistening bloodred fluid, holding it up to the single bulb in the tent. "The vampire juice? How do you know it won't make you completely crazy?"

"The hallucinogens and multimedia programs make them insane. But this stuff, it's liquid rocket fuel," Fortescue answered. "You remember my sparring match."

Bertrand nodded.

"Scared of having a shot of absolute physical supremacy?" Fortescue asked. "We are the elite, and with the power this stuff gives us, we'll be invincible."

"Now?" Romy asked.

"No. Later, when it's necessary. Wake up the brothers, tell them of Morrot's duplicity, let them know that our attack on Haiti will be for naught come the dawn," Fortescue answered. "But with the right weapon—" he indicated the bottle of "vampire" juice "—this, we will have our opportunity to raise more than an army. We'll raise a nation of superhumans."

"With one little jar?" Romy continued to ask.

"I give a sample to a chemist I can trust, and then

we'll reverse engineer it," Fortescue said. "If Morrot wants to continue with the attack on the island, then let him. None of our sacred brotherhood will fall because of his plotting."

"You're not going to kill him?" Bertrand asked.

Fortescue sneered. "That would still link us with the bastard. I'm leaving him high and dry and getting what we can for this folly. Get everyone to snatch whatever is worthwhile. Food, money, drugs and especially weapons and ammunition. The faith has to continue if Haiti is to rise again."

Bertrand regarded the zombified horde. "The original pact was made with the sacrifice of a black pig. Here, we have almost a hundred. Why not get fortune to shine brighter upon us?"

Fortescue paused, considering the implications. A cruel smile crept across his lips. "We're trying to sneak out like thieves in the night. Whatever you're going to do, make it quiet, or at least a distraction from our exodus."

Bertrand nodded. Fortescue and Romy, carrying a pack laden with Morrot's concoctions, left the corral. The Black Avenger drew his knife, a foot-long Bowie with a long, gleaming blade, scanning for a good target with which to start the show. He remembered the girls at the back of the pen, and dark thoughts whirled in his mind. Not only would the *Petro Loa* bring his offering to distant, aloof Bondye, but they would be pleased by the combination of blood and sex.

Bertrand let his chuckle escape his throat as he headed for the girls. It was eerily black, but the captives weren't moving. Indeed, they seemed to be in a deeper stupor than before, which was good. He didn't relish even the clawings of a female berserker as he spilled seed and blood in the name of Marinette and Kalfou.

Still, it was eerie stalking among the semi-living prisoners, sitting in rows that extended into the shadows of the tent. He didn't know if he preferred these soon-to-be maniacs plugged in and gradually filled with more and more madness, or a darkness where he couldn't see them.

"Marinette and Kalfou, raging spirits of the night, guide me against my fears of these mindless drones," Bertrand mumbled. "Do that, and the prettiest in this tent will come to you, emptied of blood but filled with sex."

A hand dug into the collar of his uniform shirt from behind an instant before he felt an arc of lightning rip up from his kidney. Bertrand dropped his knife as every fiber of his being pulsed with the pain of renal shock caused by the rabbit punch. As tears flowed from his eyes, crawling down his cheeks into his well-trimmed beard, he looked up to see a mud-masked figure towering above him.

"Mari and Kalfou will have to go hungry tonight," Mack Bolan said as he loomed over the stunned, paralyzed-with-pain Black Avenger.

Bertrand tried to claw for his handgun, but a ribbon of silver flickered in the darkness. He felt a great heat in his throat, punctuated by a bolt of fire that plunged into the juncture of his neck and shoulder. Suddenly, his pain and fear bled away, calmness sweeping through a body that had suffered for too long.

"Thank you, Baron," Bertrand croaked before he descended into the shadows, knowing that Samedi and the *Guédé* would take him to his reward.

Bolan let Bertrand's corpse down gently. For a moment before the man died, he seemed at peace, elated at the cruel fate that had left his throat slashed and the major juncture of arteries and other blood vessels in the crook of his neck punctured.

It didn't matter. What was important was that Bolan knew that Fortescue didn't expect his lieutenant for a while, considering his goal of mass sacrifice.

The Black Avengers and Morrot were in the middle of a falling-out, and if he didn't act fast, Fortescue would escape, laden with everything necessary to continue terrorizing the Caribbean in the name of his perversion of *Vodou*.

The conspirators and their amassed soldiers wouldn't escape. Not after the suffering they caused. This stretch of Holland Bay was going to become an abattoir.

# CHAPTER TWENTY

"Cal, the Black Avengers are planning to leave this party before it starts," Bolan called over the earpiece that Calvin James wore.

"Well, Drew, I have a few lovely parting gifts," James said, his voice dropping a few octaves into a game-show host tone. "I take it you're clear and we're weapons hot."

"Bring the noise," Bolan said.

James stuffed a 40-mm HE shell into the breech of his M-320 grenade launcher and took aim at a motorboat tied to a temporary pier. The boats would provide a link between the camp and the freighter, which was to be their primary transport to Haiti. They would also be the surest means of escape for the Haitian rebels, which meant that they were his first target.

Since the grenade launcher didn't have a significant muzzle-flash, James would be able to maintain some anonymity as he sailed the blooper onto the deck of the motor launch. Six-point-eight ounces of plastique transformed from chemical to thermal energy, the resultant blast wave shattering the craft and turning it into a cloud of splinters mixed with the frothy water of the bay. The thunderclap anchored the attention of everyone in the camp. Though he didn't have the

XM-110's sniper scope to provide the expression on their faces, James had been in enough battles to know that the hammer blow of a 40mm shell was uniquely distracting.

He broke open the M-320, the spent cartridge sliding out even as he palmed another one into its place. Once more the launcher was at his shoulder, James's aim now for the end of the dock where the escaped Grim Strokes inmates provided a pair of guards for the pier. The 40-mm microbomb landed between the two gangbangers, turning the boards that they stood on into sawdust. The pair of ragged corpses flew, landing in graceless, ungainly puddles of broken flesh and bone.

Even now, the Jamaicans and Haitians on the shore were getting their act together, scrambling for cover. There was no way for them to tell exactly where James and his cigarette boat were, but gunfire lanced over the water, since that was where the first targets had been. James was tempted to grab his light machine gun, but the muzzle-flash would make things much hotter for him in the cockpit of the boat. No, it was time to turn to quiet, though silence didn't necessarily mean neat.

The XM-110 was suppressed, so it wouldn't betray his presence, not at two hundred yards out in the surf and at night. James swept the area, looking for targets. As the crosshairs settled on a rifleman who was emptying fire into the bay, the Phoenix Force fighter pulled the trigger. The 210-grain subsonic round, unhindered by the velocity-bleeding aspects of the suppressor, crossed the distance between James and his target, striking him where his collarbones met just under his throat. The Jamaican rifleman wouldn't make much noise, but the gory crater blasted in his clavicle and his violent death spasm made everyone aware that any of them could end up as a bull's-eye.

James continued to seek out targets. A head exploded here, a gunman spun under the impact of a slug through his ribs there. Ten shots, ten hits, ten bodies strewed on the shore and gunmen were now more interested in avoiding the incoming rain of precision lead than seeking out the shooter.

James almost felt guilty for taking such easy pot shots when spotlights burned to life on the freighter. He turned to see crewmen yanking the tarps off their heavy weapons even as the spotlights scanned the waters for the source of the deadly firestorm plowing into the group on the shore. James slid back into the driver's seat and hit the throttle, accelerating even as the searing glare of one spotlight struck the cockpit of the speedboat.

There was a shout of recognition just moments before machine guns and light cannon opened up on the deck of the freighter. The rocketlike speed of the Go-fast hurled James out of the line of fire of the deck guns on the ship and made him almost impossible to hit, but there was a consequence. James, throttling along to evade incoming fire, wouldn't be able to slow down to utilize his grenade launcher against the crewmen firing at him. If he stopped, the cigarette boat would be a sitting duck, an easy target for heavy machine guns that tore jet fighters from the sky and

40-mm automatic grenade launchers capable of rendering a football field into a blast crater.

James's mind raced as fast as the craft he steered, searching for a solution so that he could return to the task of providing fire support for Bolan before he was overwhelmed.

BOLAN DETACHED the suppressor from his MP-7, not wanting to hinder the 4.6-mm bullets any more than he had to. The camp came alive with confusion and panic as James hammered the shore with a pair of grenades, turning the dock into a mangled mass, severed from the beach and burning from the ignited contents of a destroyed boat's fuel tanks.

There was a flurry of return fire from the gunmen on the shore, rifles chattering loudly in random directions over the water, but the shooters were being picked off by James's precision marksmanship. All of this bought time for the Executioner as he left the corral, heading toward the main part of the camp.

Along the way, a Grim Strokes inmate showed uncanny perception, turning at Bolan's approach. He was about to bring up his Brazilian SAF rifle, but the Executioner snapped a hard kick that jammed the frame of the weapon into the Jamaican's ribs with an ugly crunch. With his breastbone in floating fragments, he was wide open for Bolan to break his neck with the stock of the compact machine pistol. The longer he could go without making noise, the better, even though the stubby little chatterer was primed for full-volume fire.

Bolan was able to tell the Jamaicans and the Haitians apart by hairstyles. The scions of the Tonton Macoute were neatly groomed, either shaved bald or their hair closely trimmed. The Jamaicans had longer, wilder hair as befitting their Rastafarian gangster roots. Right now, a Haitian was rushing toward the corral, obviously dispatched to summon Bertrand. Even though the runner wouldn't find anything but the lieutenant's corpse, Bolan felt the need to cut down the trained soldiers among this cobbled-together terror army.

The Executioner swerved into the Haitian's path, his sudden appearance making the Black Avenger put on the brakes. Bolan grabbed the fighter's rifle, an M-4 clone, twisting it out of its owner's hands before he could pull the trigger. With the man yanked off balance, Bolan used the rifle as a battering ram. The steel tubular stock crushed the Haitian's windpipe and larynx with a deadly stab that caused bright blood to burst from his lips. With a scooping slash, Bolan used the stock to wrench his opponent's head upward by hooking his jaw. He reversed the carbine so fast, the Haitian hadn't even hit the ground before a short burst ripped through him.

Bolan took a moment to gather up spare magazines for the carbine. Out on the water, the freighter blazed to life, spotlights burning like baleful eyes. They were searching for James, and from the sound of the heavy weapons in the distance, they'd caught a glimpse of him. James would need help, as the smuggler boat wasn't armed to take down a Q-ship. Even though Bolan had upgraded from a PDW to a fighting rifle, it wasn't going to do much to help out the Stony Man commando. What he needed was something truly impressive, if only to sweep the gunnery crews off the ship's deck.

He made a mental note to keep an eye out for a suitable tool for the job even as he turned his attention toward the riflemen on the shore who were trying to tag James and the cigarette boat. The Executioner cut loose with the M-4, set to full-auto, and raked two of the riflemen who were taking potshots at James. Their backs torn open, the Jamaican gunners crashed into the sandbags that they were using to brace their weapons for long-range fire.

The muzzle-flash of Bolan's carbine was a beacon, especially as other riflemen noticed the demise of their comrades, shot in the back. The Grim Strokes gangsters whirled with their weapons tracking the basketball-size fireball released by Bolan's M-4, but the soldier had moved in the shadows, cutting away from his former position.

He also sought to keep his advantage of stealth by transitioning from the carbine to his MP-7 PDW. Since the high-powered 4.6-mm rounds had been optimized for the short barrel of the compact machine pistol, the muzzle flare was significantly less intense and less likely to catch as much attention as the M-4. Bolan put his theory to the test by ripping tribursts of armor-piercing rounds into another of the Jamaican gunmen. The gangster fell swiftly and finally as his breastbone was punctured in six places, the slender projectiles cutting through bone to ravage his aorta.

Another of the Jamaican defenders was sharper than the rest, seeing that Bolan had changed weapons, but even as he swiveled the muzzle of his SAF toward the soldier, he caught a trio of 4.6-mm rounds through the face. Brains scrambled, he triggered the auto-rifle with his dying reflex, spraying lead and fire into the night sky. The 40-round magazine of the HK PDW was an asset, allowing Bolan to take down another four men without even thinking of reloading. By the time he'd half drained the ammo box, the gangsters were scrambling, more interested in seeking cover than returning fire against the dark figure that had gunned down their brothers.

The Executioner switched between weapons again after reloading the partially spent PDW. He was in fire-and-maneuver mode, which meant that he wouldn't have time to feed an empty weapon as he engaged his opponents. He gripped the M-4 with one hand as he tore a chemical smoke grenade from his harness. A soft lob, and a thick jet of cloud burst from the canister in an ever-spreading fog. He remembered the position of a particularly large group of Jamaicans and aimed a flash-bang at them, dropping the blinding shocker into the middle of the group with a hard throw. The "distraction device" exploded in an eruption of light and sound that felt as if one had been slapped in the head by a cast-iron skillet, buying Bolan the time he needed to carve through the crowd of gunmen with a full-auto figure eight. The M-4 was left drained and Bolan tossed it behind his back, its sling keeping it with him as he drew the loaded and ready MP-7.

Through the smoke, the Executioner was able to see exactly why there had been such a sudden influx of gangsters, as they were pouring out of one of the barracks, tripping over their dead and blinded allies even as they responded to the thundering battle outside. The PDW snarled at 900 rounds per minute, 4.6-mm penetrators tunneling through one body and punching into the man behind the first target. The staccato hammering of the compact chatterbox was accompanied by the death screams of Grim Strokes gunmen who were sliced open by Bolan's relentless stream of auto fire.

Bodies toppled, and there was a pause in the exodus from the Quonset hut that had housed the Jamaicans. The pile of corpses at the door was an indication of considerable casualties, but the prefab building could hold even more soldiers. The soldier solved this particular problem by priming a Selectable Lightweight Attack Munition and tossing it through the door. As the SLAM was packed with octogen high explosives and one of its multiple purposes was to disable armored vehicles, it was generally meant more for static ambush or sabotage, not as a grenade.

Still, the considerable payload of the cigarette-pack-size bomb was more than sufficient to erupt with the fury of a god's lightning bolt. The shock wave sent Bolan staggering as he hadn't gotten completely clear of the devastated hut, but he had been out of the way of shrapnel and the pressure in his ears had been equalized so he didn't suffer aural trauma. What hit him was a fraction of the stunning impact of the flash-bang grenade he'd thrown earlier, but he was still able to fight.

Running, on the other hand, was made difficult as the blast caused Bolan to stumble, aggravating his injured ankle. His foot folded under him, but the soldier tumbled to minimize the pain and take him below the line of fire. He took advantage of the SLAM's aftermath, which had kicked up fire, smoke and debris that rolled across the beach camp.

Finding a seat against a still-standing section of prefabricated wall, Bolan took stock of how badly he'd turned his ankle. He could move his toes and pivot his foot. A test push against the ground also told him that he could handle the weight even though he'd receive a spike of pain through the ankle with each step. With a grimace, he drew the partially spent MP-7 magazine and a couple of cable ties, turning the sheet metal box into an improvised splint. By using the banana-shaped clip to limit his ankle's movement, he'd spare himself further injury, though he'd be slowed.

Bolan was aware of his diminished capabilities, and plotted the continuation of this battle accordingly.

Out in the bay, he heard an explosion. Looking up, he saw a gout of smoke coming off the deck. James had found his own solution to the problem of the Q-ship.

Good. While the Phoenix Force commando dealt with the heavily armed freighter, the Executioner had a battle to win here among the Grim Strokes and the Black Avengers. The killing field was already chaotic, and the Jamaican gangsters had suffered considerable losses, but there were still too many of them for Bolan's taste.

It was time for a beach bonfire, this one fueled by the Executioner's cleansing flames.

As the Go-fast skirted the far edges where the freighter's spotlights could reach, Calvin James was already formulating a plan to deal with the gunnery crews on board. Among the many advantages of the high-speed watercraft was its relative silence and its propulsors were able to stop almost on a dime without any need to apply reverse power. So far, the former SEAL had been extending the range between the two boats, forcing the gunners to chase him as well as the spotlights to create a larger shadow between the railing and the inky bay waters.

The strategy that James had in mind was what any small fighter took against a larger fighter with a longer reach—jam him on the inside.

With a deft twist of the helm and a blast of full throttle, the Go-fast rocketed away from the hunting beacons, disappearing into the night. Over the thunder of heavy machine guns and automatic grenade launchers, the gunners on the freighter wouldn't be able to hear the growl of his cigarette boat's engines as he swung inside the arc of the spotlights, skimming under them at lightning speed. Even as he jetted beneath the probing spray of illumination from the Q-ship's multiple spotlights, James readied himself to leave the cockpit quickly. Once more, the temptation to use the compact heavy machine gun he'd brought presented itself, but its bulk would be too much to climb with and too long to maneuver in close quarters.

No, this was going to require close quarters agility and speed. That meant the MP-7, even though he also had the sling of the grenade launcher tethered around his neck. He threw open the lid of the cockpit and maneuvered the Go-fast in front of the bow of the freighter. His target was the starboard side of the ship where a ladder and deck had been set up as a docking point for the motor launches. He killed the engines, the boat skimming to a halt with all the silence of a ghost, just in time for the thunder of the heavy deck guns to go silent.

James clambered onto the side of the Go-fast as it drifted toward the caving ladder that was hanging over the rail. He heard shouts wondering where the cigarette boat had disappeared to even as he kicked off of the side of his water rocket, snagging the rungs of the ladder. His arms protested at the sudden weight pulling on them, but the former SEAL had become accustomed to scrambling up a ladder in full combat gear. Once he got his feet under him, the climb went swiftly and he was on the deck in a moment.

"Movement off the starboard stern!" one of the crew shouted. "It's him!"

With that announcement, sailors rushed to the stern with their rifles even as a heavy machine gun swiveled. The spotlights swung down on the drifting powerboat just as streams of fire ripped at the fiberglass hull. There was a pang of regret as James watched his faithful steed torn asunder by the combined firepower of the crew, and he leveled the M-320 at a knot of sailors.

"You're not going alone, speedy," James grumbled, triggering the 40-mm launcher. The grenade had time to arm its impact fuse and struck the boat-spotter between his shoulder blades. The blast seemingly erased him and half of the group beside him out of existence, body parts spiraling into the water after the exploded corpses were once more gripped by gravity.

Panic and dismay erupted in the wake of the powerful detonation, a chunk of the stern chewed away by James's deadly charge. It would take the crew only a few moments to figure out that the empty powerboat was a diversion and its pilot was on board. He took that moment to feed the M-320 a buckshot shell, a hundred .25-caliber steel ball bearings ready to fly with a pull of the trigger.

As soon as he was ready, the ex-SEAL crossed between the two deck structures, staying low between the hold hatches. The port railing was still packed with gunmen, and there was a nest of sailors manning a Browning heavy machine gun. James shouldered the grenade launcher and fired at them, making certain that they wouldn't be able to interfere with the Executioner's work on shore now that they no longer had the Go-fast to deal with. Like a gigantic shotgun, the M-320 spit out a cloud of high-velocity projectiles that struck the machine-gun nest, stripping the flesh from the crew like a swarm of metallic locusts.

The 150-pound frame of the Browning and the twin shields bracketing its barrel proved to help James as the shot pellets struck the mass of metal and ricocheted, bouncing and spreading across the deck to cause even more mayhem. Though the rebounding pellets no longer had the ability to cut completely through a torso, they were still able to inflict deep lacerations that distracted and scattered the other riflemen on the port deck.

One of the spotlight crews swung their beacon toward the deck, and James saw the harsh, blinding beam coming. He clenched his eyes shut and aimed at where he knew the light and its users would be, firing the MP-7 on full-auto until the blazing glare cutting through his eyelids disappeared. James opened his eyes immediately and scurried to cover amid the hatches on deck. The enemy knew he was among them now, gunfire raining down from the other spotlight crew, seeking him out.

"Not going to be that easy," James growled. He unhooked a conventional fragmentation grenade from his harness, armed the bomb and lobbed it up to the second spotlight. The M-26 fragger went off, flinging notched razor wire at hundreds of feet per second. The slivers of metal were tough and fast enough to cut even through bone, and the spotlight itself exploded in a shower of sparks from the proximity to the slashing blast.

A bloodied crew member opened up with his AK-47, spraying the deck wildly. James took him out of the fight with a precision burst of 4.6-mm bullets through the face, followed with a second fragmentation grenade rolled underhand so that he would hit the metal bulkhead that held up the railing on that side of the ship. This time the shrapnel was funneled and directed by the hull of the freighter itself, spitting the deadly rain of carving wire through the ranks of the sailors.

These men had signed up to transport an army, not to fight as one. Their numbers had been depleted explosively, James's assault against them so swift and violent that two dozen of them were gone within the space of a minute. Granted, James had the advantage of surprise and high explosives on his side, but that was no consolation to his enemy. Bombs were detonating all across the deck, and sailors were torn asunder by those blasts.

Rather than gunfire, James heard the cry to abandon ship. Crew members threw themselves over the rail, splashing in the midnight waters in an effort to reach the relative safety of shore. Over the port railing, James could see twisting clouds of smoke rising from Morrot's camp, informing him that the Executioner was raising similar hell ashore.

James rushed to the deck and saw that the crew had abandoned the machine guns, still primed with belts of .50-caliber ammunition. Though he was hundreds of yards from shore, the Browning could easily reach across that chasm. The .50 BMG cartridge had an effective antiarmor range of more than a mile.

"Striker, do you have anything that requires Ma Deuce's kiss?" James asked over his hands-free set, wrapping his fingers around the handles of the monster machine gun.

"There's a Quonset hut on the west side of the camp that is full of fight," Bolan replied. "Have at it."

James grinned mirthlessly as his thumbs stabbed down the spade trigger of the Browning, the unleashed power of the Ma Deuce rolling up his arms even as two-ounce chunks of lead roared downrange at twice the speed of sound.

The Stony Man warriors had spread plenty of horror this night, but the goal of this raid was the complete crushing of Morrot and his allies.

The enemy had sown terror and murder across Jamaica. Now they reaped what they had sewn in the form of .50-caliber hammerblows at 650 rounds per minute.

# CHAPTER TWENTY-ONE

Haitian voodoo was a bastardized mixture of ancient African Vodou disguised by the trappings of Roman Catholicism. Right now, Salvatore Romy was gripped by the horrific thought that the Catholic faith he'd disguised as belief in the *loa,* a mirror image of how early Haitian slaves had obfuscated their pagan beliefs under the trappings of their white Christian masters' imagery and saint worship, had thrown him to the hounds of hell.

The Jamaican gangsters had been facing down Colonel Brandon Stone and despite their numbers being in the hundreds, the American was carving through them like a chain saw through plywood. Of course, Romy had seen Fortescue operate similarly back at the holding facility, where overwhelming firepower and blitzing surprise had combined to leave even rifle-equipped prison guards standing slack-jawed, easy targets to ruthless suppression fire. Where Romy had been on the side of the quick, smaller force before, striking swiftly and leaving behind the wounded, the confused and the dead, now he was part of the receiving end of that tactic.

Fortescue had disappeared, and Romy looked at his fellow Haitians, feeling naked in front of them as if they could see that he was only in this for the pay-check and the potential for great political power. He was no more a practitioner of voodoo than the Pope, and now he felt as though there was a sign pointed at him revealing his lack of faith, betraying his old religious principles as well as those of the Black Avengers. The carnage had inspired a quick, unnoticed sign of the cross, and his paranoia was raging between his ears as he gauged every glance thrown his way.

"Where do we go?" one of the Haitian rebels asked.

"We break for it. We weren't going to be a part of this fight anyway," Romy said. "Split up and head for the forest. Let Morrot and his Jamaican thugs burn."

"The hell you say!" Fortescue bellowed from afar. "Stone knows us. We cannot afford to let him live!"

Romy turned toward the Black Avenger leader, trying to keep the horror out of his features. Behind Fortescue, the Haitians could all see a Quonset hut full of Jamaicans beginning to disintegrate as a heavy machine gun hammered its prefabricated walls. Every time a half-inch thunderbolt struck, it produced a cloud of pulverized matter, be it brick dust or human tissue. Framed by the carnage wrought by Stone or his allies, Fortescue seemed like the incarnation of a demon, his eyes wild and fierce.

"Ogoun, hear me out! If any of these fuckers turn and run from this battle, I will give you their beating hearts as penance for their cowardice!" Fortescue bellowed. "Brandon Stone is just one man! We are the scions of Duvalier and the Tonton Macoute! A nation feared our fathers, and thousands disappeared, bodies and souls destroyed by our voodoo magic! We are the children of the pact of the black pig! Our curse hurled the mightiest empire in the world from the shores of Haiti and reduced it to the punch line of a million jokes! Live or die, we are the Black Avengers, and history will remember us!"

The Haitians, save for Romy, released a cheer of victory, even though the world around them had become a slaughterhouse with the soundtrack of an artillery barrage playing in the background.

"Oh, fuck this," Romy whispered under his breath. The opportunity to disappear from this assembly presented itself in the form of a fresh detonation, this one much closer to the Haitian group. Shielded from the blast by the bodies of the fanatics, he was unfazed by the extreme burst of light and noise that sprouted off to their side.

Romy whirled and charged toward the trees, tossing his rifle aside as he ran.

A black, crust-covered thing suddenly stepped into his path as he sought to escape. Cold blue eyes stared out from a mask carved from the earth, and Romy stopped cold, his jaw dropped in horror. Only after he'd halted did he see that the figure in front of him was bristling with weaponry.

"Stone," Romy whispered.

Big, strong hands grabbed the Haitian by the neck and clamped over his mouth. Romy was picked up as if he were a rag doll, dragged into the shadows of the forest, only put down when the back of his head bounced against a tree trunk.

"Stone?" Romy asked, his voice so low, he couldn't even hear himself over the racket of a string of explosions rocking the beach.

"You can call me that," a voice as harsh and rough as a weathered tombstone grated. "But if you talk too loudly, I'll throw you back to Fortescue."

Romy's entire frame shuddered, even though Bolan had the back of his neck in a clawlike clamp as strong as iron. "No. No."

"Suddenly you're not interested in what the *Petro Loa* have to tell you?" Bolan asked.

"It was just a job to me," Romy answered, his response more of a whimper than anything else. "He's fucking crazy, and he's going to get everyone killed."

Bolan sneered, dried mud flaking from his face like a disintegrating mask. This close, the effect was unnerving, as if this weren't a man but an elemental, a thing literally of dirt and stone risen from the earth to unleash torment upon his enemies.

"No. I'm going to kill everyone. His participation is a mere detail."

"Please...have mercy," Romy begged.

"Where is Morrot? Tell me that, and then maybe you can walk," Bolan growled. His voice was deep, inhuman, adding to the image of a demonic manifestation.

"Mother Mary, forgive me. Morrot isn't here in Holland Bay," Romy said. "He is overseeing everything from a cottage in a place called Stony Point."

There was a hint of amusement in the man-thing's features, but it disappeared as quickly as it arrived, cold fury burrowing into Romy's eyes.

"If I ever see you again, if I ever hear of you again, no one, not Bondye nor the Virgin Mary will be able to protect you. Disappear, and keep looking over your shoulder for the rest of your life."

Romy felt his bladder release. Only moments ago, he was a lapsed Catholic who had pretended to be a servant of voodoo. Now, he was firmly convinced that the creature in front of him was an almighty god of vengeance and punishment, the avatar of justice that hunted the most dangerous men in the world and ground them into dust. The god of Execution had looked him in the eye and granted him reprieve, and had imparted a dire warning.

"Thy will be done."

Bolan released the crushing pressure from Romy's neck. "Go. You have nothing to fear from Fortescue."

The former Black Avenger disappeared into the forest, his legs pumping even after his lungs burned for reprieve, begging forgiveness with every step so that the blue-eyed, coal-black god of death didn't strike him down with a thought.

WITH ONE MORE SOUL screaming into the darkness, this one on the fast path to obscurity and a life filled with dread, guilt and terror, Mack Bolan was ready to make his move against Fortescue and the remainder of the Black Avengers. The Haitians were recovering from the stun grenade that Bolan had thrown to make the frightened Salvatore Romy flee the group. He'd been observing the assembled Black Avengers, and noticed that Romy was exhibiting all the signs of shell shock and loss of will. It was a simple matter for a master of role camouflage to take on an aspect of horror even more terrifying than the dark *loa* his organization had worshipped.

Bolan snapped Romy's courage apart like a brittle sheet of ice under a sledgehammer. With that, he was able to find the final links to the mastermind behind all of this. Even so, he still had a cadre of trained enforcers to deal with.

"Cal, open up on them," Bolan ordered. "Danger close is approved."

The Phoenix Force warrior sounded hesitant on the other end of the line. "Striker, I'm working a Mk 19 automatic grenade launcher now."

"Danger close. Do it!"

The automatic grenade launcher was to the Browning heavy machine gun what the heavy machine gun was to a pistol, the hammer of an angry god being smashed repeatedly into an anthill. Where one conventional 40-mm cartridge had the firepower necessary to rip the bed off of a pickup truck, the rocket assisted shells of the Mk 19, roaring out at 350 rounds per minute, were capable of hitting targets a thousand yards away if necessary, with startling efficiency. The rain of doom had been aimed right where Bolan had marked the group with the flash-bang grenade, and the first rounds struck the ground, throwing up thick columns of smoke and fire.

The grenade launcher was like a hose, and James adjusted his point of aim higher, arcing the stream of high-powered bombs to go farther. The initial barrage suddenly sent everyone scattering, the dozens of Haitians realizing that they were on the receiving end of cosmic wrath. James's second burst landed right where the center of the group had been, ten shells landing and bursting in rapid staccato, shock waves and shrapnel cutting through the ranks of the Black Avengers who were too slow to escape the next salvo.

A corpse cartwheeled past Bolan into the darkness of the woods, a flaming, grisly pinwheel hurled by the force of a grenade's detonation with a macabre sense of whimsy to make a murderer into a flying gymnast in his final moments.

"That's enough," Bolan called.

"All yours, Striker," James returned. "You know I don't like laying down heavy fire so close to you."

Bolan was silent, emerging from the forest and tracking his M-4 at the hammered and confused survivors. He triggered bursts of full-auto into the Haitians, reaping them with a scythe of fire, copper and lead. Bodies collapsed as the Executioner strode among them. If there were some smart enough to play dead, they would live with the sight of the Bolan blitz burned into their minds, a lone man marching through swirls of smoke, spraying flame from his weapon and presenting the image of an unstoppable juggernaut. The M-4 emptied and clicked silent, but Bolan had already transitioned to his MP-7, continuing to rake anyone with a semblance of fight in them with high-velocity projectiles.

All the while, Bolan scanned for signs of Fortescue, who was either hiding or splayed out lifelessly in the middle of this killing floor. He didn't want to leave anything to chance with the Haitian leader, not when he'd proved so dangerous before. Too many dead cried out for Fortescue to receive his judgment, and Bolan wouldn't disappoint them. If he had to track the charred human pinwheel into the jungle to make certain, then so be it. Even if Fortescue was playing dead, he wouldn't be spared like the other helpless Black Avengers. He was the leader and heart of this organization, and with him destroyed, the enforcers would never be a threat again.

"Stone..." a voice croaked in the smoke. While Bolan had never heard his quarry talk, the cover name was an indication of the identity of the speaker.

"Fortescue," Bolan answered, keeping his distance. He discarded the M-4, having used up all the ammunition he'd scavenged for it. The MP-7 returned to its chest holster, most of its bullets spent, as well. He pulled his Desert Eagle, thumbing off the ambidextrous safety, turning the locked and cocked pistol into a device ready to spit .44 Magnum lead in a heartbeat.

"You were..." There was a grunt of pain. Maybe Fortescue was injured, but even a wounded beast was dangerous. "You were a formidable opponent, American."

"And you are another mad dog that just had to be put down," Bolan said. "Say hello to Kalfou for me."

Bolan circled the berm of earth where he'd expected to find his quarry. There was nothing there.

"You...have no right to speak...speak the name of my patrons, blasphemer," Fortescue returned.

"So Ogoun would murder helpless, unarmed healers like a base coward?" Bolan asked. "The *Petro Loa* have a reputation for being the most aggressive and warlike of all the spirits, but Ogoun is a craftsman and a liberator, not a cold-blooded murderer. Marinette is the guardian of single mothers, helping women scrape by, not a harpy calling for the death of thousands."

"You talk as if you understand, but you don't," Fortescue replied. "Who fed you this line of bullshit?"

The Haitian sounded stronger now. The rasp of exhaustion and pain had bled from his voice. He remembered the "vampire juice" as Bertrand had called it, the jar of ruby-red liquid that Fortescue had held up as the last hope for his plans to conquer Haiti.

The Executioner steeled himself, knowing that he was looking at the worst fight yet. He had both hands wrapped around the handle of his Desert Eagle, knowing that Fortescue had imbibed drugs that would turn him into a juggernaut, just like the berserkers he'd fought in Spaulding's surf camp, except instead of mindless rage combined with tireless fury, it would be the strength of a maniac guided by the intellect and experience of a skilled, brutal enforcer.

"I asked you a question, Stone," Fortescue taunted.

"Mambo Glorianna Davis, a true priestess, a good person," Bolan returned. "Not that a twisted psycho like you would ever give a damn about a point of view separate from yours."

"No, Stone," Fortescue replied. "Looking at you through these eyes, I can see your fear. I can see how tense you are. You know what you are facing, right?"

"Just another criminal hopped up on a drug," Bolan told him. "And I won't have any trouble with you because I don't care if you live or die, not like those poor kids you sent to do your work in Kingston."

"So you think you'll be a challenge?" Fortescue asked. "Good. I want to enjoy this battle."

Bolan narrowed his eyes. Fortescue was just to his right, about fifteen feet away, according to his uncanny sense of hearing. "Then quit skulking in the smoke, coward. Let's see who Ogoun favors, the protector of innocents, or the slime who sullies his name as he murders the helpless."

The first footstep was enough for Bolan to react. Fortescue charged with the suddenness of a bull. Standing his ground wasn't an option, and like a toreador, the Executioner lurched out of the way, bringing up the Desert Eagle, its .44 slugs booming out of the barrel to meet the Haitian halfway. Fortescue bolted through the air that Bolan had occupied only moments before, skidding to a halt and ducking low to the ground. The Executioner pivoted and opened fire on the momentarily paused Black Avenger, but Fortescue was a blur again, avoiding the third and fourth rounds in the .44 Magnum pistol's magazine.

Bolan grimaced and sidestepped, feeling a rocket of a punch graze his shoulder, numbing his right arm. He scooped the Desert Eagle out of his numbed hand with his left, twisting and putting another shot into the shadowy berserker as he retreated into the smoke. There was grunt and the soldier assumed that he'd hit something, but he recalled the maniacs released at the prison. They'd worn body armor, and constables had been forced to empty rifles into them to put them down. The commando vest that Fortescue wore was laden with ammo and gear pouches, but it was also undoubtedly armored.

The Haitian exploded from the smoke once more, charging down on the big American at a breakneck pace. With no time to reload, Bolan swung the muzzle of his massive pistol, whipping the barrel across Fortescue's face. He heard bone crunch, and blood sprayed from the Black Avenger's torn face. The strike knocked Fortescue off balance, and he staggered away from the soldier.

Reload, Bolan thought, his index finger bending to stab the magazine release behind the trigger guard. As soon as the button pushed the latch aside, the hook holding the empty box in place was gone, gravity taking hold of the metal mass.

Fortescue stopped himself with a stomp, a bestial snarl escaping his lips. He was beginning to turn as Bolan's numbed right arm bent, sensationless fingertips prying at the snap on a pouch containing another 8-round stick of .44 Magnum hollowpoint rounds. The pouch popped open and the tacky rubber pad on the baseplate of the magazine helped Bolan peel it out.

The empty box finally slid free, metal scraping metal as the spent mag tumbled to the ground. Numb muscles worked, bringing the fresh load up to the butt of the pistol, even as Fortescue turned, an insane grin stretching his lips and baring his teeth.

"One-armed," Fortescue grunted. "Not enough to

take me unarmed, but too slow to deal with me with a handgun, Stone."

The spring-loaded hook closed shut on the window in the full magazine, locking it into place, even as Bolan's index finger jammed down on the slide release. The two clicks sounded just as Fortescue took his first step toward the Executioner, his leg muscles flexing in preparation for explosive acceleration, which would have the Haitian on top of Bolan within a heartbeat, clawing fingers tearing at his throat. The battle computer that raced between the soldier's ears tracked dozens of possibilities even as his finger reached for the single-action trigger on the Desert Eagle. One miss, and the pistol would make a poor hammer for beating Fortescue from around his neck. The full eight rounds of the .44 Magnum pistol's payload in the stomach would be useless once the Haitian's fingers locked around his windpipe in a death grip.

Bolan's ankle was buckling even as he stood, his improvised splint no longer sparing him the crippling pain of putting his weight on it, so he couldn't dodge.

The only outcome for survival was a bullet through the bridge of Fortescue's nose.

The Haitian took his second step as Bolan brought the front sight to bear on his face. At this range, the millisecond it would take to send the message to pull the trigger on the Desert Eagle would be nearly as long as it would take for Fortescue to reach him, tear his left arm off and beat him to death with his own limb. The man had the strength to do it.

On the third stride, Fortescue was airborne, his long arms stretched out to grab Bolan.

The hammer of the Desert Eagle struck the primer of the .44 Magnum cartridge in the chamber. At far faster than the reactions of either man, gunpowder combusted, pressures built inside the case of the round and the hollowpoint bullet was wrenched from the neck of the casing, spinning along the cold-forged barrel of the mighty pistol.

Fortescue was still smiling as the blunt, hollow nose of the bullet flattened against the fragile maxillofacial bones that had been lain bare when Bolan's pistol whipped him. Skull bone imploded, and the deformed slug whirled through his brains like a top, drilling through gray matter and the dense clump of nerves that connected all the voluntary functions of the human body.

From supercharged maniac to 230 pounds of mindless flesh in a thousandth of a second, Fortescue smashed against his executioner, both men's bodies tumbling to the dirt in a tangle of limbs.

Bolan pushed himself out from under the corpse of his adversary, the two halves of its head flopped apart like an egg split from top to bottom.

"Striker? Striker? Do you read me?" James's voice cut through the haze inside Bolan's skull.

"A little louder, Cal," Bolan grunted. "I don't think you shouted enough to push my right eardrum over to the left side of my damned head."

"I've been calling you for thirty seconds, man," James said. "Some of those bastards got up and ran into the forest. I thought you were dead, since you were ignoring them."

Bolan shoved the Desert Eagle back into its holster. "How close are you? I can't feel my right arm anymore."

"Shit," James cursed. "I'm almost to shore."

Bolan knew that the Phoenix Force medic was aware of how bad off the soldier was if he actually implied that he might need some first aid. It wasn't quite accurate that he couldn't feel his arm—the shoulder was definitely there, blazing as if he'd received an intravenous injection of lava. Pinched nerves and dislocation were his first diagnoses, but he'd leave that to a trained professional.

"AND WHERE'S Morrot?" James asked. "Striker? You hear me?"

Bolan opened his eyes after what had felt like only a few seconds, but there was James, wrapping his shoulder. "He's at a place called Stony Point. How long have you been here?"

"Long enough to put your dislocated shoulder back in the socket," James said. "How hard did he hit you?"

Bolan looked at his dead enemy, pieces of skull laying open like the petals of a flower. "Not hard enough. I'm still here."

James nodded. "Amen."

# CHAPTER TWENTY-TWO

Dr. Killian Morrot looked at the trio of beasts he'd chosen from the crop assembled in Holland Bay. Each of them was over six and a half feet tall, averaging 275 pounds, and as fit and limber as an athlete.

They stood alert on the deck of his log cabin overlooking the valley. Stony Point was a nice, isolated place where Morrot wouldn't have encountered any trouble. As it was, he was glad that the trio of zombified thugs weren't his only line of defense. Dawn was painting the skies orange in the east, and he'd lost contact with the freighter and the Jamaican gangster Montego who had been at the Holland Bay camp. One or the other could have been attributed to neglect or a broken radio, but for them both to have remained silent since midnight, it was a sign that Stone had arrived on the scene.

Through his one good eye, he checked his watch again, then turned to the bags he'd packed.

He assumed that Stony Point was going to come under attack, and even the dozen trained berserkers on his grounds weren't going to be enough to hold off an army of constables or a contingent of MI-6 agents sent to arrest him for the planned invasion of Haiti. He examined the packet he'd prepared, just in case he was arrested.

His "friends" in Port-au-Prince wouldn't like it if he was caught with the packet, which was exactly why he'd prepared it. Covertly taken photographs were a trail of evidence that would make his friends take the majority of the heat that the world authorities would bring to bear on him.

Morrot knew that he'd spend the rest of his life in prison, even making a plea deal with Interpol or the U.S. Justice Department. How he'd rot in a cell would be determined by who he got to hang along with him. He put the envelope away, already envisioning a minimum-security prison placement.

A strange pop sounded outside. He turned, and there was nothing unusual on the deck. It had to have been one of his zombie minions. Despite his programming, each of them still had a semblance of personality, and a few of the older ones were fidgety rather than mindless.

Morrot idly wondered how Stone would fare once he reached this cabin. Considering the carnage that had been unleashed on Orleans back in Kingston, the American had grown tired of dealing with berserkers. An assault rifle/grenade launcher combination would make quick work of even the largest and strongest of his drone sentries.

He allowed himself a chuckle, which he cut off when his cell phone rang. He pulled it from his pocket. "Hello?"

"Dr. Killian Morrot, I presume," a voice answered on the other end.

"Colonel Brandon Stone?"

"Exactly."

"I take it you found my number on the speed dial of Fortescue's cell?" Morrot asked.

"Nothing gets past you."

There was that pop outside again. Morrot prided himself on being aware of his surroundings, but he couldn't identify the unusual noise. "Are you right here?"

"Give or take twenty feet," Bolan said.

"You're good. How'd you get past my zombies?" Morrot asked.

"Suppressed Beretta," Bolan explained. "Plus, I brought a friend to act as a sniper overwatch for me."

"Well, that's nice," Morrot said. "Come on in. The sliding door to my bedroom's open."

He turned to see the Executioner standing behind him, an impossibly large handgun dangling in his left hand, the right arm cradled in a sling.

"Ah, Fortescue found my vampire juice?" Morrot asked.

Bolan nodded, still remaining on the other side of the screen door.

"How was he?" Morrot asked.

"Not quite faster than a speeding bullet, but it felt like a locomotive smashed my shoulder."

Morrot's half face turned bright with a smile. "Please, come in."

"No, thanks, I don't feel like ending up paralyzed.

Nice information packet," Bolan noted, nodding toward the envelope on top of the man's luggage. "Is that everyone who was working for you, wanting you to hand them half of Hispaniola on a silver platter?"

"As bright as you are deadly, young man. Oh, to have worked with a professional like you," Morrot said. "Yes. It was my insurance against maximum prosecution should you catch up to me."

"Really?"

"You are going to arrest me, right?" Morrot asked.

Bolan lifted the muzzle of his Beretta. "Sorry. Guess you weren't that smart anyway."

"Without me, there's no chance of prosecuting the others," Morrot said, almost stammering and backing away from the door. There was a handgun on his dresser. He paused as he noticed one of his hulks loom into view behind the American. He relaxed.

"I told you," Bolan said as the lumbering giant's head burst like an overripe melon. "I brought a friend along with a sniper rifle."

The decapitated monstrosity collapsed onto the deck.

"As for prosecuting corrupt Haitian politicians," Bolan stated, "do you really think the law is going to do enough against them?"

Morrot looked toward his pistol, then the envelope. "So…"

"It's going to be my shopping list when I head to Port-au-Prince. The only prosecution will be in the next world."

Morrot's shoulders sagged. "Who are you? I deserve

that much." The words were barely out of his mouth before he lurched toward his dresser.

Bolan triggered the Beretta, that odd pop resounding one last time in the one-eyed *bokor*'s ears, then eternal silence and darkness.

"Ask Baron Samedi."

The Executioner turned and limped back to his rendezvous with James.

\* \* \* \* \*

# James Axler
# Outlanders

## INFESTATION CUBED

**Earth's saviors are on the run as
more nightmares descend upon Earth...**

Ullikummis, the would-be cruel master of Earth, has captured
Brigid Baptiste, luring Kane and Grant on a dangerous pursuit. All
while pan-terrestrial scientists conduct a horrifying experiment
in parasitic mind control. But true evil has yet to reveal itself, as
the alliance scrambles to regroup—before humankind loses its
last and only hope.

*Available November wherever books are sold.*